The Chili Queen

**Center Point
Large Print**

**This Large Print Book carries the
Seal of Approval of N.A.V.H.**

The Chili Queen

sandra dallas

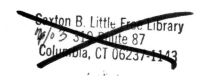
Center Point Publishing
Thorndike, Maine

For Bob. Forever.

This Center Point Large Print edition
is published in the year 2003 by arrangement with
St. Martin's Press LLC.

The text of this Large Print edition is unabridged. In other
aspects, this book may vary from the original edition. Printed in
Thailand. Set in 16-point Times New Roman type by
Bill Coskrey and Gary Socquet.

ISBN 1-58547-265-4

Library of Congress Cataloging-in-Publication Data.

Dallas, Sandra.
    The Chili Queen / Sandra Dallas.--Center Point large print ed.
        p. cm.
    ISBN 1-58547-265-4 (lib. bdg. : alk. paper)
        1. Women--New Mexico--Fiction. 2. Female friendship--Fiction. 3. Boardinghouses--Fiction.
    4. New Mexico--Fiction. 5. Large type books. I. Title.

PS3554.A434 C47 2003
813'.54--dc21

                                                                    2002073920

acknowledgments

Before you read *The Chili Queen*, please know that this book would not have been possible without the persistence of two extraordinary women: Jane Jordan Browne, my agent at Multimedia Product Development Inc., read the first draft more than a dozen years ago and never gave up on it; Harriett Dallas, my remarkable mother, taught me not to be a quitter. I miss you, Mom. I'm grateful to my family—Bob, Dana, Kendal, and Lloyd—who fill my life with joy. Thanks to the Western History Department of the Denver Public Library, the Texana/Genealogy Department of the San Antonio Public Library, and Lonnie Darnell for help with research. Thanks, too, to my lifelong friend Arnie Grossman, to Scott Mendel and Janie McAdams at Multimedia, and to my editor, Jennifer Enderlin, whose insight made this a better book.

addie

ONE

As the train pulled into the shabby station at Palestine, Kansas, the pinch-faced farmers and their wives in their rusty black-wool best lined up along the tracks like the teeth of a rake. In the Kansas heat, three boys slumped on an empty baggage cart in the shade of the depot, too listless even to tie a tin can to a cat's tail. A bitch in heat wouldn't draw a yellow dog under that sun, Addie French thought, as she shaded her eyes from the hurtful glare of the prairie, which was bleached the dirty white of worn underwear. She put a handkerchief to her nose, as if to block out the stench of sweat and barnyard and old pancakes that clung to the farmers' clothes. Although she had spent well over half her thirty-six years off the land, Addie never forgot the sour smells of the farm. She wiped her damp face and neck with a soiled handkerchief, leaving behind streaks of dirt on her wet skin.

The trip to Kansas City had been even more successful than she had hoped, financially, at any rate, and she was going home to New Mexico with enough money to buy a new cookstove and add a front porch to The Chili Queen. The gentleman friend she met there every August on his annual business trip to the city had shown her an especially good time, bought her two dresses, and paid generously for her companionship. In fact, he had been so attentive that Addie wondered if he might suggest a permanent relationship. Perhaps his wife had died at last and he was ready to propose a formal arrangement—not that she was interested, of course; still, it would do a girl good to be asked. As the week came to a close, however, he told Addie that he was moving to Montana with his wife, and he was sorry, but he wouldn't be seeing her again. He begged Addie to stay two more days; he was as hot as a billy goat in a pepper patch. As she remembered their last night, tears formed in Addie's eyes, and she swatted at them with the handkerchief. She sniffed, feeling sorry for herself that such a nice arrangement had come to an end. Feeling sorry for herself was one of the things Addie did best. She'd miss him and the yearly vacations, although she wouldn't miss Kansas. Oh my, she hated Kansas, Addie thought, catching the stink of her hot, damp body. New Mexico was hard on her hair and skin, but she'd take New Mexico's dryness over Kansas's humidity any day. She was glad to be going home.

Perhaps she should have telegraphed Welcome, telling her she'd been detained. Welcome, Addie snorted, what kind of name was that, even for a black woman? For all Addie knew, Welcome had run off with the china while she was gone—not that the china was worth anything. No sense to buy good china when the whores were likely to throw it at the customers, or each other. Addie valued

Welcome more than the dishes. None of the other domestics she hired stayed for more than a few days, but Welcome had been there for four weeks, and rascally and outspoken as she was, she liked the job and planned to stay, or that was what she'd told Addie, at any rate. The first time she met her, Addie had had a feeling about Welcome, and for no reason she could put her finger on, she trusted her—trusted her enough to leave her in charge of The Chili Queen while Addie was away. She could have closed down the hookhouse, but she was afraid she'd come back and find the girls gone. So she hadn't had any choice but to trust Welcome.

The woman had shown up one morning asking for work, speaking in that funny way she had; Addie thought it was a mixture of slavery talk and high-class language Welcome had picked up somewhere. Addie was desperate for hired help. Plenty of whores came through looking for work, although not when she needed them, it seemed. But not many women looked for jobs backstairs in a parlor house, cooking and washing for as lazy and ungrateful a group of human beings as ever lived. Addie'd have given the job to a blind man, and she didn't expect much out of Welcome. But in a week, the portly, fine-looking black woman, who was big enough to go bear hunting with a switch, had taken over as if she owned the place. She cooked and cleaned and kept the girls in line. Welcome even faced down the drunks with no better weapon than a fry pan. Addie wasn't sure why Welcome had come to Nalgitas; probably, she was drifting through, just like the girls. Maybe she was tired of moving around and wanted a place to call home. Addie hadn't asked. Why question good luck? When it's raining porridge, hold up your bowl. Addie just hoped that Welcome had kept the whores in line and was still there when she got home.

As Addie tucked the handkerchief into her fine bosom, the train stopped, jerked once, then shuddered as it settled into the depot. The conductor climbed off the car, holding a metal step, and set it down. He held out his hand to a woman who struggled with a heavy satchel. A farmer came forward and took it from her, and the two walked off, the woman following a few steps behind him. None of the half-dozen passengers who got off the train was greeted with hugs or cries of welcome. It wasn't just the heat. These were dour people, Addie knew. They rarely showed emotion; maybe they didn't have any. The crowd thinned out as the last of the passengers left the train. Those who remained on the platform gathered around the steps, anxious to board.

A man who stood out because his suit was too well tailored to be home-sewn—a banker, Addie decided with interest—pushed onto the train ahead of everyone else. Hoping the man was bound for Nalgitas, Addie leaned forward in her seat as he stopped in the aisle near her, forcing the other passengers to wait behind him. "Here. Ticket to Holden," he said, holding up a twenty-dollar gold piece so that everyone could see it. "Two dollars seventy," he added, as if the conductor didn't know the fare. The conductor pocketed the coin and gave the man a ticket. He counted the thirty cents out loud, then handed over a fistful of bills. Two of the dollar bills were folded, Addie observed. The conductor had shorted the passenger by two dollars. He'd done the same thing earlier with a woman in a shapeless coat and dirty scarf tied around a face as lumpy as a potato. Two little girls had held onto her skirt as she'd shifted the baby in her arms and taken out a bill. Anyone who'd cheat a poor immigrant was mean enough to whip his own grannie, and Addie had grabbed the conductor's wrist and pinched it hard. Then she'd told him in a low voice that if he didn't give the woman the correct change, she'd announce to the entire car what he'd done. The conductor handed the woman the rest of her money, but he'd given Addie a hard time after that, opening a window to let the dust blow in on her and taking liberties when she went out on the observation deck for air. Addie's left breast was sore from where he'd grabbed it and wrenched it hard, and she wondered if he'd left a bruise.

As the banker passed Addie, he curled his lip and moved to the far side of the aisle, kicking the hem of her dress out of his way. Did he think she was contagious? The gesture cost him two dollars. He could get swindled out of the whole damn gold piece for all Addie cared. She looked the conductor full in the face, then slid her eyes to the mark, letting the conductor know that even though she kept her mouth shut, she hadn't missed the cheat.

The conductor might be good enough to fool an immi-grant woman and an unctuous banker, but not Addie French, the queen of the sleight-of-hand artists—the former queen, at any rate. Nobody gave short change like she did. There wasn't a man or woman in the Southwest who was better at palming, the switch, or the thimblerig than Addie French, and she didn't cheat poor foreign women, either. She'd tricked the best in the business.

She might still be at it if she hadn't picked the wrong mark, and he'd clubbed her. Addie still had a hurting in her bones sometimes from where she'd been beaten. After she recovered, she had taken a good look at her career and decided scamming was too dangerous. She'd learned her lesson. As good as she was, there was always someone out there who was sharp enough to catch her. Whoring wasn't as chancy, and the work was steady, easier on the nerves, too. Not that men wouldn't knock you around sometimes, but they didn't try to kill you out of meanness. By now, of course, Addie wasn't a whore herself anymore, except when she chose to be. She was a businesswoman. She owned a house. If the banker had been going to Nalgitas instead of Holden, she might have slipped him her business card. Men who snubbed you in the daytime didn't mind calling after dark.

Remembering the card, Addie fished in her reticule until she found the pasteboard, pulled it out, and admired it:

THE CHILI QUEEN
NALGITAS
MEN TAKEN IN AND DONE FOR
FOUR BOARDERS, FIRST RATE
MISS ADDIE FRENCH, PROP.

Actually, the four boarders included Addie herself, who filled in only now and then.

She had replenished her supply of cards in Kansas City and this time had added a gold border. It gave a touch of class. Addie ran her finger over the raised black letters and was about to return the card to her purse when she heard an angry male voice.

"Sit here. You shan't ride beside a man. You are foolish in the ways of the world, Emma. A traveling man isn't to be trusted, and you've not sense, but would let him start up a conversation with you. You're fool enough to talk to strangers. He won't take you if you're mauled, you know." He pushed a woman into the seat next to Addie, much to Addie's annoyance. The train was not crowded, and she'd expected to have the seat to herself.

Addie narrowed her eyes to take in the man, who wore black pants that ended above his shoe-tops and a coat that showed two inches of wrist. The coat was stretched across his broad back, and when he reached overhead to place a box on the brass rack, Addie saw the half-circles of sweat staining his underarms. Still, he was tall and lean, with thick black hair that was streaked with gray, and he was handsome, with high cheekbones and pale eyes, but his face was mean, and he snarled at the woman. "You're not to change seats. You hear me?"

"John," the woman pleaded. "Please. People are staring." She glanced at Addie, then turned her head away when she saw Addie watching her. The woman was a little younger than her husband. Under a large hat, her hair appeared to be the same glossy black. Her skin was whiter than his, and she had startling blue eyes. Addie, who was an expert in knowing what was hidden under corsets and petticoats, sized up the woman's body. She was tall and slender, girlish even, with small breasts and hips—not a body a customer would find at The Chili Queen, not a body like Addie's own generous, cottony one, with a bosom a man could sink into. But some men liked scrawny women, just as some men picked chicken wings over drumsticks.

"You're to pay mind to him. Don't sass him like you do me. If your opinion doesn't agree with his own, keep it to yourself. Don't act so pert, either."

Addie snorted and gave John the fish-eye. He sent her a hard look, then slid his eyes down to take in her silk dress, which was the shade of a brass watch—the same color as her hair. If he were as smart as he thought he was, he'd recognize her as a whore and order his wife to move, which would give Addie back the seat. Instead, he looked at Addie with such hatred as she had never seen on a man's face and told her, "Mind your business."

Addie raised an eyebrow and continued to stare.

"You know if you go, you can't come back. You wouldn't be welcome. I'd be shamed. This is your last chance," said the man in a voice so low that only the woman and Addie heard him. When the woman didn't reply, John sighed and said, "I told you already you were a fool, but you made your bed. Now you've got to sleep in it." He paused again, and his voice was even lower when he said, "Keep a sharp eye for investment. If it suits me, I'll pay him five percent. Might be he'd think better of you if you were to bring in a little money. He couldn't hardly think worse after what you've got yourself into."

"But that's our money, John. It's not just yours," the woman whispered fiercely.

"Well, I guess if it'd been meant for you, it'd been left to you, wouldn't it? 'Twas left to me to spend as I see fit."

"You know why that was."

John started to reply but when he saw Addie still

watching, he pressed his lips together in a hard, straight line.

By then, the boarding passengers had found seats, and the conductor was looking up and down the tracks. "All aboard," he called.

John glanced up. "I got to git."

He took a step down the aisle, but the woman grabbed his coat. "Aren't you going to wish me luck?"

John stared at her for a long time, chewing his lip. Then without a word, he turned and left the car. As he jumped off the observation deck, the train lurched, and he landed on one leg and fell to the ground. Without looking back, he got up and limped away. Addie glanced at the woman, who leaned forward with alarm. Then a smile flickered across her face.

Neither woman spoke until the train slid away from the platform and moved onto the dry prairie. Emma—that was what the man had called her—got up and shoved a portmanteau onto the overhead rack, then pushed a hamper under the seat. The hamper interested Addie. She'd eaten the dinner she'd brought with her from Kansas City, and the only food available from the train butcher was meat sandwiches that were dotted with fly-specks.

Emma took off her bonnet, a shabby black silk that was too unattractive ever to have been fashionable, ironed the strings between two fingers, and carefully set the hat on the empty seat across the aisle. "He put my hatbox over-head, but it's already got two bonnets in it, so there's no place for this old thing," Emma told Addie.

Addie blinked and turned to her. Without the awful hat,

the woman was a little prettier, although not what anybody would ever have called a beauty. She had strands of gray in her hair.

"They're stylish. One's pink. *He* doesn't know I have them."

"You going on a trip, are you?" was all Addie could think to say. John was right. His wife talked too much to strangers.

The woman nodded and introduced herself. "My name's Emma Roby."

"Where you going, Mrs. Roby?"

The woman laughed. "Oh, you think John's my husband. He's not. He's only my brother. I'm *Miss* Roby."

"Well, I'm Miss French. Miss Addie French."

"We're just like two maiden ladies on an adventure, then."

Addie thought that was an interesting way to put it.

"Do you want to see the hats?" the woman asked. Before Addie could answer, Emma jumped up and removed the hatbox from overhead. She unbuckled it and lifted the lid. "This is the pink one." Emma reached into a cloud of paper and brought out a bonnet the color of a baby's bottom, with ruffles and couching and long satin streamers, and thrust it into Addie's hands. "And there's this one, too." She removed a tiny round red hat that reminded Addie of a tin of Enameline the Modern Stove Polish that Welcome used to polish the stove at The Chili Queen. Even her girls wouldn't wear such silly bonnets. "I made them myself," the woman said shyly. "Even John says I'm an unusual smart woman with my fingers."

"Where are you going to wear a hat like that?" Addie

nodded at the tin of stove polish.

"Nalgitas. It's in New Mexico."

Addie jerked up her head. "Nalgitas?"

Emma nodded.

"Hats like them wouldn't last a single dust storm. We get fierce dust."

Emma ran a deep blue ribbon on the red hat through her fingers and asked if Addie was from Nalgitas. Addie acknowledged that she was.

"Why, isn't that the best thing? You're the first person I've met who lives there. I hope we'll be friends," Emma said. She set the hat carefully into the box, then reached for the one Addie held, tucking it in beside the first and arranging the tissue paper on top. She returned the box to its place on the rack. "Isn't this a wonderful coincidence?"

Addie didn't think so. She inquired of the woman if she were visiting.

Emma flushed and looked away. "I'm going to live there. If you must know . . ." The pause was a little too coy, Addie thought. "I'm getting married," Emma added.

"Oh," was all Addie said. Wives weren't so good for business. Sooner or later, most of them tried to shut down a whorehouse.

"I won't actually live in Nalgitas. My husband, that is my husband-to-be, owns a ranch near there—a big one. He says it's the biggest in a hundred miles, but you know how men brag—except for John, that is." Her face turned hard.

"What's his name?"

Emma looked confused. "John."

"The rancher, I mean."

"Oh, him. It's Mr. Withers. Mr. Walter Withers."

The name was not familiar, and Addie was glad she wouldn't be losing business. Marriage didn't keep men from a whorehouse, but bridegrooms weren't such good customers. Then she wondered if Mr. Withers used another name at The Chili Queen. Men did that sometimes, although she often told them, "What I do best is forget names." She asked, "What's he look like?"

Emma looked down at her hands and muttered something.

"What's that?"

Instead of answering, Emma reached into her bag and pulled out a tiny tintype not much bigger than Addie's thumbnail. Addie took the picture and squinted at it. The image was so dark and out of focus that she couldn't tell even if the subject were a white man. "He doesn't show much, does he?"

Emma shook her head.

"Tall or short?"

Emma shrugged.

Addie snorted. "What's that? You're not sure? Sounds like you never met him." She laughed at her little joke, but when Emma looked down at her hands and began fidgeting with the strings of her bag, Addie blew out her breath. "You never met him? Are you one of those mail-order brides?"

"Certainly not," Emma said quickly, glancing around as Addie's voice rose. She snatched the picture from Addie and put it into her purse. "No, I certainly am not."

"Well, what are you then?"

"I'm not a wife you pay for like something in a wish-book. I have my pride."

Not so much, Addie thought. She studied the worn velvet on the back of the seat in front of her as she waited for the woman to explain.

In a minute, Emma cleared her throat. "We have corresponded for a long time. I believe that by doing so, we have gotten to know each other better than if he'd courted me in person."

Addie stared at the tobacco juice stains on the floor of the car and tried not to smile.

Emma explained, "We were not distracted with physical things, you might say." She cleared her throat again. "We have gotten to know each other's souls."

Addie had never known anybody's soul and wasn't much interested in hearing about Mr. Withers's. So she asked how the two of them had gotten acquainted.

"He placed an ad in the newspaper at home, saying he would be pleased to correspond with a good Christian woman, as there are none in Nalgitas." Emma thought that over and added, "I mean I'm sure there are some, such as yourself, but he said he wasn't personally acquainted with any."

"No doubt," said Addie, who wasn't acquainted with any, either. It seemed curious to her that Emma hadn't married before, and she wanted to ask about it, but that was too rude a question even for Addie, so instead, she inquired how long the two had been writing.

Six months, Emma told her. "He wrote two weeks ago and invited me for a visit and said that if I were agreeable, we should consider matrimony. But he said if I didn't like him, I was not bound. I can always leave."

"But you can't go back home, can you? Your brother said as much," Addie pointed out.

Emma frowned, thinking that over. "No, I suppose not. But it doesn't matter. I've made up my mind I'm going to like him."

"What if you don't?"

"I will, that's all," she replied so sharply that Addie felt rebuked. Emma unhooked the collar of her wool jacket and stretched her neck. "Anybody has to be more likable than John," she added more agreeably.

That one was not fit to associate with hogs, Addie thought. Then she asked, "What if *he* doesn't like *you?* Have you thought about that?"

Emma bit her lip and looked down at her hands. "I hope to be up to the mark," she said, a catch in her voice, and Addie felt a little ashamed of herself. The woman had enough trouble without borrowing more. Besides, Addie thought as she glanced at the hamper, there was no need to offend her. "Well, I'm sure he'll like you just fine. I never knew an old batch who wouldn't be happy with just about any woman. They're not too particular, you know." She thought that over. It wasn't much of a compliment, but Emma didn't seem to mind.

Emma unfastened another button, then another, and in a moment she took off the jacket. When Emma reached up to put it onto the rack, Addie noticed there were no wet spots under her arms. Maybe the woman didn't sweat. Addie felt the perspiration on her own face, and as she reached for her handkerchief, she dropped the calling card. She'd forgotten she was holding it.

Emma picked it up and read it. Well, it couldn't be

helped, Addie thought. The woman would give her a horrified stare and move as far away from her as possible. Addie would lose out on the supper, but she'd get the seat back. That was some consolation.

Emma looked puzzled as she studied the piece of pasteboard. Then she smiled. "Oh, I am double-lucky." She put the card into her purse.

"What?" Addie stammered. Emma wouldn't be the first woman who was disappointed in love and decided to turn out. Still, Addie couldn't see this particular woman becoming a whore if things didn't work with the rancher. Besides, there wasn't much call for a gray-haired woman in a hookhouse. The Chili Queen was no old-ladies' rest home.

"I mean, you running a boardinghouse. If Mr. Withers doesn't want me, I can stay with you at"—she glanced down at the card—"The Chili Queen." She laughed.

She might be an unusual smart woman with her fingers, but in other ways, she was dumb as a barrel of hair. Addie was tempted to shock the silly woman into silence by telling her just what went on at The Chili Queen, but Emma might complain, and the conductor was just mean enough to put Addie off the train at the next stop. So instead, she replied, "You just do that."

After a while, Emma got up and removed a cloth workbag from the portmanteau, then took out several scraps of fabric that had been cut into shapes. She threaded a needle with cotton and began to sew the little pieces together. Addie fanned herself with her hand as she watched Emma stitch. In a few minutes, Emma snipped off the thread with a pair of scissors shaped like a crane and held up her work for Addie's inspection. The design, worked in calicoes that were bright blue and brown the color of stiff coffee, was called Double Pyramids, Emma explained.

Addie didn't understand women who named their sewing. She didn't have a hand for it herself. Besides, Addie always put store-bought spreads on her beds instead of quilts. A quilt reminded a man of home, and that was not a good thing in a whorehouse. She muttered a compliment, then turned and stared out the window.

The train passed a hardscrabble farm, the buildings plain and unpainted, the field so poor the homesteaders couldn't raise a row with a pitchfork. A woman slouched in the barnyard, shading her eyes as she watched the train. Three little girls in raggedy dresses and drooping sunbonnets stood next to the tracks, the biggest child holding a baby. One of the girls waved, the others just stared at the train, their heads turning to watch it out of sight. Without thinking, Addie waved back.

She used to be the girl with the baby—the oldest one, who'd had to mind the others when they came. She'd known all about babies. Her mother had one every year—except in the year after her father died, before her mother remarried—and Addie had helped deliver them. She'd known from an early age how a baby got started, too. There was only one bedroom in the house, and it was partitioned off with rough boards that had big cracks between them. Addie'd lain awake at night, listening to her step-paw root around in the bed, grunting like a pig in slops. Addie cringed when her mother begged her husband to keep away from her, then gave into him. Addie half-pitied her and half-hated her for satisfying the old man. Finally, the worn-out woman with skin the color of smoked ham slid an old bureau in front of the bedroom door at night to keep him out, and he slept on the floor in front of the fireplace, wrapped in a blanket.

But then he had come for Addie, a great big half-grown girl. She kicked him pretty hard the first time, and the next day, he cowhided her. But he didn't stop pawing her, and her mother didn't seem to mind. So Addie took the money her step-paw kept hidden in her mother's scrapbag—not all of it, just enough to buy a ticket and a little more for expenses. Then she flagged down the train and told the conductor she wanted to go to San Antonio. It was the farthest place she'd ever heard of. When she got there, she changed her name from Adeline Foss to Addie French, because that sounded like a long way from the farm, too. Sometimes Addie felt guilty about leaving her sisters behind and wondered if the old man had gone after them after she left. Maybe they'd run off and turned into whores, too. Addie thought about them whenever a girl turned up at The Chili Queen asking for work, a girl who looked as if she'd come from soul-stomping poverty. Addie hardly ever turned away a girl with a sad story.

She stared back at the brown-yellow farm long after the girls had become specks and then nothing at all. The train passed another farm. A boy rushed to the tracks, a dog at his heels. Addie waved at him, too, but he stared at her with a hostile face and didn't wave back.

"It's a cruel life," Emma said, startling Addie, who hadn't realized she was looking out the window, too. "They're worn out from being poor."

"Sand on one side of the house, clay on the other," Addie replied. "It reminds me of home. We were turkey poor—poor enough to eat wallpaper, if we'd had wallpaper." Addie stopped herself. She didn't much talk about her childhood. She turned to Emma, who had a look of hate on her face, as if she were remembering something unpleasant. "You come from such, do you?"

"Oh, no," Emma said quickly. "Oh, no. But I've known men bereft of human decency, men every bit as mean as those farms. Oh, yes." Her face twisted then turned stony, and Addie stared at her, wondering what had brought on the outburst. But in a minute, Emma got control of herself and gave an embarrassed smile. "I mean, I've heard of men like that. I don't know any personally, of course. We have a very prosperous farm. John's a good farmer. I have to say that for him. And our folks had money. But I could have been a poor farm woman, I suppose. There but for the grace of God . . ."

"But for the grace of God what?" Addie asked.

"Oh, it's just an expression. It means the luck of the draw."

"There but for the grace of God," Addie repeated. She'd always been drawn to fancy words.

"My mother was from New Jersey. She was quite refined," Emma continued, running her fingers over her stitching. "She taught me to do hand sewing. Mother studied at Elizabeth T. Stephens's school in New Jersey."

"Did your mother read? Myself, I can read, you know."

"Oh my, yes Mother could read. She read French, too. Miss Stephens ran a finishing school. Mother made a beautiful sampler there when she was very young. I even remember the verse:

Now while my hands are thus employ'd
May I set out to serve the Lord
While I am blesst with health and youth
Help me O Lord to Obey the Truth

"Isn't that lovely?" Emma asked.

Addie didn't care about obeying the truth. "There but for the grace of God . . . ," she said.

Emma looked puzzled as she returned to her sewing. She worked the needle up and down, taking half a dozen stitches before she used a silver thimble on her finger to push the needle all the way through the fabric. She straightened the seam so that it didn't pucker, and examined the patchwork. "I probably shouldn't have stitched it in black. They say if you sew a quilt-top with black thread, you'll never sleep under it with your intended. But I don't believe in such things. Do you?"

Addie knew better than to tempt fate, but she didn't care to talk about sewing, so she shrugged and said, "I guess you're so prosperous you've got money in the bank." A mosquito landed on her arm, and she flattened the pest, but not before it drew blood. Addie flicked away the dead insect and licked her finger, placing it on the welt. "We got mosquitoes in Nalgitas the size of grasshoppers and grasshoppers the size of chickens," she said with a touch of pride.

"And how big are your chickens?" Emma asked.

Addie frowned. "They're the size of chickens, same as any place. Don't you know that?" She wondered if Emma would think her nosy if she asked about the bank again, but she didn't care. She considered other people's money her business. "You got money in the bank, do you?"

Emma didn't seem to mind the question. "John does. I don't have a pin. I suppose you heard what he said, that it's all his money."

"Most times that's the way of it, leastways with man and wife, but you being brother and sister, I thought you might own something yourself."

Emma turned the stitching right side up and smoothed it with her hand, then she examined the corner where three pieces came together. One was off just a fraction of an inch, and she pulled out the thread. Then she set the quilting in her lap and leaned back and closed her eyes, pressing her fingers to them. Addie stared at her. She'd never before spent this much time with a good Christian woman. Her mother was a Bible reader, but Addie had decided a long time back that she hadn't been much of a Christian if she'd let her husband have his way with her own daughter. It was pie-crust religion, all crust and no filling.

"Half is mine. Half is rightly mine," Emma said, her eyes still closed. "Father meant for the farm and the land—we have a good deal of it—to go to both of us. He trusted me. He said I had a better head for investment than John, who is too greedy for his own good. But Father didn't think so highly of my ability to attract an acceptable husband, and he feared I'd marry a man who was after the money. So he left everything to John, with the understanding John would share with me. Of course, John didn't, and there was nothing I could do because Father hadn't put it in writing. It's not that I have been hard used. I don't want for anything, but John begrudges spending money on me. John's stingy, except when it comes to spending money to make more money, but that's greed, not good investment. The thing of it is, John doesn't believe he's cheated me. He thinks he has treated me fairly. You heard him: He even wants me to look for a New Mexico investment for him."

Emma paused, but Addie didn't say anything, hoping the woman would continue, and she did. There was a catch in Emma's voice when she said, "To tell you the truth, I think John's glad to see me go. Now he can do as he pleases with the inheritance and not have me there to reproach him. Well, I'm glad to be gone, too. We never had much use for each other, and toward the end, we came mighty close to hate. He has ten thousand dollars in the bank, and half is rightly mine, all of it, really, for John has the farm, too." She gave a dry laugh. "All I got out of it was the makings for two bonnets and a one-way ticket to Nalgitas."

Emma was indeed foolish in the ways of the world and much too talky. Addie leaned close to her and said, "You ought'n to tell people things like that. There's men who'd kill you for less."

"Well, it's not what I've got that I'm talking about. It's what I haven't got, so it doesn't matter."

"Still, I wouldn't tell it about in Nalgitas. There are bad men there. Buck Sorrell for one."

Emma opened her eyes wide. "Oh!"

"Well, not anymore," Addie admitted. "But there are others. Ever heard of Butch Scanga?"

Emma sat up straight.

"And Ned Partner?"

"Ned who?" Emma asked.

"Partner. Ned Partner."

Emma shook her head. "I guess not. Is he anybody?"

"Anybody?" Addie snorted. "Ned Partner's the smartest outlaw in New Mexico is all. He robbed a bank in Santa Fe of five thousand dollars, they say, and the posse went after him with dogs. Those dogs, they picked up a scent, and they followed it to a line shack. They shoved in the door and commenced to howl in the worst way. The sheriff and his deputies drew their guns and surrounded the place and called out to Ned to surrender. When there wasn't any answer, they shot their guns into the place, then ran up close and looked inside. But all they found was those dogs fighting over the leavings in a scrap bucket. Ned Partner wasn't there, and the bank never got the five thousand dollars back. I guess Ned made fools of them. Everybody in New Mexico talks about it." Addie shook with laughter, then daubed at her eyes with the handkerchief. "Oh, he's the best there is, I tell you."

"He got away with five thousand dollars?"

Addie started to nod, then stopped. She'd become as loose with her talk as Emma. "It might have been four thousand or maybe two thousand. Maybe there wasn't any money in the bank at all. How would I know?" She shrugged and waved her hand, dismissing the subject of Ned Partner. "There's outlaws all over New Mexico and Colorado and Arizona, too. Why, some of 'em are women. Did you know that?"

Emma looked alarmed.

Addie chuckled. She was enjoying herself. "There's Ma Sarpy, only she's in the Breckenridge jail up in Colorado, and Cross-Eyed Mary Foster, and Little Bit, and Anna Pink." The last three actually were prostitutes since Addie couldn't think of any more female outlaws. "I can't remember every and all of them."

"Why, that's so—depraved," Emma said. She put her hand to her throat and fingered a brooch pinned to her collar.

Addie felt a twinge of guilt at having alarmed Emma and said, "Oh, I shouldn't worry if I was you. I never personally saw a woman outlaw in Nalgitas, and the men, when they come into town, they keep to the saloons and hook—" She stopped, searching for a better word than *hookhouse.*

"Other dens of iniquity," Emma finished for her. "I suppose it wouldn't hurt to see an outlaw, but I wouldn't care to be acquainted with one." She threaded her needle and picked up the sewing in her lap. "Would you?"

Addie cast a sideways glance at Emma, who was restitching the plucked-out seam and didn't look up. "I would like a bath," Addie said. "My bones need easing. The first thing I'll do when I get home is tell the servant woman to heat water on the cookstove and fill up my bathtub." She leaned back in the seat, thinking about lying in her tin tub filled with hot water.

Emma seemed surprised that there were servants in New Mexico.

"Oh, I've got just one. Tomorrow, when I get home, I'll have her to cook me up a big beefsteak and bake a custard pie."

Emma said a custard pie sounded mightily good, then reached for her jacket and opened the little watch pinned to it. "It's past suppertime. When does the dinner car open for business?"

Addie snorted and told Emma there wasn't any dinner car on the train. Passengers brought their own or bought from the train butcher. "But it looks like you brought yours with you." Addie pointed to the hamper and restrained herself from licking her lips.

"Oh, that's not supper," Emma laughed. "Those are my cinnamon-rose starts. I was known all over the county for my cinnamon roses." She lifted the lid and showed Addie the wilted clippings wrapped in damp rags and newspaper. Then Emma offered to give her one, since Addie had been so friendly.

"Oh no. Thanks to you anyway," Addie said. "Land in Nalgitas is so poor it won't sprout peas."

Emma insisted and even offered to plant it for her.

Addie waved her hand. "I'm not much at tending things."

Emma put away the clipping and asked if the train stopped for supper, then.

"Where would we stop in the middle of Kansas?"

"Well, we have to eat something. I was so nervous about missing the train that I could not eat a morsel from the time I got out of bed this morning. I surely would like fried chicken and gravy or maybe a chop. And a slice of peach pie. Now that's eating."

"Go 'way! It makes me hungry just to hear you talk about it," said Addie. "You won't find any of that here. You'll have to make do with what you can buy, and you

29

can't be too particular about it. The food'll keep you from starving is about all I can say for it. I guess I could see what he's got." She straightened her dress and stood up, as Emma turned aside so that Addie could squeeze past her. "I feel the need for some air anyway."

Emma returned to her sewing, as Addie moved up the aisle, her silk skirt rustling. A man got up and followed her out of the car. He returned in a minute, his face red. After a while, Addie came back, giving the man a contemptuous glance as she passed him. She had made up her mind to act the lady for the rest of the trip and didn't welcome the advances of a traveling man. Addie handed Emma a pork sandwich wrapped in newspaper and a piece of gray cake, saying supper was her treat. The two women chewed silently until Emma gave up and wrapped the remains of her sandwich with the cake and put it under her seat.

"It's not much, is it?" Addie asked. "I'll tell you what I'd like is a nice bowl of chili."

"Chili?" Emma asked. "It's too hot for chili."

"Not San Antonio chili, not the chili they sell from the stands in the Plaza de Armas. There's nothing in the world that satisfies so good. If you'd ever had a bowl of that, you wouldn't say no."

Addie finished the sandwich and turned away from Emma to stare out the window at the sky, which was ruffled with pink and black and purple. The sky reminded her of San Antonio, too, the soft darkening evenings when the scents of coffee and chocolate, chili and sizzling fat filled the air. Addie had loved the peppery smell of the chili as she scooped the beans and meat and gravy into dishes and handed them to her customers. Some of the men refused to buy from any other vendor, giving their business only to her. Other chili queens worked there, too, selling tamales and enchiladas, tacos, menudo, and chili, but Addie was the favorite and best. Her customers stood shyly under the trees, smoking cornshuck cigarettes as they watched her work in the smoky lantern light, or sat on benches at plank tables, staring boldly at her as they ate. Sometimes they brushed their hands against her big breasts as they took the bowls or touched the ribbons in her hair. White men were rough with her, as though they were entitled to rub against her, but the others, the men whose skin was the dusky color of the night itself, had hands that were soft and gentle. Their touch made Addie's insides feel warm and liquid, like lard on a hot stove. They were generous, those brown and black men, handing her dimes and quarters and sometimes even bills and never asking for change.

She loved the life of a chili queen and considered herself fortunate that one of the vendors had employed her, since the girls were almost always Mexicans. She could have stayed there forever, but a gambler who saw how quick she was with her hands taught her card tricks and told her she could make as much in a day as a chili queen did in a month. She was ambitious, so she went with him. The two had worked the sleight-of-hand games together, until he'd left her for another woman. But he had taught her well, and she could make the pass, force a card, palm, ruffle, and slip the cards. She could make a card vanish from the table and be found in a man's pocket or under his handkerchief or hat. There was little she couldn't do with a deck of cards, until that night she was found out and beaten.

When she healed, she gave up card games and turned out, walking the streets by herself and picking up men. After her experience with the gambler who had clubbed her, she was a little scared of men, however, so she accepted the protection of a fancy man. But he was the worst man there was for taking her money, and when she held back, he threw her out, and she drifted through Texas and into New Mexico. She worked at houses then, because even though the madams took half her earnings, Addie felt safe. She liked Nalgitas right off because it was filled with miners and cowboys and railroad workers, few of them with wives, and they were generous. When the madam she worked for decided to move on, Addie bought the house. She'd run it for eight years.

That was too long, Addie thought, staring out into the darkness. It was time for her, too, to move on, maybe go back to San Antonio, perhaps even get married. She could buy a stand and hire girls to work for her, then expand into the other plazas. She'd serve first-rate chili, all beef, no pigeons or dogs or horse meat. Perhaps she'd even open a restaurant and become the queen of the chili queens. That was her dream, anyway, but it would take money. All of Addie's money was in The Chili Queen, and where was a buyer for a whorehouse in Nalgitas?

The train rounded a curve, and Addie made out a horse beside the tracks—a black horse. She shuddered as she leaned against the window and watched the animal fade into the darkness. She'd been uneasy around black horses ever since a chili queen in San Antonio had sworn to her that seeing a black horse meant death.

When Addie turned away from the window, Emma was still sewing, squinting in the dim glow from the kerosene lamps on the ceiling of the car. "You'll waste your eyes. You'll go blind as a mole," Addie told her.

Emma took a few more stitches then pulled the needle through the fabric and straightened the seam. She anchored the needle in her sewing and put it away in her bag. "Sewing calms me. I guess I've quilted a hundred miles of thread in my life and could quilt another mile or two before we reach Nalgitas."

"You don't look nervous," Addie told her. In fact, Emma was calmer than Addie. Her back was straight and her face serene. Addie curled up against the window, and when she awoke several hours later, Emma looked as if she hadn't moved. She sat bolt upright with her hands folded in her lap, as she stared out the window into the darkness. Addie reached over and patted her hand and muttered, "You might could sleep. I never saw a thing that was improved by worrying about it." Emma turned to her and nodded once, then looked out the window again. Addie didn't know if Emma followed her advice, because she was looking out at the countryside when Addie woke up in the morning. The train was at a standstill.

"Breakdown," Emma told her. "We've been here"—she opened the watch pinned to the jacket she had put back on to ward off the prairie cold and peered at it—"two hours and twenty-seven minutes."

"Oh, hell-damn!" Addie said, then glanced at Emma to see if she'd heard, but Emma was watching a workman walk down the track, swinging his lunch bucket.

"I wanted a bath and a good supper before I opened up tonight. If this train doesn't hurry, I won't have time for even a quick wash," Addie complained. She straightened up and smoothed the golden dress, rubbing a soot stain on her satin sleeve where it had brushed against the window. The stain turned blacker. "I should have worn black. Who cares if I look like a farmer?"

Emma chuckled. "There's something to be said for ugly," she replied, smoothing her own skirt.

"Oh, I didn't mean—"

"It's all right. I never paid much attention to clothes before. Perhaps I will now. Is there a dress store in Nalgitas?"

Addie snorted. "No dress store, no bonnet shop, just a general store with a shelf of calico, red mostly. I myself shop in Kansas City." Addie liked the way that came out. It made her sound cosmopolitan, and she repeated it. "I buy in Kansas City. They got nice stores."

Emma stretched her arms then stood up and said it was her turn to forage for food. As Emma walked down the aisle, Addie took in the woman's slim waist and hips, wishing she herself weren't spread out in back like a cold supper. Emma returned in a few minutes with two apples and a handful of walnuts.

Addie hadn't seen them at the train butcher's the night before and asked where Emma had acquired them.

"Off a track worker. They were in his dinner pail. He wouldn't sell his sandwiches or the pie but said he'd take a dollar for the rest. They'll have to last us to Nalgitas, I guess, since the train butcher's out of food," Emma said.

She took the scissors from her bag and gave one of the walnuts such a sharp crack with the handle that Addie's head jerked back. The nutmeat inside was withered. "Well, damn!" Emma said.

Addie smiled at the swear word, but Emma didn't notice because at that moment the train jerked, then jerked again and began to creep down the tracks. Addie ate her apple, then fell asleep again against the window. She slept most of the day until, in the late afternoon, Emma nudged her to say the train was approaching Nalgitas—six hours late.

Addie squirmed, then stretched, letting her arms hang in midair when she saw Emma. The woman sat rigidly in the buttoned-up black suit. The brooch was pinned to the neck of her shirtwaist, the watch secured to the jacket. She looked just as she had when Addie first saw her—except for the pink hat on top of her head. Addie stared as she slowly lowered her arms.

Emma's face turned the color of the hat. "Do I look too bold?" Emma asked.

"Oh, no." Foolish, addle-brained, Addie thought, but not bold.

"I'm a plain woman, as plain as homemade soap. I wanted to make a good first impression."

"It's a nice touch," Addie told her. She was too good-hearted to tell the woman how silly she looked. Instead, Addie retied the bonnet strings so the bow was on the side of Emma's face, not under her chin. And she adjusted the hat to sit on the back of Emma's head.

By the time Addie was finished, the train was slowing. Addie tried to see the town through Emma's eyes. It was mud brown, dusty—the streets, the storefronts, the houses. Even the cottonwoods seemed dirty, their leaves listless in the still air. The two blocks of false-front buildings that made up the main street needed paint. Several structures were boarded up, a few ready to fall down. Spread out from the street were blocks of squat houses, many of them made of adobe bricks and plastered with dirt. Addie found them homey, but she thought Emma would not be impressed. She'd prefer the frame houses with curlicues of sawn lumber for trim, although they were shabby, their paint peeling from the sand that blew against them. Addie looked for The Chili Queen and felt such a touch of pride when she spotted it, off by itself, close to the railroad station, that she pointed it out to Emma. But Emma was distracted, scanning the faces in the depot, as the train slid to a stop.

"You see him?" Addie asked.

Emma shook her head. "All I have is the picture. But he'll recognize me. My photograph is a better likeness than his."

"Maybe that one." Addie pointed to a man who stood off on one side. "Kind of short, isn't he? Is your gentleman short?"

Emma looked startled. "I don't know."

Addie rolled her eyes, and Emma blushed. "I guess you'll find out soon enough," Addie said.

She stood up, but Emma touched her arm and nodded at a man leaning against the depot. "Do you think he's Mr. Withers?"

Addie squinted at the big man who stood with one foot braced against the wall. "Not likely. That's Charley Pea.

He's the blacksmith. He's got him a wife. I know it for a fact. Mayme's her name." Charley had taken a trip to Texas the year before and had returned with a bride, who'd put on airs, pretending to be a lady. But Addie had told it around town that Mayme was a whore from Ft. Worth, a hussy so depraved she'd been thrown out of the whorehouse where Addie'd worked—for corrupting the other girls. Mayme had picked a fight with her once and had broken Addie's nose and pulled out a chunk of Addie's hair. Although the fight wasn't Addie's fault, she'd been docked by the madam. So Addie had been all too happy to expose Mayme, although Addie had paid for it. Now she had to take her horses twenty miles away to be shoed. The blacksmith still fairly hated her. In fact, when Addie passed him on the street not long before she went to Kansas City, he had spit tobacco juice on her skirt. And he was the one who'd thrown two kittens down her well. Addie was sure of it.

Addie and Emma made their way down the aisle and onto the platform, which was crowded with men dressed mostly in rough clothes. Ranchers and miners stood beside the freight cars, waiting for shipments. Mexicans silently moved around them as they unloaded barrels and boxes. Men and a few women milled about the tracks waiting for passengers or just watching the train to see who got off. Addie knew some of them, but it wasn't wise to greet customers in public, so she merely looked them over, raised an eyebrow at one, smiled at another. She touched Emma's elbow and pointed her head at a neatly dressed man holding a hat in his hand and smiling in their direction. But just then, a woman made her way past them and joined him.

Emma's eyes darted about, and she seemed to lose her composure. "He's not here," she whispered.

"Oh, you don't know that. Maybe he's inside, waiting for folks to leave. He might be shy," Addie replied. "Or he went to the saloon for his dinner. Train's awful late, you know. Now, you go sit on the bench in the shade and wait for him. He'll be along directly." If Emma was sitting in the shadows of the depot, the man might not see right off how old she was.

"Will you wait with me?" Emma asked.

Addie was tempted, since she was curious to see this Mr. Withers. But she didn't fancy having the man recognize her and explain to Emma that she'd been keeping company all night and day with a whore. That wouldn't bother Addie so much, but she didn't see any reason to turn the woman into an enemy. And if Mr. Withers were as upright as Emma believed, he wasn't likely to approach Emma with Addie sitting beside her. Besides, it was late—and a Saturday night, Addie realized with a start. She had to find out what had gone on at The Chili Queen since she'd left. She wanted a tub and her supper before customers arrived. So she shook her head. She tipped the stationmaster to store her trunk until one of the Mexicans could deliver it to The Chili Queen, then picked up her valise. "Luck to you," she told Emma.

Emma was too distracted to reply. Addie squeezed her arm. Then she started down the road to The Chili Queen. When she looked back, Emma was sitting on the bench beside the depot, the pink hat in her lap. Except for Charley Pea, who was still watching the train, she was alone. There but for the grace of God, Addie thought.

TWO

W here you been? I darn tired of looking at whores," Welcome said by way of greeting as Addie came through the kitchen door. "You was supposed to come home two days ago. I skillet the ham and pan the biscuits when I heard the train whistle blow that day, but you didn't come, so I ate them myself. I thought maybe you got kilt." The big woman grinned as she used one hand to lift a huge cast-iron wash pot and set it on top of the stove. Addie couldn't have hefted the pot with both arms. The servant woman was strong enough to play marbles with a cannonball.

"You certainly don't live up to your name, do you?" Addie asked.

"I hired on to cook and wash, and I work early and quit late. But I never agreed to tend three whores," Welcome said. "Two now. Miss Broken-Nose Frankie ain't here."

"What?" Addie dropped her things on the floor and slumped into a chair.

"Miss Broken-Nose run off. That leaves Miss Belle Bassett and Miss Tillie Jumps. They're upstairs sleeping. Might be they're fixing to leave, too, and you'd have a whorehouse with no whores." She laughed. "Ain't been nobody come around looking for work, neither."

That didn't surprise Addie. In the past year, Nalgitas had slumped, and bad times didn't bring hookers looking for work. She sighed. It was Saturday night, and if business were decent, she would have to pitch in. Her bones ached too much. "Any other good news you got for me?"

"The window's broke out in your bedroom. Don't ask me who done it. I'm not allowed to sleep in the house." There were three rooms for girls upstairs. Addie's room was off the kitchen, which was connected by a hallway to a large parlor. Welcome had a shack out back, a converted chicken house.

"You can take Miss Frankie's room if you'll help out. You know what I mean. There's more than one man that's asked about you. Most places don't charge the same for dark meat as white, but that doesn't go with me. I always did like a Negro man as much as a white one. I guess that goes for a woman, too. You can keep half, just like the other girls." Addie didn't know if the men who'd inquired about Welcome wanted her because she was a Negro or because she was a big, bold woman. They might not even know Welcome was a Negro, because her skin was the pale brown of dried prairie grass.

"I'm not much more Negro than you are," Welcome said. "But no matter. This old flesh and bones is a Christian woman, and I won't share my tender parts for pieces of silver."

Addie wondered why her employees always talked back to her. The servants were brash, the girls uppity. She sighed. "Well, fix my supper then and heat up water for a bath. I expect you could smell me coming from the station."

"Yes, ma'am. I could."

Welcome built up the fire in the cookstove, then she pumped water and poured it into a kettle. She set a place for Addie at the kitchen table, and went to the icebox, peering inside. "We had purty plenty to eat two days ago when you was supposed to be here. Now we got just leavings," she said. "I guess you'll be wanting your bath first." Welcome went outside and fetched the little tin tub from the back porch, and by the time she hauled it into Addie's bedroom, Addie had taken off the silk dress and thrown it onto the bedroom floor. She was wearing only a wrapper.

Welcome picked up the pile of yellow satin and held it out at arm's length, wrinkling her nose. "It looks ruint, but I'll see if it'll clean up." She tucked the dress under her arm. "The money from the customers is in your bottom drawer. I was going to hide it away in your Bible because them girls weren't likely to look there to steal it, but I could not find your Bible."

"Most likely I took it with me."

"Most likely." Welcome snorted. "You got more than one hundred dollars. That's after I took out for going to market. And I paid myself ten dollars extra for running things while you was away. Those whores wore me out good." She left the room, calling over her shoulder, "I'll fetch you a glass of whiskey before I heat up the hot water."

Addie sighed and rubbed her face. Then she examined her fingers. The nails were broken and the cuticles raw. But that didn't bother her as much as the backs of her hands. There were half a dozen brown spots on each one, and the veins stuck out like meandering streambeds. She was fortunate customers didn't pay much attention to hands.

Welcome returned with the liquor, and Addie took a long sip. It was the first good thing that had happened to her since Kansas City. With a bath and supper, she might make it through the evening. As she set down the glass, she heard a sharp ring of the front doorbell and sighed. It looked as if the fooling around would commence early that night. "You get it," she told Welcome. "Tell him we don't open till nine. If he's here at nine sharp, he can have his pick of the girls. Don't tell him we got only two." She glanced at the clock on her bureau and was surprised to discover it was nearly eight. "And get those girls up and bring me my bathwater."

"You want me to black the stove and fix a turkey dinner while I'm at it?" Welcome asked, as she shut Addie's door and went to the front of the house.

Addie finished the whiskey and was about to get the hot water herself when Welcome banged the door open.

"Is he coming back?" Addie asked.

"He's a she. Somebody asking for you."

Addie brightened. Perhaps life was looking up. "A girl? She could start tonight, and then I wouldn't have to help out. Is she a looker?"

"She's no likely-looking girl for you. If you ask my opinion, this one's hustling for the mite society."

Something pricked at the back of Addie's mind, and she rubbed her hands over her face. "What's she look like?"

"I said it once, and I say it again: Not like no whore."

"Does she have on black?" Addie paused. "And a pink hat the color of my backside?"

"Only smaller," Welcome replied.

"Katy, bar the door!" Addie shook her head back and forth. "I don't guess you sent her away."

Welcome shrugged. "You said you was looking for a

girl. You didn't say you wanted a comely one. She's setting in the parlor, just like a biddy hen."

"Well, get her out of there. Put her in the kitchen. Tell her I'll see her as soon as I get some clothes on." Addie stood up and stripped off the wrapper, amused that Welcome averted her eyes. "And watch your tongue. Don't tell her what kind of a place this is. She's a maiden lady that thinks The Chili Queen is a boardinghouse." Addie chuckled.

After Addie had wrapped her tired body in a house dress and brushed out her hair, pinning it sloppily on top of her head, she went into the kitchen, where she found Emma seated at the table, in the place Welcome had set for Addie. Emma had finished the piece of cold fried chicken and was wiping her mouth with a napkin. Addie wondered where the napkin had come from. Welcome never put out napkins for the residents of The Chili Queen.

Emma turned to Addie. The dirt on the woman's face was tear-streaked, and her hair was snarly. The pink hat sat on a chair, the bonnet strings wadded up. "I didn't know where else to go," she said, a catch in her voice. "I mean, I don't know anybody else in Nalgitas, and you were so kind on the train. I hope you don't mind. After all, you said I could come here."

Maybe so, but she hadn't meant it. In fact, Addie minded considerably more than Emma could guess. The woman was just one more problem she'd have to deal with before she could open The Chili Queen. Still, Addie's heart went out to Emma. Addie was nosey, too. She patted Emma's black-gloved hand and said, "Well, dearie, let's have it. Tell me your story." She stopped when Welcome came to the table with a piece of pie and a glass of milk. Addie pulled her chair up to the table, but the servant ignored her and set the plate and glass in front of Emma, who picked up her fork. Heartbreak didn't seem to affect the woman's appetite.

"You can bring me my dinner now, Welcome," Addie said curtly.

"I gave her the leavings from the girls, and that's all there is. She got the last of the hereafter, too." *Hereafter* was what Welcome called dessert.

"What about me?" Addie almost wailed.

Emma had started on the pie, but she put down her fork and shoved the plate toward Addie. "Oh, I'm so sorry. I thought since this was a boardinghouse, you had eaten, and I was having the leftovers. I wouldn't want to rob you."

Addie sent Welcome a stern look that she hoped would tell the hired woman to keep her mouth shut. She only fluttered her hand at Emma. "Go on. You eat it. Welcome will fry me up some side meat and eggs."

Welcome seemed in no hurry and regarded Addie for a long time. "Yes, ma'am." She didn't move.

"Now."

"Uh-huh."

When Welcome turned to the stove, Addie asked again, "What happened?" As she leaned forward, she brushed her sore breast against the edge of the table and sucked in her breath. When she'd undressed, she'd noticed the bruise, now an ugly purple, that the train conductor had inflicted. She thought about asking Welcome for ice, but she guessed Emma might go distracted if Addie bared her breast, right there at the kitchen table. Besides, it was too late to do any good. So she ignored the throbbing. "Did he turn you down?" Addie realized that was the wrong thing to say, and she added quickly, "Or maybe you didn't like him. Is that it? Tell me everything."

Emma shook her head and began to sniff.

Addie hated whimpering, unless she was the whimperer. "Well, what was it?"

Welcome butted in. "You look like a plague of misery. You tell Miss Addie every and all the incidents."

"What's this got to do with you?" Addie asked, angry that Welcome seemed to be taking charge. "You work for me, remember?"

"I quit. You want me to quit? Almost am I ready to leave." Welcome reached behind her back to untie her apron strings.

"Just fix me my supper."

Welcome patted Emma's shoulder and turned to the stove.

"Oh, dear, I've come between you and your hired girl," Emma said.

Addie waved away the apology. "Tell me what he said," she ordered.

Emma took a deep breath and let it out. She searched her bag, finding a handkerchief, which she held to her nose. To Addie's relief, Emma didn't cry. Instead she sneezed. She put away the handkerchief and sighed again. Then she said quickly, "He wasn't there." The admission wore her out, and she sank back into the chair as if done with the story.

But for Addie, that was only the beginning. For all the inconvenience she'd gone through for Emma, Addie was owed a good story. She reached for Emma's hand and held it between her own. "I told you he was having his supper, or he could have got drunk and passed out. Maybe his horse bucked him off, and he had to walk to town." She was warming up. "He could have got washed away in a flood and killed."

"It ain't rained since you left," Welcome said from the stove. She cracked an egg on the side of the frying pan. It sounded like a shot.

"Well then, he might have been run over by a freight wagon or killed by outlaws—" She stopped because Emma was shaking her head back and forth.

"No. None of that," Emma said. "He was there at the depot, all right. I didn't see him, but he saw me. He left a letter. It wasn't more than a few minutes ago that I thought to inquire for a message. And there was his dispatch, lying there." Emma reached into her bag and took out a sheet of cheap paper that was folded in half, then folded again. *Miss Roby* was written on the outside. Emma straightened the paper, and set it on the table.

Addie snatched it up and began to read the pencil script to herself, nodding her head at each word as she sounded it out. Then she glanced up at Welcome, who was paying no attention to the skillet. "All right, you can hear it," Addie told Welcome, and as Emma cringed, Addie read the salutation: *"Dear Emma Roby."*

Addie smoothed the paper on the table and pointed to each word as she pronounced it.

"You are older than your picture, and I believe you are

not a suitable match for a man such as myself." Addie read each word distinctly, and when she got to the end of the sentence, she looked up at Emma, but Emma was staring stoically at the stove. *"I did not bargain for an old maid. I am not cruel but am a coward, so I will leave this with the station man. It is better if you go on back home and forget about*
"Your faithful servant,
"W.W."

Welcome set down a plate of fried eggs and fatty meat in front of Addie, raising an eyebrow. "She's a mail-order bride," Addie explained.

"No such a thing!" Emma said indignantly.

Addie shrugged. "She's not a mail-order bride. She just came out here looking for somebody she never met to pick her off the platform at the depot and marry her."

Welcome went to the cupboard and came back to the table with a fork, which she handed to Addie. The black woman had big hands. And her feet in their brass-toed brogans were big, too. Once, when a man had gotten rough at The Chili Queen, Addie had called Welcome, who came to the room, holding a frying pan in one hand, slapping it against the palm of the other. The man bolted before Welcome had a chance to use it. Addie wondered how many other men Welcome had taken on. Maybe she'd chunked around her husband when he went after her. The servant had told her she'd been married, but "we abided poorly, so I let him go. He whipped me for any misdemeanor dislikeable. I guess he's in hell now, if the devil can stand him." Addie had been a little afraid to ask Welcome if she had dispatched him there.

"I was to meet a gentleman here to get married. We had corresponded," Emma explained to Welcome.

"For no reason you should be sorry you missed out on such a devil on earth," Welcome said.

Addie was surprised at the outburst and waved her away. "It's not your business. Don't you have chickens to kill?"

"It's too dark to kill chickens," Welcome said. She withdrew into the shadows of the kitchen but didn't leave. Well, Addie thought, if Emma didn't mind Welcome listening in, why should she?

"I didn't have any place to go. I thought I could stay here. You said I could," Emma repeated.

"Ha!" said Welcome. Addie turned to her, but all she could see in the dark corner was Welcome's white apron.

"You do take women, don't you? Your card says, 'Men taken in,' but I hoped . . ." She left the sentence hanging in the air as a question.

"There isn't room," Addie said. "We're full up."

"Let her taken Miss Frankie's room, but she can't call me 'nigger.' Miss Frankie did, and I told her 'git.' "

"That's my business to put her out," Addie protested.

Welcome chuckled in the darkness. "You take Miss Frankie's room, Miss Addie, and give up yourn to the lady. Since it's off the kitchen, she won't be bothered by any goings-on."

"Who are you working for?" Addie asked her.

"Put her upstairs, then," Welcome suggested.

"It's just for tonight. I'll look for a housekeeping room in the morning," Emma said. "But if you have a vacancy, I'd be pleased to be your roomer."

"You're staying on?" Addie asked.

"What else can I do?" Emma shrugged. "You heard my brother. I can't go back home. And I wouldn't if I could. I thought . . ." She paused and looked down at her hands, embarrassed. "I thought maybe I could set up a hat shop. I think I have a talent for trimming hats."

Addie gave her an astonished look and was about to reply when the bell on the front door rang. Welcome came forward, and she and Addie exchanged glances. "You got you a caller," Welcome said.

"I can hear that."

"If you have company, I can go on upstairs." Emma stood up and reached for her hat. "If you would just tell me which room."

"You want me to show her?" Welcome asked. She appeared to be enjoying herself.

"I could go back to the depot. There's a bench there that I could sleep on. I don't want to intrude," Emma added.

"No," Addie said quickly. "You let me get my things, and you can stay in my room. I'll go upstairs."

Emma yawned. "I'm so grateful. I'm awful confused and so tired I could sleep until the roll's called up yonder."

"You do that," Addie said.

"That's a real nice thing you done," Welcome told Addie, who was surprised at how she was warmed by the compliment.

Welcome picked up Emma's valise and took it into the bedroom, Addie following behind. "Get the door and show him into the parlor. I'll take my clothes upstairs. And make sure those lazy girls are ready. You tell them I'm home, and I don't tolerate slackers," Addie told Wel-

49

come. She glanced at Emma to see if it had dawned on her what she was talking about, but the woman had sat down on the bed and leaned her head against the bedpost. She was almost asleep. Addie sighed, wondering why things never seemed to work out quite right for her. The Chili Queen was hers, paid for by her hard work. But she was headed upstairs to a hooker's room while Emma was about to go to sleep in her bed. Addie'd always thought of herself as kindhearted. Now she wondered if she were just an easy mark.

Business was good at The Chili Queen that night, so good, in fact, that Addie herself had taken care of three customers. When the last one left, she locked the front door and sent the girls upstairs to bed. In the kitchen, she found Welcome still awake, scrubbing out the little bathtub. "You was working, so I give her the bath," Welcome said. "You want one?"

But Addie was too tired to wait for Welcome to heat fresh water. She started toward her room.

"Uh-uh. Where you going?" Welcome asked. " 'Member, you got a lady in there. You're sleeping in Miss Frankie's room." She pointed to the ceiling and laughed out loud.

Addie turned around and made her way to the stairs. Broken-Nose Frankie's room was the smallest in the house, but it didn't matter where she slept, Addie supposed, as she threw her clothes onto the floor. Like Emma, she could sleep until judgment day. Addie climbed into bed and sank down, nearly to the floor, it seemed. In the morning, she'd ask Welcome to help her tighten the bed cords. She shifted around on the cornshuck tick to get comfortable. The tick crackled and scratched, and Addie wished she had her own feather mattress under her. But she found a comfortable spot and closed her eyes. Then she sniffed. The odor from the sheets made her gag. It wasn't just the smell from the night's activity, either. Miss Frankie had been none too clean, and the sheets hadn't been washed since she left. Maybe they hadn't been washed in all the time Miss Frankie had worked there. And the room was close. Addie got up and opened the window as wide as it would go, which was only a few inches. Parlor house madams, even those whose establishments were as fine as The Chili Queen, nailed strips of wood to the window tracks in the boarders' rooms to keep men from climbing in and the girls from sneaking out.

Addie got back into bed, but something hard in the mattress poked her, and she moved around like a nesting bird to find a satisfactory place. She was nearly asleep when a horsefly buzzed about her head. Addie swatted the fly, and it flew off, but in a minute, it was back. In the moonlight that filled the room, Addie saw it land on the iron bedstead, and she smashed it. Then she picked it up by a wing, got out of bed, and flung it out the window, stopping to watch as Welcome walked from the back door of The Chili Queen to the shack where she slept. She was an odd one, but Addie was too tired to think about Welcome. She glanced at her hand and saw that the fly's wing was stuck to the palm, so she went to the washstand and poured water into the bowl, rinsing off her hands. The towel was gone, and Addie dried her hands on the sheet.

The bed was hot, so Addie took off her nightdress and

lay down on top of the sheet, banging the pillow to fluff it up. She hoped Emma had had just as much trouble falling asleep, but she doubted it. Addie felt a bite on her leg and hoped Miss Frankie hadn't left behind bedbugs. She spread her nightgown over the top of the bed and lay down again. There was yelling and a gunshot from the direction of the saloons. Then a horse galloped past The Chili Queen. Those were comforting sounds, and lulled by them, Addie at last fell asleep.

She did not know how long she'd slept, but the sky was light when a woman's scream made her jump out of bed. Probably, one of the girls had had a bad dream, most likely Miss Tillie, who had been in a sour mood all evening and so unpleasant with a cowboy from Raton that Addie had returned Miss Tillie's half of his money. Addie settled back in the bed. But the woman screamed again, and Addie sat bolt upright, as she realized the sound wasn't from one of the girls. It had come from downstairs: The mail-order bride was the one having a nightmare. There was nothing Addie could do about it, and she settled back in bed. But the woman screamed a third time, making so much noise that Addie knew she'd have to shut her up or she'd awaken the whores, and they would go downstairs, and Addie was too tired to explain to Emma what a pair of hookers was doing in a boardinghouse. So she got out of bed again, wrapped the soiled robe about herself, and barefoot, she made her way down the dark stairs, stepping on something wet. She prayed it was water but didn't think so.

As she reached the kitchen, Addie heard a key in the back door, and she picked up the poker from the stove in case of an intruder. But it was Welcome who came through the door, muttering, "That noise pesters me. It's louder than a skeleton dancing on a tin roof. Is it Miss Tillie again?"

Addie was glad Welcome had come. If Emma had the hysterics, it might take two of them to calm her down. Addie jerked her head toward the bedroom door. "No, it's that damned old maid, probably dreaming about her wedding night—which is as close to it as she's going to get."

But just then, they heard a swack and a man cried, "Ouch!"

Addie swore softly, starting toward the room. But Welcome got to the door first, opened it, and rushed in ahead of Addie. Emma, clutching a hairbrush, was standing over a man, who had his hands to his head. "Addie, by zam, it's me," he said.

Welcome gave a deep, throaty chuckle. Then Addie, too, began to laugh. Emma raised her arm to strike again. "He came through the window. I believe he is a masher."

Addie grabbed the hairbrush from her. "Naw, he's no masher. He's Ned."

"Who?" Emma asked, looking around for a second weapon. The man on the floor had lifted his head and was staring from one woman to another.

"He's Ned. Ned Partner is who he is," Addie said.

A look of terror crossed Emma's face as she recognized the name. "The outlaw?" she asked, drawing back against the bed, her hands crossed over her chest.

"Oh, Ned won't hurt you. He comes here all the time. He's my—" Addie stopped, suddenly shy in front of Emma. She tightened the belt of the wrapper and pulled the lapels over her chest. "He's my brother." She couldn't say why she'd become self-respecting all of a sudden.

"What?" asked Ned, as he got to his knees. "What the hell are you talking about?"

"Oh, she won't tell anybody about you. This here is a maiden lady I met on the train. She doesn't know anybody in Nalgitas. I gave her my room," Addie explained, then added, "just for tonight."

Ned got to his feet, gently touching the spot on his head where Emma had hit him, then checked his fingers for blood. There wasn't any. "You picked a maiden lady with a good arm," he said. "You got any ice for this goose egg?" he asked Welcome.

"Any gentleman would have come in at the door, but I guess you ain't one of them. Now come along," Welcome told him, and the two went into the kitchen, followed by Addie and Emma, who had slipped a robe over her night-dress. Addie wondered, with the heat, how Emma could sleep in a long-sleeved bedgown that was buttoned up to her neck, especially with all that hair hanging down her back. Emma's hair might have gray streaks, but it was long and thick and curled prettily around her face. Addie twisted her own scraggly hair into a knot at the back of her neck.

Welcome used a pick to chip off a piece of ice, then wrapped it in a towel and placed it on Ned's head. "You hold that," she told him. "I'd be guessing you'll want eat-ments."

"I guess," Ned said.

Welcome stirred up the fire in the cookstove, then picked kindling from the box and fed it into the coals. She sliced bacon into the skillet and mixed up batter for hot-cakes. "You want I should fix your breakfast, too?" she asked Addie.

Addie had had too much whiskey the night before, which had caused a hurting in her head, and the idea of food made her stomach churn. She shook her head. Welcome turned to Emma, who replied, "I would, if it's not too much bother. I could help."

Welcome shook her head, and Emma sat down at the kitchen table as far from Ned as possible, staring at him.

He stared back, amusement in his eyes. Ned's eyes always laughed, even when he was angry, Addie thought. Ned was the best-tempered man she'd ever known—and the handsomest. He was just under six feet tall and muscular, and he had green eyes and curly brown hair that turned a little red in the sun. Women could just hardly keep away from him. Still, with all that temptation, Ned was loyal. He was loyal to a hooker, and that made Addie feel good.

"You have the advantage over me," Ned said to Emma. "You know my name, but I don't know yours."

"Oh, she's Emma Roby, and she's a mail-order bride from Kansas, only her intended thought she was too old and left her at the station," Addie said. Emma bit her lip, and Addie felt ashamed of herself. It wasn't necessary to be so cruel. "If you ask me, she's better off," she added lamely.

"So you're going back home?" Ned asked.

"She can't. Her brother won't take her back."

"You got a tongue, or just a right arm?" Ned asked Emma.

The corners of Emma's mouth turned up a little, and her eyes, almost the color of forget-me-nots, got bigger. She seemed less frightened when she glanced at Addie, who nodded for her to answer. "I thought I'd stay here a few days, with Addie, with your sister," she muttered.

"My what?" Ned asked.

"Your sister," Welcome said. The sound of batter poured into the hot skillet didn't quite drown out her chuckle. She browned sugar in a saucepan and added water.

Addie wondered why Welcome went to the bother of making syrup, since she'd always set a can of molasses on the table for Addie and her girls and for Ned, too. Then Addie realized Welcome was putting on airs. Most likely, she had worked for gentry once. Addie didn't know, because in the business she was in, you didn't inquire into a person's background. For sure, Welcome thought Emma was more refined than a house full of whores, and Addie was offended. "We don't need napkins."

Welcome didn't reply. She flipped over the hotcakes and put them on a plate, pouring syrup over them. Then she set down the plate in front of Emma.

"I expect that's Ned's plate," Addie said.

"Ladies first," Welcome told her.

"Then it'll be for me." Addie hoped she'd made it clear that this was her house, and she came first. She wasn't sure she had.

Emma smiled and pushed the plate toward Addie, but the smell of food gagged her, and she felt foolish, remembering she had told Welcome she didn't want breakfast. "No, you take it," Addie said. The plate sat between the two of them until Ned put down the ice and reached for it and began to eat.

Welcome set down another plate before Emma, then brought coffee. She picked up Ned's empty plate and stacked half a dozen flapjacks on it and handed it back to him. While Ned and Emma ate, Welcome leaned against the kitchen wall, watching Emma, who took tiny bites and chewed delicately. When she finished, she put the fork upside down, the tines in the center of the plate.

"When do the other boarders eat?" Emma asked as Welcome removed her plate.

Welcome shrugged. "They sleep till noon. Sleep after noon, too. Sleep all the time except when they're working."

"That's very accommodating of you. If I ran a boarding-house, I would insist people ate at regular hours."

Ned laughed and looked up at Addie. "I know you got boarders, but I never knew you to call The Chili Queen a boardinghouse."

Addie mouthed the word "no" at him.

Emma looked confused. "It's a boardinghouse. The Chili Queen takes in boarders. What else would you call it?"

"A hookhouse," Ned said with a grin.

"A what?" Startled, Emma looked at Addie, then back at Ned.

Addie shook her head at Ned, but he ignored her. "Honey, you must know what this place is," he told Emma, as he moved his empty plate aside. He folded his arms on the oilcloth that covered the table.

"Ned!" Addie said, but Ned ignored her. Maybe he was getting even for the knot on his head.

"Ma'am, you just spent the night in a whorehouse and no mistake," he told Emma.

"Addie here's the head—" Ned stopped at last when he saw Addie glaring at him and finished, "She's the madam is what she is."

Emma didn't move a muscle, but the blood drained from her face until Addie wondered if the woman might faint dead away. Being left at the railroad station would be nothing to her compared to spending a night in Nalgitas's only whorehouse. Addie glanced at Ned, who seemed pleased with himself. He put the tip of his finger into a drop of syrup on the oilcloth, then licked the finger. Emma continued to stare at him, then slowly she turned to Addie, who quickly glanced away. Emma looked at Welcome then. The big black woman folded her arms across her chest and grinned. "I guess you are bad mortified," she said.

Emma blew out a breath. "I am. I am mortified, indeed," she said. "What will people think of me?"

"What do you expect they think of you anyway, coming here like you did to marry a man in a picture?" Addie asked, offended.

Emma's lip trembled. "You should have told me. Yes, you should have."

"You expect me to stand up in the train and announce what I do and maybe get thrown off? You chose to sit next to me. I didn't ask you. I didn't invite you to The Chili Queen, either. You did that yourself. I fed and homed you. You had my bath, and you were so busy feeling sorry for yourself that you never once said thanks to you." Addie was feeling plenty sorry for herself, too, and she leaned forward to say more, clutching the robe that gaped open.

But Emma broke in. "No, I did not, and I say it now. Thanks to you for the hospitality. If there is fault to be found it is with me."

"Oh," Addie said, a little deflated.

"And I'm sorry about the bath. I didn't know. I intend to pay you board and room. I do."

"Oh, that's all right. I wouldn't know what to charge."

"Hell, Addie, it's not like you didn't ever charge anybody before," Ned put in.

"*You* never paid," Addie shot back, then added, "I never charged a *woman*. And I never charged for *supper*."

"I shall certainly find a room elsewhere," Emma said.

"There ain't hardly nobody in Nalgitas that'll take in such as you," Welcome told her, "only bad women would."

Emma shivered a little. "Then I shall find a little store and live there. I am thinking of setting up a millinery shop. Miss French says there is none in Nalgitas."

"A what?" Welcome asked.

"A hat shop. I fancy I am rather good at making hats." She looked down modestly.

Welcome snorted and went to the stove, stirring up the fire. "Well, if you made that hat you brung with you, you won't find nobody here to buy it. Even Miss Addie's whores wouldn't wear one of those. Ain't that a fact, Miss Addie?"

Now Welcome was the one being cruel, although Addie agreed that someone had to disabuse Emma of the idea of a hat shop. "Mind your business," Addie retorted, but Welcome only laughed and asked Addie if she wanted some fried-up eggs.

Addie ignored her and stared at Emma, wondering what to do with her. It was a dilemma, because there was only one thing Addie knew to do with women. In the morning light, Emma wasn't so bad. At the moment, Addie supposed, Emma looked better than she did. Emma appeared younger than the day before, and from what Addie could tell, Emma's body was firm, even if it was scrawny. But although Addie was short one whore, she didn't believe Emma was much of a prospect. She'd surely be insulted at the offer, although it paid considerably better than anything else in Nalgitas, certainly more than making hats. As Addie stared at Emma, the woman looked up at her and smiled. Then she began to chuckle.

"What?" Addie asked.

"I was just thinking how John would respond to this. What would he do if he knew I'd spent my first night in Nalgitas inside a . . . a . . ."

"A hookhouse," Ned said.

"Yes."

"Who's John?" he asked.

"My brother. He has a farm in Kansas. He's the reason I can't go back. She knows." Emma dipped her head at Addie.

"Yeah." Addie didn't elaborate. She leaned back in the wooden chair and rubbed her eyes. She was tired enough to sleep sitting up.

"What am I going to do, Miss French?"

Addie slowly focused on Emma, wondering why the problem had been turned over to her to solve. "I'll sleep on it," Addie said.

Ned yawned, then stood up and stretched. "I'm going to bed, too."

He started for Addie's bedroom, but Welcome gave a warning, "Uh-uh." When Ned stopped, Welcome asked Addie, "You want your brother to sleep in the barn?"

Addie looked confused for a moment, then said, "Oh, yeah." She looked at Emma. "My brother always sleeps in the barn. He came through my bedroom window because the back door was locked."

"Aw, come on, Addie. She knows who you are. She knows who I am, too," Ned protested.

Addie stood up and drew the wrapper around herself, sashing it so tightly that she looked like a mattress-worth of feathers stuffed into a pillow tick. "The barn," she said stubbornly.

She didn't care if she annoyed Ned, but she hadn't. He rarely got angry. He grinned at Addie and gave a mock bow. Then he turned to Emma and touched the sore spot on the top of his head. "Ma'am," he said. "Good night to yourself and to my sister—my older sister." He went outside, the screen door banging behind him, and called over his shoulder, "My *much* older sister."

Addie went back to Miss Frankie's room and fell asleep. When she got up, it was dinnertime, and she went into the kitchen, where Welcome was working at the stove. "The girls are fed and gone to town. *She's* out back taking wash off the clothesline. A man brung your trunk from the station, and I unpacked it, and she washed up your things, the sheets on your bed, too. Maybe she expects to stay. She earns her keep."

"Doing your work, you mean," Addie said.

Welcome ignored the remark. "I got the kettle on. You smell like chickens. Tub's in there." Welcome nodded at Addie's old bedroom.

Addie had enough dirt on her to grow beans. She went into the bedroom and stripped off her robe, then got into the tin tub and scrubbed herself until there was a thick scum on the water. Addie toweled herself and put on a clean gown and told Welcome she was going into town and would be back by suppertime. When she returned, Ned and Emma were sitting at the table, drinking coffee, waiting for her.

"I told them I wasn't dishing up till you come back," Welcome said.

Addie blinked at the hired woman's sudden deference. "Oh," she said, waving her hand graciously. "Well, you can see I am here." She sat down at the head of the table.

"Miss French—" Emma began, but Addie stopped her.

"Addie'll do. You call me Addie. I'll call you Emma. We'll both call him Ned."

Ned smiled at her, and Addie felt warm to her bones. "We've been talking about what she ought to do," Ned explained. "She told me all about her brother and why she can't go home. She even told me about the family money that's hers by rights. But I guess she can't do anything about that. There isn't any school in Nalgitas where she can teach, and you already got a cook. Hell, I don't know what to tell her. I haven't worked a real job myself since I left Iowa." He turned to Emma. "That was twenty-and-one years ago, during the war. My father was a devil for work. He cuffed me every day for no good reason." He glanced at Addie and winked. "Our pa, I guess I should say."

"I guess," Addie said.

"You've been an outlaw since then?" Emma asked, her eyes wide.

"Well, I just rightly never held a job, except now and then," he said. There was a touch of pride in his voice. "I didn't have to. I've had a rambling time."

Addie gave him a warning look, but Ned said, "Oh, that's all right, Addie. You told her yourself that I work the other side of the law." He explained to Emma, "There's not much law in Nalgitas. Seems like half the people in town have a price on them. The only folks who think they're quality are the blacksmith and his wife." He winked at Addie.

"Emma here could make herself two hundred dollars turning you over to a U.S. marshall," Addie warned him.

"Oh, she wouldn't do that." Ned turned his sleepy grin on her, and Emma smiled back a little uncertainly. Addie felt a tiny shock of jealousy. "Besides, anybody who turned on me wouldn't have long to spend the money," he added. He continued to grin, but Addie knew he spoke the truth. Emma studied Ned for a long time, then exchanged a glance with Welcome, who set down three plates of food on the table.

Addie looked down at the potatoes and some kind of meat on her plate. She figured it was best not to know what the meat was. The first week Welcome was at The Chili Queen, one of the girls asked about the supper, and Welcome told her it was hog jowl and black-eyed peas. "You ought to study on how to get at that money of yours," Welcome said.

"Go about your business. You're not supposed to be listening," Addie told her.

"Then stay out of my kitchen. You expect me to plug up my ears with chicken grease? Besides, it rightly don't matter what I hear. It only matters what I tell."

Addie had to agree with the wisdom of that. Welcome was no gossip. But then, there wasn't anybody for her to gossip with. She left The Chili Queen only to buy fixings, and as far as Addie knew, the woman hadn't made any friends in Nalgitas. Besides, Addie trusted her. She liked her, too.

Welcome poured hot water from the teakettle into a basin and began to hum softly as she soaped the pots.

"You got how much coming to you, was it?" Addie asked Emma.

"Oh, I don't know, maybe a thousand dollars," Emma said, looking wary.

"I thought you said five thousand," Welcome put in.

"It doesn't matter to me. I'm not after it," Addie said, hurt that after all she'd done for Emma, the woman didn't trust her.

Emma at least had the grace to blush. "I guess five thousand dollars is about right."

"There ought to be some way for her to get that money. Then she wouldn't have to make hats. Shoot, maybe we could help her. We could all come out a little bit richer, you know, get our cut from her brother," Ned said. He winked at Addie.

She returned a faint nod. "You got your name on his bank account?" she asked Emma.

"Oh, no. It's all in John's name." Emma took a tiny bite of potatoes and looked over her shoulder at Welcome and nodded her approval.

Addie furrowed her forehead as she thought. "I could take him in a card game easy." Ned had never seen her work a sucker at cards, had never seen her perform sleight of hand at all, and Addie thought it would be a fine thing to show him how good she was.

Emma swallowed the potatoes, then wiped her mouth with a napkin. Addie noticed the napkin lying next to her own plate and put it into her lap.

"John doesn't play cards," Emma said.

"You say he's greedy, do you?" Addie asked.

"Yes, he's greedy."

Ned stopped eating, and with his fork in the air, he studied Addie.

"'Times a man gets so greedy, he don't think good," Welcome put in.

"I was going to say that." Addie used her hand to wipe her mouth, then remembered the napkin and touched it to her lips. "Didn't he tell you to watch out for an investment? Didn't I hear him tell you that?" Addie asked.

Ned put down his fork, while Welcome turned her back to the dishpan and folded her arms in front of her. Addie was on to something, and the three of them waited for Emma to answer. It was so still in the kitchen that when Ned scraped the floor with his boots as he leaned back in his chair, Addie jumped.

"Well?" Addie asked when Emma didn't reply.

Emma nodded, glancing furtively at Ned, then at Welcome.

"Then I guess the way to get your money is to find something for him to invest in." Addie nodded once to emphasize her words, and forked a piece of meat into her mouth. She studied the way Emma held her fork between her thumb and forefinger, then looked at her own utensil, which was held in her fist like she was grasping a bucket handle. She changed her grip, then glanced around to see if the others had noticed, but only Welcome was watching her.

"But what?" Emma asked. "That's the question, isn't it? What could we get John to put his money into? He won't just send me the cash, you know. He's not stupid."

"Oh," Addie said. "I guess that's right."

Ned pursed his lips together as he thought. "Why don't you tell him you found a gold mine."

Emma laughed and set down her fork in the middle of her plate, the knife beside it. Addie wondered how she could eat so fast taking those little bites. "There's no way in the world John would invest in a gold mine."

"Maybe he'd set you up in the hat business. How about that?" Addie asked.

Emma shook her head. "No, I don't want to give him the satisfaction of knowing I didn't get married. Besides, the only thing John likes is land. He bought so much after Father died that I warned him we'd be land poor."

The three of them studied on it, while Welcome brought a pie to the table and, using a butcher knife, cut it into slices.

"What's that?' Addie asked.

"Custard pie. She said you wanted it." Welcome pointed at Emma with the knife, then slid it under the pie and dished up the dessert onto the dirty plates. Addie wondered whether she should ask for clean dinnerware, but she didn't want Welcome to chide her about putting on airs. She held her fork awkwardly as she cut a piece of her pie that was steeped in gravy.

"Maybe you say you found you a farm to buy, a good one," Welcome said as she licked the sharp knife.

Emma ate slowly, thinking. "John trusts my judgment on land, but I don't know if he'd buy me a farm."

Welcome snorted. The three looked at her as she set the knife on the table and pulled out a chair and sat down. "I guess I'm better at figuring than you white folks. You tell him you found good land, and you'll pay up half iff'n he'll put up the other half. All he has to do is send you the money."

Emma's mouth fell open. "Why, that might work. Yes, I think that would work."

Ned looked to Addie, who studied Welcome, wondering whether the black woman was just smart or if she had a little larceny in her. Then she realized that Welcome must be on the run from the law, just like Ned. She'd come to Nalgitas because it was a safe place to hide. She wondered what Welcome's game was. "How come you know so much about cheating people?" Addie asked her.

Welcome studied Addie for a long time, then replied, "I got my reasons. I wouldn't ask about them. No sir, I would not."

Addie decided Welcome's reasons could wait for another time. Addie nodded at Ned. "It might work."

Ned looked skeptical. "Your brother would turn over the money just like that, just for the asking?"

Emma frowned. "That's the question, isn't it? And I don't know the answer for certain." She spoke slowly, as if she were thinking out loud. "John doesn't really believe he cheated me, and he doesn't know how much I hate him. He always trusted my judgment before."

"Wouldn't he want to see the land for himself?" Ned asked.

"It's harvest time. He wouldn't want to leave. And I don't believe it's in John to think his own sister would cheat him." She looked up and smiled at Ned, then at Addie. "I think it's worth a try."

Ned grinned back. "Hell, why not ask him for ten thousand dollars while you're at it?"

"No, John would never agree to that. Besides, five thousand is mine. It wouldn't be right to cheat my brother out of what's his."

"No?" Addie asked.

"It wouldn't be right," she repeated. There was an edge to her voice that surprised Addie.

"How about fifty-five hundred, then. You get five thousand. Ned and I can get five hundred for helping you out. It's only right, what with me taking you in like I did. Seems like he wouldn't mind paying for that." Addie smiled at Ned, who beamed at her in admiration.

Welcome stood up and tightened her apron strings. She picked up the dirty plates, balanced the butcher knife on top of them, and started for the dishpan. Then she stopped. "I guess you better make that fifty-seven fifty, so's I get my cut, too." She turned and gave Addie a lopsided grin, but Addie could see the woman was dead serious.

Addie smiled back. She felt better about Welcome now

that she understood her.

Welcome had gone out back to the chicken coop where she slept, but the other three were still at the table when Miss Belle and Miss Tillie returned. The two boarders went through the front door and down the hallway to the kitchen, chattering. They stopped when they saw Emma.

"That's the one," Miss Tillie told Miss Belle. Miss Tillie was a sizeable girl, short with orange hair and freckles that she powdered over with flour, and she was so bowlegged, she couldn't pen a pig in a ditch. "I knew she was here last night. I told you I had a feeling something was different. I always get feelings."

"She's old," Miss Belle whispered, loud enough for Emma to hear. Miss Belle was tall and buxom with dark hair and eyes that smoldered when she looked at men. She was very popular. "We heard about you in town," Miss Belle told Emma. "Lordy, everybody knows. I wouldn't be in your shoes for a wooden nickel." She frowned, not sure that had come out right.

Addie shook her head. Those two were dumb enough to drown in a hoofprint of water. They needed looking after. Maybe that was why she had taken them in. "You wouldn't be in anybody's shoes for a wooden nickel," Addie told her.

"You're not to take the cowboys from the Rockin' A. They're mine, all of them," Miss Tillie said, then added, "not that they'd want you, you being old and all. But men are curious, Lordy yes, and they might want to give you a try, but you tell them no." Miss Tillie was rarely anybody's first choice at The Chili Queen, and she guarded her few loyal customers with a fury. "You wouldn't want to cross me," she warned.

Emma blushed and looked as if she wanted to disappear. But she said nothing. Instead, Addie spoke up. "Miss Emma is a guest of mine. She isn't a whore, and you treat her proper. And don't you gossip about her in town, or I'll snatch you bald-headed." The girls giggled. They knew that Addie was fond of them and that her threats didn't mean anything. And Addie knew that whatever the girls picked up at The Chili Queen, they would spread around town, no matter what she said. She'd have to keep them away from Emma—just as she'd always kept them away from Ned.

Miss Belle sat down on a kitchen chair and sulked. "She'll give us a bad reputation is all. Men don't want no turned-away mail-order bride."

Addie glanced at Emma, who had slunk down in her chair. "I told you to mind your manners, Belle," Addie said.

"I bought new ribbons for my hat," Miss Tillie said. She looked at Ned as she spoke, but she couldn't catch his eye.

"I'll sew them on for you," Emma spoke up.

But Addie shook her head. "Welcome's the only servant around here, although she's no better with a needle than a hen with a thimble. You sew them on yourself, Tillie. You do a good enough job with your needle; they'll look mighty pretty. Go on upstairs and take Belle with you. We have business taking place at this table."

"What kind of business you got with an old maid?" Miss Tillie asked.

Addie sighed. "I brought perfume from Kansas City,

and I'll give it to you presently if you mind your manners." She waved the girls away.

"Come on, Belle. I'm not too good to sew on bonnet strings." Miss Tillie slammed the door as the two left the room.

Addie went over and opened the door to make sure they were not listening. "I'd get rid of those two whores, but their heads are as empty as their pocketbooks," Addie said, although she knew she was too soft ever to fire anybody. "I guess they'd starve if I threw them out. Besides, I've got nobody else. There but for the grace of God . . . ," she added, remembering Emma's phrase.

Emma stood up and went to the bucket of water by the door. She took a dipperful and sipped, throwing what was left out the back door. "I guess it's time for me to go to my room," she said.

"Not just yet," Addie told her, standing up herself. "I got a hookhouse to run, and you got a letter to write. Welcome will post it for you. You write it, and I'll look it over." Addie wanted to make sure Emma didn't write anything that would give away their scheme. Emma was not wise in the ways of cheating; Addie was, she thought with pride. She set sheets of paper and a pencil on the table. Then she went into the bedroom and picked out a dress from the wardrobe and took it upstairs with her. She didn't fancy sleeping another night in the hot little bedroom, but there was nothing to be done about it. At least, it was Sunday night, and business would be slow. She wouldn't have to do her part. As she left the room, she looked over her shoulder at Emma and wondered if the woman appreciated what she was doing for her. Then she glanced at

Ned, who winked at her. He, at least, was grateful for the scheme she'd dreamed up.

Emma reached for a sheet of paper and squared it in front of her on the oilcloth. The paper was wrinkled, and she flattened it with her hand.

Ned picked up the pencil, examined its broken tip, and took out his penknife, feeling the blade with his finger before he sharpened the lead. When he was finished, he handed the pencil to Emma and pushed the shavings into a neat pile on the table. "What are you going to say?" he asked.

Emma shrugged. "He's my brother, but I never wrote him a letter in my life." She frowned at the paper and reached for the pencil, touching Ned's index finger as she did so. Ned looked up quickly, but Emma didn't see him. He rubbed his index finger with his thumb.

"Dearest Brother John," she began, then stopped. "I would never call him that," she said. She crossed out *"est,"* then thought again and crossed out the entire word. "This will have to be a practice paper."

Ned folded his hands on the oilcloth. "You two don't have much to say to each other."

"No." Emma didn't elaborate. Ned started to say something, but Emma held up her hand. "I have to concentrate."

It took her more than an hour of writing, blacking out words and crossing out sentences, rewriting, adding words here and there. At last she put down the pencil and held up the sheet of paper, moving her lips as she read the words to herself. "I think this will do," she said.

Ned reached for the paper, but Emma shook her head. "You won't be able to read it. I'll copy it over. Is there ink and a pen?"

Ned shrugged. "Not that I ever saw, but I wasn't looking."

"It would be better with ink. John always writes his letters in ink." But she took a fresh sheet of paper and carefully copied the letter in pencil. She read it through, then went to the stove and used the lifter to remove the lid and dropped the first draft through the hole. "We wouldn't want to leave this lying about where one of Addie's girls might find it," she explained. She stirred the fire with a poker until the paper caught and flamed up. Then she went back to the table, where Ned was reading the letter. He didn't move his finger along the words when he read as Addie did.

When he finished, he set the paper on the table and stared at it, while Emma studied him anxiously. "You are a man. I would value your opinion."

Ned leaned forward, his arms on the oilcloth, then he examined the cuff of his shirt where it had settled on a spot of gravy. He wet his finger and rubbed at the gravy, then gave up and rolled up his sleeves so the spot didn't show. "Well, one thing, if I was your brother and disliked you as much as you say he does, I wouldn't care what your husband thought of you. I'd just care what kind of money I could make. So I'd take that part out."

Emma picked up the pencil and crossed out a line.

"And here's another thing," Ned said, squinting at the letter. "You don't say in here why this rancher wants to sell you the land at half the price. I'd suspicion the deal if

I could get twenty-thousand-dollar land for eleven thousand five hundred."

Emma thought that over. "Yes, I think that's right." She scribbled something.

Ned squinted as he read the corrected letter. He read it through a second time, then grinned at Emma. "I'd say you got her."

Emma looked relieved. She copied the letter onto another piece of paper, and when she was done, she pushed it across the oilcloth to Ned. He read it through, then looked up slyly. "You spelt 'written' wrong. It's got two *t*'s."

Emma looked startled, then embarrassed. She picked up the letter and squeezed in a second *t*. "Where did you learn to spell?"

"I had a fair bit of schooling before I left home. I'm not as dumb as people think."

"No, I can see that," Emma said.

Emma began to fold up the letter, to turn it into its own envelope, but Ned put his hand on hers. "Better wait till Addie sees it. She wants to read it. You best do what Addie says."

Emma stiffened. "I believe I know how to write to my own brother."

"I said best let Addie read it."

She nodded. "All right."

Ned leaned back on two legs of his chair and called out the back door, "You, Welcome, come on in here." In a moment the servant came through the door. "Go fetch Miss Addie. Tell her she's wanted."

Welcome eyed him. "What'll I tell her's so important

she has to come?"

"Tell her anything you want. Tell her the truth. You've been listening in."

Emma jerked her head around to look at Welcome, who met her eyes, then went through the kitchen to the parlor. In a minute Addie was back, looking displeased at being summoned. Emma handed her the paper, and standing up, Addie read it.

"How come you didn't tell him you want your husband to think good of you?" she asked. "That's what I'd do."

"Yeah, she's right," Ned said, not looking at Emma.

Emma didn't reply. Instead, she took the letter from Addie, picked up the pencil, and wrote something. Then she got out another sheet of paper and began to copy the letter once more. Ned looked at Addie over Emma's head and winked. Addie's eyes lit up, then she glanced at Welcome, who was staring at her. Addie put her hands on her hips. "Go about your business. I don't pay you to stand around and eavesdrop," she said.

" 'Tis my business," Welcome told her. "I got two hundred and fifty dollars on it." Welcome went outside, her laugh following her across the backyard.

As she watched the servant disappear, Addie clicked her teeth. It was a sound her mother used to make, and Addie wondered when she'd begun doing it. Sometimes she felt she was getting old, and that was a terrible thing in her business, even for a madam. At least, Addie thought, there wasn't any gray in her hair—not any gray that hadn't been colored with a nice gold, that is. She stood a little straighter and pulled in her stomach, arching an eyebrow at Ned. But he was looking at Emma, who had just set down the pencil. Addie studied him until he looked up at her and blushed, as if he'd been caught doing something wrong. Addie wondered what he'd been thinking. "Read it," Addie said.

Emma cleared her throat. *"Brother John,"* she began, then lowered the paper and explained to Addie, "He's as economical with words as he is with money. He wouldn't like anything flowery."

Addie nodded.

Emma raised the paper so that it was close to her nose, and Addie wondered if she had bad eyesight. Perhaps she was too vain to wear spectacles, but anyone as plain as Emma wasn't likely to be vain. Addie was glad her own sight was still so sharp she could see a knothole in the barn door fifty feet away.

"Brother John. You will be glad to know that marriage suits me. My husband is like you, plainspoken and hard-working, and he saves his money. He suits me, too."

"Why'd you say that?" Addie asked.

"So John will trust him," Emma replied. "If I said he was handsome and made me happy, John would think my mind had gone weak. John doesn't believe in love."

Addie knew the type well enough. "Go on."

Emma cleared her throat. *"You said upon my departure to keep an eye out for investment. I believe I have found one, and so I have written to you. My husband has the opportunity to purchase 20,000 acres adjacent to his ranch for $11,500 cash. It is good cattle range, worth almost twice that, but as it cannot be reached except through my husband's property, the market for it is limited, and the owner is willing to sell it cheap."* Emma smiled at Addie. "I thought that was good reasoning."

Addie didn't reply, and Emma ducked her head and continued. *"Mr. Withers would buy it himself, but he does not have all the money. Here is what he proposes: You and he will each put up half the cash. Mr. Withers will run cattle on the land. He will charge you for your half of the calves but defer payment until the cattle are sold. Then he will deduct the cost from your share of the sale price as well as the five percent you promised me if I should find you a suitable investment. As an act of good faith, he will not charge you interest on the calves, nor for your share of the operations for the first three years. I believe it is a fair arrangement for both of you. You said my husband would think better of me if I showed a good head for business, and I desire his good opinion—as I do yours. Time is of the essence, as there is talk in town that minerals have been discovered just across the river from the land in question, and we believe if the owner hears the news, he will raise the price. The law requires access be given where mineral rights are concerned.* I made that up. John wouldn't know otherwise," Emma said, not looking up. *"Send your money order to me in care of general delivery. I am residing in a respectable ladies' boardinghouse in town while Mr. Withers completes the house he is building for me. You may trust me.*

"Very respectfully,

"Your sister

"Emma Roby Withers."

"I still don't know why he'd trust you," Ned said.

"Oh, you don't know him. He's a fool to make money. It clouds his judgment," Emma said. Then she added, "I

77

believe John would consider it a blot on his character to think his closest kin would cheat him."

Ned shrugged. "Maybe so."

But Addie knew men like that, and she nodded her approval of the letter. She watched as Emma took out another sheet of paper and began to write the final draft. Addie produced a two-cent stamp from a drawer in the cupboard and set it on the table.

"I'll take it in to the post office in the morning," Emma offered when she had finished the letter, folded it to form its own envelope, and put the stamp on it.

Addie didn't want to risk Emma having second thoughts. "Welcome will put it in the postbox tonight. Come on in here, Welcome," she said in a quiet voice. For some reason Addie felt comfortable knowing that the servant was always lurking nearby, as if she were protecting her. In a few seconds, the back screen opened and Welcome entered the room noiselessly. Without a word, she took the letter and put it into her apron pocket. Then she turned around and went back out, and Addie watched through the kitchen window as Welcome took long strides down the dirt road and disappeared in the darkness.

THREE

Miss Tillie and Miss Belle had tromped off to the saloons, telling Addie they didn't care to tarry with a woman who looked just like an old-maid schoolteacher, not that they knew much about teachers since neither had ever been to school. Welcome was hanging up the wash on clotheslines stretched between the barn and the privy.

Emma fussed with the cinnamon-rose starts she had planted all over the backyard. She was as tender with the roses as if they were her children, and every hour or two she watered them. Addie sat in a straight chair in the shade on the back porch, fanning herself, watching Emma as she carried a heavy bucket of water with one arm; the other arm was outstretched to balance herself. Emma had earned her keep, all right. Addie had to hand her that. In the five days she'd been at The Chili Queen, Emma had taken a working fit. She had scrubbed the parlor carpet, sewn curtains for the kitchen windows, weeded Welcome's garden, and repaired the broken window in the bedroom. Whenever she sat down, she picked up her piecing and had completed half a dozen quilt squares. Still, Addie couldn't shake the feeling that something wasn't quite right with Emma. She couldn't put her finger on it, but it made her nervous.

"That woman's busier than a two-tailed cat. It makes me tired just to look at her," Ned observed. He was sitting on the edge of the porch next to Addie, his feet planted in the dirt, his elbows resting on his knees. Neither one of them had moved in the past hour.

Addie resisted telling him that everything seemed to make him tired. "You ever hear such a thing as rosebushes at a house of joy?" she asked instead. "Next, she'll put out a fountain and an iron dog."

"Might look nice. My sisters always planted flowers at home on the farm," Ned said, "You could name the dog Rio. I had a dog named Rio once. He was a shaggy black-and-white dog about this big." Ned put out his hand even with his knees.

Addie looked at him curiously. "I never heard you talk about home before, except to say you were glad you left it."

"I am glad." Ned didn't look at her but kept staring straight out into the yard. "I guess I never thought much about it before. I'd like to see Rio again. I suppose he's dead. He'd be twenty-five years old if he wasn't."

"What made you think about those way-back days?" Addie put down her paper fan and found a handkerchief, which she balled up to mop her neck. She reached inside her dress to dry her shoulders and bosom. "You could fry eggs on me, I'm that hot."

Ned turned to watch her and grinned as she held the front of her dress open and flapped it back and forth to push the air inside. "Maybe it's because I just got me a sister I never knew I had."

"Get me a drink of water, will you?"

Ned stood up and walked lazily to the well. You could whistle a chorus of "Listen to the Mockingbird" in the time it took him to lift one foot, set it down, and lift the other. Ned drew a bucket of water and scooped out a dipperful, sloshing the liquid over the sides as he carried it back to Addie. She drank and handed the dipper to Ned, who sipped, then carefully poured the rest of the water over a rosebush Emma had planted alongside the house. "I wish you hadn't told her we were kin. I never knew you to have an attack of respectability before."

Addie picked up the fan and swished the hot air. She didn't know herself why she hadn't set Emma straight, and she was a little surprised the woman hadn't figured out how things stood. Or maybe she had and kept her mouth shut for fear Addie would demand she give up the bedroom. "When you busted in like you did Sunday morning, she thought this was a boardinghouse. Maybe I didn't want her thinking I was sleeping with an outlaw. I got my pride, you know."

"Oh, zam, Addie! When did you ever care about pride?" Ned sat down again. "You ought to tell her now. You and me could take back the bedroom." He raised an eyebrow.

Addie thought that over. There was nothing she'd like better than a sweet time with Ned. He was an uncommon handsome man. Just looking at him with that little smile on his mouth and his green eyes that slid over her then made her insides feel like a caramel candy left in the sun. There'd been plenty of men in Addie's life before, and she'd loved some of them pretty good, but none the way she did Ned. La! He was easy on the heart.

Addie felt a hammering inside her the first time she saw him, and he was smitten, too. She'd opened the door of The Chili Queen, and there he was. After she'd looked Ned up and down to take in all of him, Addie had invited him inside. She hadn't had to remind him of his manners, asking, "Won't you rest your hat?" the way she did most of the cowboys, because Ned had removed his hat as he came through the door. She'd ushered him into the parlor and introduced him to the girls, but he hadn't even looked at them. Instead, he'd sat on the sofa and talked to Addie. Whenever a customer arrived, Ned sat politely while Addie introduced the man to one of the girls, took his money, then returned to Ned. When the last customer left, Ned went into Addie's bedroom with her and had been coming back to The Chili Queen ever since. That was four years ago. He was always welcome, whether he stayed a night or two or for weeks at a time. He hadn't paid the first night, and Addie had never asked him for anything since. She let him be a loose horse, going where he wanted to, and always welcomed him back. She never asked where he'd been, although she usually knew. In fact, she sometimes suggested robberies, picking up information from customers who talked too much. Of course, Ned did the planning and pulled off the jobs. And it didn't bother him that Addie earned her living running a parlor house, either. He never looked down on her, never reproached her for sleeping with other men. There was something to be said for that.

Ned, of course, was the reason Addie wouldn't have married the man in Kansas City, even if he had asked her. She'd thought plenty about marriage on the trip home, however, although she and Ned had never talked about it. She'd told Ned once about her idea of going back to San Antonio and setting up a chili operation, perhaps opening a restaurant. Maybe if she could get the money to make the move, Ned would go along—as her husband. She'd take care of him. Ned wouldn't have to find work, unless he wanted to, and Addie was pretty sure he didn't. He was tired of being on the run and had begun talking about settling down with the money from his last robbery. He'd taken a little more than five thousand dollars, and he hadn't let it get away from him this time, either. At least that was what he'd told her. Addie'd never seen the money, never knew where Ned hid it. The only problem that Addie could see was that she didn't know if Ned wanted to marry her. Maybe leaving him out in the barn by himself at nights would make him realize how much he wanted to be with her. No, Addie wouldn't tell Emma she and Ned were lovers.

"She won't be here for long, just until her brother sends her that money," Addie said. "Besides, where else would she sleep? She can't stay upstairs in Frankie's room, and I don't suppose she'd sleep in the barn. I guess if you get bothered, you could come here like a regular customer."

And ask for Belle? Ned asked, but Addie had shifted her attention to the road. Two men were riding slowly toward The Chili Queen. One of them pointed at Emma, who had her foot on a shovel, digging a hole. The men laughed and rode on. "Look at that." Addie frowned. "She's given me a hurting. Men see her and think she's one of my girls. No wonder my business has slowed down."

"It's always slow in the middle of the week. You've said it yourself," Ned said. "Besides, the cowboys at the Rockin' A are digging postholes. You won't see those boys until Saturday night."

"No, it's that woman," Addie insisted. "She's doing first one thing and another, and if she doesn't stop her foolishment, she'll crochet a mat for the front door with 'Welcome, Jesus' on it." Addie stopped fanning herself and leaned toward Ned. "At night, she stays to her room, but in the day, she's outside working in the garden or sitting right here in this chair where everybody can see her. She works her quilt, just like this was an old-ladies' home. She even asked me if I had a rocking chair she could bring out." Addie had worked herself into a bad mood.

"I wouldn't mind a rocking chair to sit on," Ned said. Addie swatted him, and he added, "We'll just have to wait her out. You said it will be only a week, two at most. It's not as if I can do something about it."

"Maybe not," Addie said, thinking it over. "Or then again, maybe you can. It's about time you earned your keep."

Ned looked up suspiciously. "Now, don't go and spoil a fine thing," he warned.

"A fine thing for you," Addie retorted, then held her tongue. She'd always done for herself, never suggested Ned nail up a clothesline or fix the broken hinge on the wardrobe. That was one of the reasons he loved her. She was different from other women. Ned was a man who didn't like to be needed. If he helped out, it was because he wanted to. But this wasn't a job Addie could do herself or hire done, like stringing barbed wire or whitewashing the kitchen. This was something nobody but Ned could do. "You just look at her out there talking to Welcome. She's in everybody's way." Addie took a deep breath and said, "I want you to take her out days."

Ned chuckled.

"I mean it."

"Aw, Addie."

"I want you to get her out of here."

Ned stood up and went behind Addie, putting his arms around her and kissing the tip of her ear. "Now, honey, you settle down. Before you know it, she'll be gone, and except for those roses, which you are going to like when they bloom, and two hundred and fifty dollars you didn't have before, you won't even remember she was here," he said.

Addie leaned against Ned, then thought better of it and

straightened up. A few days with Emma was likely to make him even more appreciative of Addie. "Don't you sweet-talk me. I got a business to run, and I expect you to do your part."

Ned began to massage Addie's neck and shoulders. "What am I supposed to do with her, take her to church?"

"If it suits you. But Sunday isn't for three more days. We got between here and then. You take her for a buggy ride."

"For three days?" Ned pinched the fat on Addie's plump arm, and she winced.

"Every day until that money comes."

"What if she doesn't want to go?"

"I expect you'd know how to make her want to."

Ned took his hands away from Addie's shoulders and leaned against a post. The two of them didn't say more because Welcome came across the yard and set her big wicker laundry basket on the porch, sitting down straggly-legged next to it. "I got the wash done up, unless she finds something more dirty." Welcome nodded her head at Emma. "She's wore me out good."

"The way she works is a caution, all right," Addie said.

"You could wash my shirt," Ned said, straightening up and starting to unbutton the front. "And polish the buttons. I had it brightened up with brass buttons, but they got dull."

"I don't do for you," Welcome said.

Ned frowned and looked at Addie, but she only laughed and said, "I don't do for you, either, because you don't do for me. You want your buttons shined up, you can mix up salt and vinegar and polish them yourself." Then she turned to Welcome. "Ned wants to shine himself up to take Emma over there on a buggy ride."

Welcome narrowed her eyes at Ned. "How come you was to have tarry with her?"

"'Cause I said so," Addie said. "I got to get her out of here before she kills my business dead."

"I could keep her patching around the place, and maybe find her more work to do in the garden," Welcome offered.

The garden had been Welcome's idea. She had planted it the day after she'd arrived, and while Addie thought a vegetable garden had no more place at a whorehouse than rosebushes, she'd changed her mind when Welcome brought in the first weedings of lettuce. Addie wondered if Welcome had been a field hand during slavery—she'd seen scars on Welcome's powerful arms and one shoulder when the woman was bent over the scrubboard—or perhaps, like other Negroes Addie had known, Welcome was always a little worried about where her next meal would come from. But then Addie'd been worried about that a time or two herself. "Emma's already tended to the garden. You shouldn't have planted it if you couldn't care for it yourself."

Welcome shrugged. "I'm satisfied with what confronts me." She stood up. "Gimme that shirt. I'll go mix up the salt and vinegar."

Ned removed his shirt and handed it to Welcome, who looked him over and laughed.

"What's so funny?" he asked.

"You look part Negro. You got a white chest on you and hands and a neck as dark as me. That makes you half black and half white."

Ned didn't say anything, but went off to the barn for a clean shirt. Addie laughed however, and said, "I guess I never minded a man that was half black and half white."

Welcome, who had been watching Ned, slid her eyes around to Addie and muttered, "That's packs of trouble."

"Well, I guess you'd know," Addie replied.

"I guess I would," was all Welcome said. She put the basket on her hip and went inside, muttering, "Lord have mercy on me, yes."

Addie sat on the back porch, fanning herself, until Ned reappeared, dressed in a white shirt. He'd put on clean pants, too, and his boots looked as if he'd shined them. He went to the well and poured water over his head, slicking back his hair with his fingers. Then he ambled over to Emma and said something to her. Emma looked startled, studied on it, then smiled and nodded. As Emma started toward the house, she smoothed her hair, then rolled down her sleeves. Suddenly, Addie felt a twinge of jealousy and wished she were the one who was going off for a buggy ride with Ned. Maybe she hadn't been so smart after all. Before Emma could reach the house, Addie got up and went inside. "Here," she told Welcome. "Give me that shirt. I'll polish the buttons."

"I got the misery in my footses," Welcome said the next morning when Addie came down to breakfast and found the hired woman sitting on a chair at the kitchen table, her feet propped up on a second chair.

Addie looked at Welcome's splayed feet, which were splatter-bare. "I got the misery myself, so don't expect any sympathy from me," Addie said sourly. "Where's my breakfast?" She was sore that Ned was enjoying himself, rambling over the countryside with Emma, while she had to stay behind and work. In fact, Addie had slept poorly for stewing about it. She had all but forgotten that getting Emma away from The Chili Queen had been her idea, not Ned's.

Welcome moved her feet to the floor and covered them with her long, striped skirt, but she didn't get up. "I already fixed breakfast for him and her. Flannel cakes. Then I mixed up the flapjacks again for them girls, but I might as well have fed them chicken heads, pigtails, and parsnips for all the thanks I been given. I didn't hire on to cook breakfasts three times a day, particularly for them as does not appreciate it. Not nary a lick more will I cook this morning, no."

"Where's Ned?"

Welcome looked at her glumly. "Oh, I tied them up some eatments in a checkidy cloth and put them in a carryable basket, and they lit a rag, going Lord knows where, him in another clean shirt and her all Jenny-Linded up in a riding dress. They left hours ago. If you ask me, there's deviltry about."

"I guess I didn't ask you, did I?" Addie replied. "And what do you care?"

Welcome shrugged.

"Are you going to get my breakfast?" Addie asked.

"No, ma'am, I am not."

Addie sighed. "You ever going to mind me?"

"I'll move on if you ain't happy. Just say the word." Welcome grinned and gripped the table to push herself up.

"But I'll fetch you bread and jam. *She* brung a jar of quince jam in her trunk, handed it to me this morning and said give it to you. I wouldn't let those girls have it. I ought to crumble up corn bread with peas and pot liquor and pour it in a trough and let them eat it like Adam, without no spoons, just the way they fed the little children in slavery days."

Addie leaned forward and tapped one fist on top of the other. "Was that the way you were raised?"

Welcome's face went stony. She adjusted her bright red head rag and turned and shuffled to the drain board, where she picked up a butcher knife. Then she took out the remains of a loaf of bread and sliced off a piece, setting it on a plate. She carried it to the table, along with a dish of butter and the jar of jam.

"You were a slave, weren't you?" Addie asked.

"I was still in my young days when freedom came," Welcome replied, not answering the question.

Addie let it go. She spread a fulsome amount of jam on the bread and ate it, while she thought. Then she asked Welcome if Emma kept her trunk locked.

Welcome didn't reply but asked, "How come you let him take her off like that, and not in the buggy? She was wanting to ride a horse, and she wouldn't do it sidesaddle, so she went off astride, just like any man. It don't look right."

Addie looked at her curiously. "I ask you a second time why you care?"

"I say again it don't look right. It sorely does not. She looks common as pig tracks."

"This is a hookhouse," Addie snorted, "or didn't you

know? We're not as refined as Mrs. President Grover Cleveland."

"That one is no hooker."

"It's her choice to stay. I wouldn't stop her from leaving."

Welcome sat down again and began to rub her foot. "I don't like it."

"Nobody asked you. Besides, you're not always right about things. No you're not."

Addie spread butter across the bread, then put several spoonfuls of jam on top and took a bite. "Quince jam. Why would anybody make a jam out of quinces? Why not plums or peaches?" she asked.

"Maybe she left before plum-ripening time in Kansas."

"You know anything about plums?"

"No. You know anything about quinces?"

Addie laughed and shook her head. Welcome had made her feel some better. "I guess we don't know why she made quince jam, then." She shoved the rest of the bread into her mouth, then licked the jam off the side of her hand and announced she was going to look inside Emma's trunk.

Welcome stopped as she picked up the plate and looked at Addie. "How come you're to snoop?"

Addie was wounded. "I'm not snooping. Maybe there's something I ought to know about in there. What if she's a morphine fiend? She might murder us all in our beds. You, too. Or maybe she smokes opium. She could burn down the house and me and those girls along with it. I'm responsible for those girls. She could be a doper, she's that scarce-hipped," Addie continued. "Why, she's so thin her ribs rustle against each other like cornstalks drying in the wind. Dope does that, you know."

Welcome tried to keep a straight face but couldn't and began to chuckle.

"Well, it might could be so. Yes it could," Addie said, but she laughed, too, suddenly feeling a warmth for Welcome. "It's my house, and I got the right to see anything in my house, don't I? If you want to have a look yourself, you can come along." Addie stood up and brushed crumbs off her wrapper. Some of the crumbs were from yesterday's breakfast. Welcome followed her into the bedroom.

In all her days put together, Addie had never seen a room so neat. Emma's brush and comb, nail buffer and toothbrush were laid out neatly on the bureau, with a row of hairpins so tidy and straight that they looked like little toy soldiers lined up. The floor shone as if it were a mirror, and the furniture must have been dusted that morning, since it didn't have the film of dirt that blew in through the window every day. The spread was pulled tight across the bed, which did not sag as it usually did. Emma must have tightened the ropes that held the tick. Beneath the bed was a pair of shoes that were worn and repaired, but had been cleaned and polished. The black dress hung neatly on a peg on the wall. "I don't suppose you did up this room," Addie said.

Welcome shook her head.

"It's nervousness. What's she got to be so nervous about?" Addie said.

She tried the lid of the trunk, but it was locked. "She doesn't trust me. Is that any way for a guest to behave?"

Addie asked. "I am greatly insulted."

Welcome turned to leave but stopped when Addie said, "What's your hurry? I guess I know how to pick a lock or two." Addie extracted a hairpin from the row, leaving a little gap between the soldiers, and held it up. Then she knelt down beside the trunk and carefully inserted the hairpin into the lock, wiggling it around. In a few seconds, there was a click, and Addie sent Welcome a look of triumph. She lifted the lid.

Welcome nudged Addie aside so that she could look in first.

Addie struggled to keep her balance as she wondered why Welcome was in such a hurry.

"This ain't right," Welcome said.

"Oh, la!" Addie began removing the items in the trunk—dresses, petticoats, drawers, a corset. There were scraps of material for quilts and a supply of bonnet strings and soft fabrics for hats, some silk rosettes. It looked as if Emma planned to set up a millinery all along, Addie observed.

"Or make a whole supply of hats for herself. Maybe she'll make me a hat." Welcome grinned, and Addie crunched up a piece of green taffeta and held it over Welcome's head. "This looks better than that old rag you've got on. Your hair's got red in it. Take it if you want. She won't miss it."

"No, ma'am. The devil will not have my soul for a piece of green silk."

"Suit yourself." Addie rummaged around inside the trunk, tossing out shoes and stockings and an 1879 bound volume of *Peterson's Magazine*. She flipped through it and stopped to study a woman wearing a Saratoga dress and bonnet. "Maybe that's where she gets the ideas for those hats. Why, this one's been out-of-date for years." Having gone to Kansas City every year, Addie considered herself an expert on fashions. She looked into the trunk again. "That's odd. You'd think she'd have a Bible and one of those cooking books."

"She already knows how to cook. And maybe they had but one Bible, and her brother kept it. Besides, she's no cheerbacker."

"No what?"

"Preacher. I never heard her say one word about the Lord, yet. Or you neither."

Addie snorted and got on her knees to peer into the bottom of the trunk where something was wrapped in a piece of silk. She lifted it out, removed the material, and found herself staring at the likeness of the man who had gotten on the train with Emma. "This is her brother," Addie said, handing the picture to Welcome.

"He's a fine-looking man," Welcome observed.

"Oh, I don't know. You wouldn't say that if you saw him. He's too mean."

"So she say." Welcome held the picture closer to study it, then handed it back.

Addie wondered why Emma had brought along a picture of her brother, when she hated him so. Maybe she'd wanted the frame for her husband's picture, and now that there wasn't any husband, there was no reason to remove John Roby's likeness.

Addie put the picture back into the trunk and began to pile Emma's things on top of it.

Welcome chuckled. "You think she won't know you snooped when she opens this trunk and finds it as messy as an owl's nest?"

Addie threw up her hands. "You straighten it, then." She went into the kitchen and sliced herself another piece of bread and ate it plain. Then she stood in the doorway watching Welcome as she carefully folded each garment and returned it to the trunk. When she was finished, Welcome closed the lid and extracted the hairpin, straightening it and returning it to its place on the bureau. "You're a regular lady's maid," Addie observed.

"You want some breakfast now?" Welcome asked.

"Naw, I want a glass of whiskey." Addie started for the parlor, then turned and cocked her head at Welcome. "You coming, or is that against your religion, too?"

"The Lord comes down on drunkness," Welcome said, then smiled. "But I suppose He don't mind a little nip to help the hurting in my footses."

Addie grinned at Welcome and decided she must have been a liver in her time. Maybe she still was.

In fact, Addie had two or three glasses of whiskey, or maybe four or five, before she went to sleep on the sofa. She was bad to drink sometimes, and when she woke up, she couldn't remember if Welcome had drunk as much, or more important, what the two had talked about. By then, it was late afternoon, and Addie was alone in the house. She threw aside the coverlet that Welcome had spread over her and padded upstairs, glancing into the rooms, but the girls hadn't returned. Maybe they'd pick up a cowboy or two in the saloons. Addie hoped they wouldn't be too drunk to work. She felt bad about neglecting them lately. After all, she'd always considered herself to be a mother to her girls. After the business with Emma was done, Addie would throw a party for her two boarders.

Addie went into the kitchen looking for Welcome, but the woman was nowhere to be found. Maybe she'd gone to the chicken coop to sleep off her drunk. Addie wouldn't begrudge her that. In fact, Addie had developed a warm feeling for Welcome. She went back upstairs to Miss Frankie's room and poured tepid water from the pitcher into a basin, soaped and rinsed herself, brushed her hair, and put on a cotton dress. She wandered around the house again, but Welcome had not returned. So she sat on the back porch, wondering what Ned was up to.

Perhaps he was right. What was wrong with telling Emma that Ned and Addie weren't brother and sister? He should be getting back soon, although there was no sign of horses in the west. Welcome had said they'd ridden in that direction, probably to avoid going through Nalgitas. Addie was thankful for that. She wouldn't have to endure teasing from customers telling her that Ned had thrown her aside for a woman who looked old enough to be his mother. She fidgeted on the chair. Usually Addie liked lazy afternoons with the girls gone and nothing to do, but today, she was nervous all over. She examined her hands, picking off a hangnail and leaving a raw spot that oozed blood. Addie stuck the finger into her mouth and sucked on it while she shaded her eyes with the other hand and looked across the prairie again.

A bee buzzed past her ear and landed on a wild aster that

had taken root in the naked ground beside the house. When the bee flew off, Addie got up and plucked the lavender flower, smelled it, and stuck it into a buttonhole. She looked at the barn. Maybe Ned and Emma had returned while she was asleep and had gone inside so as not to disturb her. She looked around, but there were still no signs of riders, so Addie crossed the brown grass to the big structure. She opened the door and peered inside, letting her eyes adjust to the darkness. She'd built the barn herself after she bought The Chili Queen. Besides room for a buggy, a phaeton, and a wagon, the barn had four horse stalls and a tack room, as well as a hayloft above. Addie loved horseflesh, although she no longer liked to ride a horse herself. Fine horses were a sign of prosperity. They were good for business. She liked to dress up the girls and drive them around town to stir up attention. Addie had sent a three-dollar money order to Currier & Ives in New York City for a picture of Lexington, a racehorse, which she put into a gold frame and hung in the parlor. Even her shelf for whatnot things had three horse figurines mingled with the collection of colored glass slippers and toothpick holders.

Two of the stalls were for her horses, one for Ned's, and the fourth held saddles and bridles, since Ned had taken over the tack room. Usually Ned stayed with Addie in her room when he was at The Chili Queen, but she'd furnished the tack room with a bed and a light so that he could go there when things in the whorehouse got too noisy.

Ned's horse was gone, along with one of Addie's horses. She walked over to the remaining animal and let him nuzzle her. The boy who cleaned the stable and cared for the animals had come in that morning and swept out the stalls. The smell of fresh hay reminded Addie of the farm she'd left when she was hardly grown. The recollection made her feel neither good nor bad; the only time she thought much about her childhood was when she was on the train, passing through dirt-farm country.

She patted the animal's neck and turned to leave, then caught sight of the tack room. It was Ned's domain, and Addie never went inside unless he was there. She stared at the enclosure for a long time. Going through Emma's trunk was one thing, but Ned's belongings were sacred. He didn't like snoops. Still, she had the right to spy on him, didn't she? It was her barn. Everything in it was her business. And what harm was there in looking, as long as Ned didn't find out? Addie reached behind a post for the key. She went to the barn door and peered out at the horizon just in case Ned was returning, but there was no sign of anyone.

Addie unlocked the door and went inside, stopping to light the kerosene lantern that hung on the wall. Ned wasn't as tidy as Emma, but nonetheless, the room was neat. The blanket was pulled up over the bed and pillow, and Ned's clothes hung on nails on the wall. Besides the bed, the room held only a straight chair and Ned's trunk. Addie looked at the trunk for a long time, then took a couple of steps forward and yanked at the lid. It was unlocked, and Addie lifted it, bending over to see inside. The trunk wasn't even full. There were Ned's clothes— extra pants and shirts and a heavy coat he wore in winter. A schoolboy's primer was under the clothes, along with

three newspapers with front-page stories on bank robberies. Addie knew Ned had committed two of them; she
wasn't sure about the third but thought it probably was
Ned's doing. Under the newspapers was a piece of brown
cardboard, and at first, Addie thought it was part of the
trunk. But she lifted it out and turned it over and found
herself staring at a prosperous farm family. Addie took the
photograph to the light to get a better look. In the center
of the picture was a stern-looking couple. The woman
looked worn out, and no wonder, with the brood of children around her. The tallest boy, the one holding a dog in
his arms, might have been Ned, but Addie wasn't altogether sure because he was so young. Behind the family
was a two-story frame house, with a veranda and what
appeared to be a trumpet vine growing over it. She was
pleased that Ned had come from a good family, for it
meant that she had traded up.

"There never was any such picture took like that of the
Foss farm," Addie muttered to herself. If she'd lived in a
house like this, she'd have had a bedroom door to lock,
and she might not have left home. Addie studied the boy
again, to see if his ears stuck out a little, like Ned's. But
she couldn't tell. She turned her attention to the two older
girls, one with a quilt in her hands. They'd be grown up
now. Addie wondered what they'd think if they knew their
brother was an outlaw. But maybe they did know. And
what would they think if they knew he was keeping company with a hooker? A madam, she reminded herself, for-
merly the most popular chili queen in San Antonio. Ned
could have done worse. Still, Addie had a feeling they'd
be a whole lot easier in the heart knowing their brother

was married to someone like Emma.

Addie did not know a tear had rolled down her cheek until it splashed onto the photograph. She wiped it off with her sleeve, then turned the picture over. On the back was scribbled *Old K. farm, Ft. Madison.* She wondered what *K* stood for. Maybe this wasn't Ned's family after all but just some picture left in a trunk he'd bought. Or maybe the photograph was with something Ned had stolen, although she didn't know why anybody would steal a picture. She studied the boy again and thought she saw how his nose was flattened a little, like Ned's. He'd told her it was broken when his father slammed him against the barn. Maybe Ned's name wasn't Partner at all. Maybe it was something that started with a *K.* She'd never asked him about his name, and he'd never said. Well, she'd never told him her name was Adeline Foss.

With a final look at the family, Addie blotted the wet spot on the photograph again and put the picture face-down in the trunk. She felt all around inside the empty trunk, but there was no sign of money. Mindful of the way Welcome had repacked Emma's trunk, Addie folded Ned's things and closed the lid. She was about to search the rest of the room, but the horse in the stall neighed. Addie quickly left the room, locked the door, and replaced the key. Then she stroked the horse for a moment and left the barn. Welcome was sitting beside the chicken house, watching her.

"You been in there a long time," she observed.

Addie started to tell Welcome to mind her business, but she stopped. Welcome was her friend now, maybe her only friend, she thought with a surge of self-pity. Besides, after the two of them had gone through Emma's things, Addie's snooping in Ned's trunk didn't seem so bad. Of course, Welcome didn't know that's what she'd been doing. Addie didn't reply.

"Looks like you forgot to put out the lamp."

Addie spun around and saw light coming from between the cracks of Ned's room. She hurried back for the key, opened the door, and blew out the lamp. When she returned to Welcome, Addie said, "I guess it's my business what I'm doing in my barn."

"Guess it is," Welcome replied. "What you want for supper? I was thinking sage tea and chicken gruel." She laughed good-naturedly.

"How about a beefsteak? You feel like beefsteak?"

Welcome grinned at her. "I always feel like beefsteak. It fits my insides easiest. I'll make you a cake, too. You come along, and I'll let you sop out the bowl, just like in your coming-up time."

"I never had anything to sop in my coming-up time," Addie said.

Welcome gave a short bark of a laugh. "Neither did I, child. Hell and damnation, by God, neither did I."

Addie didn't see Ned for two more days. She didn't see Emma either, although at night, whenever Addie went into the kitchen, she noticed the bedroom door was closed and knew the woman was inside. Then on Sunday noon, after a slow Saturday night that she blamed on Emma's presence at The Chili Queen, Addie locked up the house, sent the girls to bed, and went into the kitchen, where she found Ned and Emma waiting for her.

"I wondered maybe you moved out," Addie said to Emma.

Emma eyed her, then said with a hint of annoyance, "I know I am a burden to you. I will leave as soon as my brother sends the money."

"We got an idea," Ned said.

Addie considered him a moment, then said, "Let's talk about it in the parlor. I could use me a drink."

The three of them started for the front of the house, followed by Welcome. "You're not wanted," Ned said.

"Oh, I don't have secrets from her. She can stay," Addie told him.

Ned started to protest, but after looking from Addie to Welcome and back again at Addie, who had put her hands on her hips, Ned said, "Suit yourself, honey."

Addie sat down, taking up the entire sofa, which was red and slightly soiled. Ned and Emma seated themselves on chairs facing her, while Welcome blended into the semidarkness next to the long plush curtain that spread out on the floor like the train of a dress. Addie poured herself a glass of whiskey and handed the bottle to Ned, who poured one for himself. Emma reached for the bottle and two glasses, filled one and handed it to Welcome, then filled another. Before Addie could raise her glass, Emma had drunk hers.

"You don't usually see ladies take their whiskey like that," Addie observed.

"You don't see ladies take whiskey at all," Emma replied. She added softly, "I suppose I do not fit the classification of a lady anymore. You said it yourself."

"What are you going to do with that money when you

get it?" Addie asked her.

Emma lifted her glass to her lips, then realized it was empty and set it down. Addie pushed the bottle toward her, and Emma filled it again, but this time she only sipped the liquor. "I have not decided," Emma replied. "I have always fancied seeing San Francisco."

Addie nodded. "Me, too."

Ned cleared his throat, and the three women turned to him. He seemed nervous, but Addie didn't especially care about putting him at ease. She toyed with a strand of hair that had come out of the knot at the back of her head, then pinned the loose hair in place. "Well, what is it?"

"Me and Emma have an idea, about that bank in Jasper you told me about."

Addie had indeed told him about the Jasper bank. She had had it in mind that Ned should rob it ever since the bank president had visited The Chili Queen in the spring and sweet-talked Addie into giving him a free time with Broken-Nose Frankie, promising to let Addie have a business loan at a favorable rate. Addie had wanted the money to do a little work around The Chili Queen, so she'd dipped into her own pocket to give Miss Frankie the fifty percent she would have earned from a paying customer. But when Addie had taken the train to Jasper and called on the banker to make good on the loan, he'd denied he was ever at The Chili Queen and refused her. Of course, Addie shouldn't have asked him for the money when his wife was visiting the bank, but how was she to know he was married to the sharp-nosed woman in black merino? No matter what the circumstances, there'd been no call for him to say she was "the spit of the devil."

Addie'd been itching to get even ever since, and she'd told Ned about the bank, but Ned hadn't been keen on robbing anything that close to home. Now, however, after spending all that time with Emma, Ned must have figured out a way to get away from her—by going off to Jasper to rob the bank. Addie almost smirked as she cocked her head and leaned back against the settee. "And?"

"Me and Emma thought we'd take it."

"What!" Addie jerked upright and stared at Ned. "What do you mean you and Emma?" Welcome let out a sound like a growl.

"Me and Emma, we're going to take it," Ned repeated. He glanced at Emma for confirmation, but she was staring at Welcome.

"Emma doesn't know as much about robbing a bank as a dog does about Sunday," Addie snorted. She glared at Emma.

"You said it would be as easy as honey to knock over," Ned persisted.

"Yeah, as easy as licking honey off a thornbush—with her along." Addie gestured with her head to Emma. "Oh, that's a fool idea all right." She stood up, but the room was too small for pacing, and she sat back down and asked Emma, "What do you know about taking a bank? You think it's as easy as getting a money order, do you? You just walk in and say, 'Give me your money, if you please?' "

"Ned will do the robbing," Emma said quickly. "I'm just going along with him so people won't be suspicious. I'll pretend to be his sister. Who'd expect a bank robber to take along his sister? Ned says there's no danger in it at all. At all." Before Addie could reply, Emma added, "I am of a mind to do it. I have already strayed. One more transgression won't matter much. You need not worry about my soul."

"I won't."

Ned set his glass on the table, sloshing the liquor over the side. He had not touched it. "We talked it out. We'll say we're farmers going into town to buy supplies. If it looks too dangerous, we'll turn around and come on home."

"It's against my wants," Addie said. "You'll get caught."

"We'll be careful. I'll be all right since I won't leave the wagon," Emma said. Then she added with a touch of iron in her voice that Addie had not heard before, "I believe I can do anything I set my mind to."

"I'm not so worried about you getting caught. I'm worried about Ned."

Before Emma could reply, Welcome blurted out, "No! God, my deliverer, no!"

The other three turned to her in surprise. "Oh, hush up," Ned said. "It's not your business."

"'Tis," Welcome replied. She twisted her dark hands in her white apron. "'Tis if you get caught. Then where's my two hundred and fifty dollars?"

"We won't get caught, neither of us," Emma told her softly.

Welcome stepped forward so that they could see her better and shook her head. "It's devilment. You will get caught, and they'll come after us, come after me."

"What have you done that you don't want anybody to

find out about?" Ned asked.

Welcome stared him down. When Ned looked away, Welcome said, "The only real sin I committed was I was a dancer." She looked at the others to see if they would challenge her. They didn't.

"I will not be found wanting," Emma said quietly, looking at Welcome. "I performed in amateur theatricals at home and believe I can act a little. I'm not so good, but I'm not so bad, either." She looked down at her hands. "I—we—will not get caught. I promise you."

"Oh, promise, la!" Addie said. "How can you promise? I bet you never did anything in your life against the law."

Emma didn't answer.

"You'd risk everything—?" Welcome asked, but Emma interrupted.

"I'm not risking anything," Emma said, sending Welcome a look Addie didn't understand.

The four of them sat there for a moment, not saying a word. Addie could hear Miss Tillie and Miss Belle upstairs arguing and knew she should see what the fuss was about. Miss Tillie could turn mean, and when she fought with Miss Belle, she would commonly smack her over. Something dropped on the floor above them, and Addie raised her eyes to the ceiling. She sighed. The business overwhelmed her sometimes.

"Then I guess it's settled. Me and Emma will leave at sunup tomorrow."

"What?" Addie asked, forgetting the two boarders. "We have to think on this some more. Besides, you don't have to leave so soon."

"I'm done thinking," Ned said.

"We want to be back by the time John's letter arrives," Emma added. "I shall not impose any longer than I have to."

Before Addie could respond, there was another thump on the ceiling. Addie turned to Welcome. "You go up there and swat their behinds."

The hired woman straightened her long skirt, then smoothed her apron. "Don't you mess this up," she said, although it was not clear whether she was talking to Ned or Emma. Then she took the stairs two at a time as she called, "You stop that racket or I'll cut your ears off."

Addie glared at Ned and Emma. "No good will come of it. No good at all."

"Oh, I feel lucky," Ned told her.

"Well, I don't," Addie said, thinking she had the damndest luck of anybody she knew.

ned

Ned was always an admirer of sunrises. From his first days in the West when he was a runaway boy, he had been gladdened by the dawn over the prairie. He loved the beauty as the day began to break, the black sky softening into gray, the faint streak of yellow light, then flash following flash of violent color—rose and purple and magenta—as far as the eye could reach. He never failed to hold his breath as the sun slid over the horizon like a giant gold watch. If he rode late at night, he waited until sunrise to bed down. And when he stayed at The Chili Queen, he sometimes rose at dawn just to watch the day begin, going back to bed only when the color in the sky faded into blue, the pale shade of a shirt that had been washed again and again. Once, when the sunrise filled the heavens with streaks of pink and orange, Ned awakened Addie to see the wonder of it, but she muttered she had never seen a sunrise that was worth missing two minutes of sleep. She'd take a sunset any day. Not Ned. Sunset was the beginning of darkness; sunrise meant a whole new, glad day ahead, filled with the gift of surprise. From the first time Ned had seen the western sunrise, with the daylight washing over the prairie, turning the brown grasses to gold, he had felt his boy's heart lift and was filled with a sense of freedom he'd never even dreamed about at his father's farm on the Mississippi.

Ned turned to look at the sunrise over his shoulder that morning, as he drove west in the wagon with Emma beside him. He didn't say a word, but gestured behind him with his head, and she twisted about to see the spectacle.

"The orb of day," Emma said, as the orange ball popped up over the horizon, all but blinding Ned when he turned to look again.

"What's that?" Ned asked.

"It's what the poet calls the sun," Emma explained.

She was a smart one. Ned liked sitting beside a woman who read poetry, not that he'd ever read any himself. Still, he appreciated an intelligent woman.

"It's the best time of day. The world is deserted. I can believe I am the only one about," Emma continued.

"Well, you are," Ned said, "except for me." He turned to smile at her, but it was too dark for Emma to see his face. Besides, she was looking straight ahead now, down the road, away from Nalgitas.

They had been in the wagon for two hours. Ned told her they would leave early because the drive was a long one. That was true, but he was anxious to be on the road before Addie awoke with another reason why robbing the bank at Jasper was a bad idea. So he'd gotten up at three, put on a new shirt, hitched the horses to the wagon, then gone to The Chili Queen to awaken Emma. When he reached the house, he found her fully dressed, arguing in heavy whispers with Welcome. The two grew silent when they heard Ned's footsteps on the back porch, and he wondered if they had been talking about him.

"I'm short of gladness to see you here," Welcome told him.

"She had hoped you'd oversleep and not awaken until it was too late for us to leave," Emma laughed. "But never mind her. I, for one, am glad to see you, glad to be going."

"You haven't no right to taken her," Welcome told Ned.

"You just want Emma around to do your work," Ned replied. He was even more cheerful than usual.

Welcome sniffed. She finished packing a dinner in a basket and gave it to Emma. Then she picked up Emma's carpetbag and handed it to Ned. "If you let her be captivated, I'll raise revolution."

"I reckon she's not your concern," Ned said. "For a hired woman, you sure do mind other folks' business."

"It's terrible dangerous what you are setting out to do, and I got money on her," Welcome responded. "What if she don't come back?"

"Welcome is only being protective. Women alone are like that. They look out for each other," Emma explained to Ned. She had put on the black traveling dress and bonnet she had worn on the train, but had draped a cape over her shoulders, since early mornings on the prairie were cold.

"Why's that?" Ned asked, wondering how Emma knew such a thing. He started for the door.

Emma seemed to read his mind. "A woman knows," she replied vaguely. She turned to Welcome. "Now don't worry. We shall come back as good as ever."

"And quicker than a chicken can fly, I expect," Welcome muttered sourly. She followed the two out onto the back porch and watched them make their way to the barn, wringing her hands under her apron.

"You tell Addie not to worry, either," Ned called softly, so as not to awaken her. He knew Addie never worried about his safety, but it seemed like the right thing to say.

In the end, Addie had agreed to Ned's plan, maybe because she realized there was no way to stop him. But she'd refused to let him take her horses. Somebody might recognize them and then where would she be? Ned knew that wasn't the reason. Addie hoped that if he had to arrange for horses himself, Ned would reconsider the robbery. But he was stubborn, and his pride was at stake, not just with Addie but with Emma. He wasn't much of a man if he let the madam of a whorehouse tell him what to do. Ned wasn't sure why, but it mattered to him what Emma thought. So, he'd gone into town the night before and bought a couple of nags—black ones. Addie shuddered at the sight of them, although Ned didn't know why.

Addie hadn't said anything about not using her wagon, so Ned had hitched the horses to it.

He opened the barn door and led the horses out. Then he helped Emma onto the wagon seat. She turned and waved to Welcome as they pulled out, but Ned couldn't tell if Welcome waved back, for the woman was hidden in the darkness with only her white apron visible. He could see the apron like a flag until The Chili Queen disappeared from view.

Ned and Emma didn't talk much the first couple of hours, and when they did, they kept their voices low, as if they were afraid someone would overhear them. Ned felt Emma shiver beside him, and he reached for a blanket and handed it to her. She took off her bonnet, and wrapped herself in the blanket, with the fold over her head. When he glanced at her, Ned thought she looked purely Mexican. It was a good thing she could change her looks like that. When you were on Ned's side of the law, you wanted to confuse people about your appearance. As good-looking as he was, Ned, too, could make himself unmemorable. That was why he was daring to rob a bank so close to home. With the Santa Fe bank, he'd been foolish to brag about the haul. This time, he would keep his mouth shut, and no one would connect him with the robbery.

The horses plodded along, and Ned remarked that he did not believe they would out-travel even a man on foot. He explained to Emma that they had been the only animals available. The blacksmith had just bought a pair of fine horses, but he'd run them to ground before he'd sell them to Ned or Addie, even at a good profit.

Emma didn't ask why. Instead, she said, "I am reposed in the belief these horses are fine. People would wonder about dirt farmers with animals as good as Addie's. And a wagon is the ideal mode of travel. It would be unseemly to arrive on horseback." It was uncanny that Ned was also thinking there was an advantage in traveling as they did. He nodded and slapped the reins over the animals' backs, although the horses kept on plodding.

"You can change your mind anytime," Ned told her. He'd been saying that ever since they'd agreed to rob the Jasper bank. "I mean, you can change your mind right up till we walk up to the bank door. I wouldn't hold it against you."

Ned had expected Emma to back out even before they left Nalgitas. But she had told him, "You shall not find me a reluctant companion." He was surprised that she had agreed to the plan in the first place. But then, he had already decided Emma was not altogether what she seemed.

Ned had been thinking about the Jasper bank for several weeks and had brought it up because talking about a thing helped him think about it clearly. Usually he sounded out Addie, but they hadn't had much time alone since she'd returned from Kansas City. He was shocked when, after she heard him out, Emma said it was a job for two, and nobody would ever suspect a man and woman. "I suppose I shall go to hell for robbing my brother. The devil will be just as happy to see me if I have committed two offenses," she explained. "I'm of a mind to join with you temporarily in your life of crime."

Ned didn't think much about heaven and hell, but he did think about jail, and he was not comfortably safe with the idea of a woman as a partner. He told her straight off, no. Why, he'd never even heard of a woman robbing a bank. But after he thought about it, that was precisely why he found it an interesting idea and began to reconsider. "What happens if somebody shoots at you?" he asked.

"Then I shall shoot back. I can handle a gun, you know. I'm not helpless. No, I am not." Emma had laughed then and said, "I crave adventure. If that were not so, I would not have left Palestine, Kansas, to come to New Mexico in the first place. I think I have a level head and that I will not let you down."

He hadn't brought up the bank the first time they'd gone out riding together. In fact, the drive that day had started out so poorly that Ned expected he'd never exchange a civil word with Emma again. She sat on the buggy seat as far away from Ned as possible. Ned slumped forward, to make it clear he did not want to talk. He drove the horses too fast, giving them their heads and letting the buggy jerk and snap on the poor road. He hoped Emma would be too scared to ride with him after that. Then he'd tell Addie he'd done his part; she couldn't blame him if Emma refused to go out with him. But Emma hadn't seemed to notice how fast they were going—until the buggy lurched, catching Ned off guard, and he dropped the reins. Feeling their freedom, the horses began to run. Ned reached for the reins, but Emma grabbed them first, and standing up in the buggy, bracing herself against the seat, her skirt swept back against her legs, she pulled until the animals were under control. Emma doubtless felt exhilarated with the exertion, her body taut, her bright eyes flashing. When the horses stopped, she handed the reins to Ned, who looked at her in awe. He'd never seen a woman react so coolly to danger.

"I have lived my life on a farm and know as much about horses as any man," she said. "If you are trying to frighten me, you will have to find a better way to do it."

Ned lowered his head and looked sheepish.

Emma laughed. "I know you are showing me about not out of the goodness of your heart, but because Addie has ordered you to do so. Of course, I don't blame her. I am not unmindful that I am an impediment to her business." Despite the pretty speech, Emma did not seem in the least contrite. "I am not a twit. I am used to keeping my own company and often prefer it to tolerating fools. So I am happy to sit here on the prairie the day long, whilst you entertain yourself elsewhere."

"What's that about fools? Do you think I'm a fool?" Ned asked.

"Not at all. It is an expression only. I hoped to make the point that I do not mind being alone. You are neither of you fools—you and Addie. I do not underestimate you."

While Ned thought that over, Emma stepped down from the buggy. She opened the little watch pinned to her jacket. "Go about your business, and come back for me at five o'clock. I shall entertain myself until then, and no one will be the wiser. Tomorrow, I will bring along my sewing. I propose that neither of us tell Addie about the arrangement."

She started for a tree some distance from the road.

Ned hadn't wanted to spend his time with Emma, but now that she made it clear she didn't care to be with him, he was hurt. Women generally didn't avoid his company. "Hey," he called. "Come on back. There's snakes out there."

"There are snakes in Kansas."

"Rattlers. They're fierce."

"Then I shall look for a stout stick."

"It might rain. You'll get wet."

"Welcome says it hasn't rained in weeks."

"It's dangerous out here," Ned yelled, but Emma walked on. "There's outlaws. You wouldn't want to meet up with one."

"I already have."

"Hey," he called again.

Emma stopped but didn't turn around. She waited.

"I've got cookies."

Emma was still a moment longer, then turned around. "Now, I believe you have hit upon something."

Ned held up a small basket. "I'm going to eat in the shade, and since there's only one tree out here, you'll have to sit with me, unless you want to be in the sun."

At that, Emma laughed. "You have the advantage of me," she told him.

Ned led the horses to the tree, unhitched and hobbled them, then he sat on the ground while Emma found a rock to perch on, and they took turns sipping from the bottle of water he'd brought along, too. Ned took out a handful of cookies and handed one to Emma.

"If we are to go out again tomorrow, I would like to ride on a horse instead of in a buggy. Do you think Addie would be shocked?" she asked, then broke off a piece of the cookie and ate it.

"Addie's a whore."

"You are unkind. She is your sister, or so she says—and a friend to me."

"No, ma'am, I am stating facts. Addie is what she is, just like I am. We don't make excuses."

Emma nodded. "I suppose I must get used to this new world I have chosen." She ate the rest of her cookie, then brushed crumbs from her skirt. "She would not mind, then, if I rode a horse?"

"I wouldn't think so."

"Astride."

Ned glanced at her. "Well, maybe not astride."

"A sidesaddle is cumbersome. I always rode astride at home. I prefer it."

Ned shook his head. "Addie might not like it. She's funny about some things." He finished the cookies he'd taken out, then reached into the basket for more. They were a different kind, with raisins in them. Ned picked out the dried fruit. "I don't like raisins. Never did."

"I'll remember," Emma said. "If we leave before Addie's awake, she'll never know about the saddle."

"I like nuts better," Ned said.

They didn't talk about the saddle again, but the next day, Ned put a man's saddle on Addie's horse and led it out of the barn for Emma, who was wearing some kind of skirt that was split in the middle like pants. Emma was right. She was as good on a horse as any man. In fact, when they returned to The Chili Queen after their ride, he was more tuckered out than she was.

That day, Ned showed Emma the ranch country around Nalgitas. The following day, he took her to What Cheer, a deserted mining town on the rail line between Nalgitas and Jasper. The tracks had looped north to What Cheer because of the area's once-promising gold discoveries. The deposits proved to be shallow, however. The precious metal played out, and the miners moved on. But the railroad still jogged north through the old town, then turned abruptly southwest to Jasper.

Now, not so many years after the town was founded, What Cheer was rotting into the earth. A depot, a store, and a saloon built of milled lumber sagged; their windowpanes were broken out. The only other buildings were a few log cabins that squatted along the single street, weeds growing on their dirt roofs. They had been thrown up hastily, without windows. Their doors were open, as if the occupants had been too anxious to leave to close them. Only one of them had a front porch, and Ned and Emma stopped beside it, tying their horses to the porch post. Emma found a chair with three legs and sat down on it, carefully leaning her head against the wall and rubbing her hands over her face. Then she leaned foward, balancing herself on the chair, and looked down the street. She seemed to find What Cheer an interesting scene. "I always liked a mining town," she said.

Ned, seated on the porch at her feet, asked, "When did

you see one before now?"

Emma's chair wobbled as she looked down at him. "Oh, I haven't. I've just seen pictures is all. Mining towns always appear so . . . so haphazard, you know, as if people didn't care what they looked like, as if the life itself was more important than the place they lived in." She gave up on the chair and stood up. "I have lived with too much order."

"I never liked farming myself."

Emma took off her hat, and unpinned her hair, shaking it out. She separated it into strands with her fingers and began making a single fat braid. "You were a farmer?" she asked.

"Like I told you, I ran off when I was kid. It was during the war, and I tried to join up as a drummer with the Union. But my father found out about it, and he whipped me. So I just lit out west instead, all the way from Ft. Madison, Iowa."

"And procured a new name. 'Ned Partner' is much too grand to be real."

Ned grinned. Even Addie hadn't figured that out. "I kind of liked the sound of 'Ned Partner.' It's better than 'Billy Keeler,' at any rate." Ned had never told anybody his real name, but after all those years, what did it matter? Besides, there was nobody Emma could tell.

"Do they know where you are?" Emma extracted a piece of string from a pocket and tied it around the end of her braid.

"Nope. I've got a sister, Alice. I write to her every now and then, but she doesn't know how to reach me."

"Maybe she's dead."

Ned thought that over. He reached for a stem of dried grass and stripped it. "I wouldn't like to think so."

"Perhaps it doesn't matter. Perhaps it is the writing alone that matters. Have you thought about seeing your family again?"

Ned shook his head. "I'm not much for going back. Now take Addie, she's different. She's all the time talking about going back to San Antonio. She loves San Antonio."

"But not Iowa?"

"Now why'd she want to go to Iowa? Far as I know, she's never been there."

Ned thought about what he'd said and looked at Emma to see if she'd caught it. She gave him a wry smile, and he wondered how long she had known he and Addie were not brother and sister, maybe from the beginning. He threw away the stem and reached for another, pulling it out by the roots. "I never wanted to farm, leastways not along the Mississippi. You could drown in your own sweat back there. But ranching, now there's something different."

Emma didn't seem to hear him. She shaded her eyes as she looked out over the town. Then she stepped off into the dirt and began to walk slowly down the street, peering into the houses. Ned followed, and in a minute, they reached the depot and stopped. There was no platform, and the train station itself was just a board shack with a sign above it that read WHAT CHEER. The sign was as warped and faded as the town.

"There's no stationmaster. Does the train stop here anymore?" Emma asked.

"I suppose, if somebody wanted it to, that is. But why would anyone want to stop at What Cheer?"

Emma shrugged. "Maybe a cowboy." She peered into the dark building. "Does anyone still live here?"

"Not that I know of. Every now and then an old prospector says he's coming out here to find the mother lode. He never stays long."

Emma stepped into the depot, Ned behind her. The room had been stripped except for a bunk built into one wall, and a broken table that was overturned. Weeds grew between the broken floorboards. A piece of ragged muslin hung from a string stretched across the single window. There was a rustling in the far corner, and Emma shivered. "It's just a rat," Ned told her. "A pack rat."

"I hate them," Emma said, taking a step backward and bumping into Ned and losing her balance. Ned caught her and held her. Emma's arms were lean and corded, not like Addie's mashed-potato flesh. Except for helping her onto a horse or into a wagon, Ned had never touched Emma. And he felt a shiver go through him.

"It's cold in here," he said, but he didn't move. Emma stood where she was for a full minute then she turned, and without looking at him she stepped out into the sunlight. Ned followed, fighting off the urge to touch her again. He didn't want to grab her. He didn't even care to hold her, but he wanted to touch her arm again.

As they walked back through the town, Emma stopped to pluck a dead flower from a thorny bush. "It's a rose, a climber. A woman lived here. She planted a rosebush." Emma let the brown petals fall from her hand as she returned to the horses. But she didn't seem to be in any hurry to leave. She took the canteen from Ned's horse and sipped, then handed it to Ned, who drank.

"What's so different about ranching that you like it better than farming? It all seems the same to me," she said.

"What?" Ned asked.

"You said you wouldn't mind ranching."

Ned was surprised. He'd thought Emma hadn't been listening. "Well, for one thing, ranchers don't have to raise pigs. I hate pigs."

Emma laughed, and Ned liked her laugh. It was a medium laugh, not high and shrill like most women's. But neither was it whiskey-deep and throaty like Addie's.

"And you don't have to plow. I promised myself when I left home, I'd never plow another row."

"I guess you wouldn't be much of a farmer then."

Ned returned the canteen to his saddle, then went through his saddlebags until he found some hard candy and gave a piece to Emma. She dusted it off on her shirt and put it into her mouth, then sat down on the porch step, sweeping her split skirt to one side.

"There's a ranch I could buy," he said suddenly. "I never told anybody about it before. It's in Colorado, up around Telluride. I figure I could sell beef to the mining camps."

Emma bit down on the candy, then tilted her head as she asked, "Why don't you—buy it, that is?"

Ned leaned on the porch post and looked down at her. "Well, for one thing, it costs twelve thousand dollars, less if I paid cash, but I haven't got it."

"I thought you had five thousand dollars. Addie said you got that when you robbed a bank."

"Addie talks too much. Besides, that's less than half of what I'd need." He was silent for a moment, looking out over the prairie. "Anyway, Addie, she'd never live on a ranch, and I'd get lonesome by myself."

"You might find a woman who was partial to ranching," Emma said softly.

"Yeah," Ned said, thinking it over. "But it doesn't matter since I don't have the money."

"You could borrow it."

Ned laughed. "You think a bank would loan to me?"

"You could rob another bank, then," Emma said.

"It's not that easy," Ned replied. He stood and untied the reins of Emma's horse. "I expect we better get to home."

Emma stood up and mounted her horse. Ned untied his reins, then looked down at the dirt at a red flower that poked out from under the porch floor. He broke it off, and without a word, he handed it to Emma. She looked startled, then reached for it. But instead of giving her the flower, Ned put his hand over hers and held it for a minute. Then he let go, and grinning, he fixed the flower to her horse's bridle. He felt a little foolish then, and mounted quickly, spurring his horse into a gallop and leaving Emma behind. She followed at a slower pace, and after a mile, Ned stopped to let her catch up.

"There is a bank not so far from here, at Jasper. It would cost only the taking," Ned told her, as they walked their horses. "Addie's after me to try it, but the farmers at Jasper are dirt poor. I don't guess it's got more than two dollars in it."

Emma thought it over. "Who's to say how much a bank has? It's a bank, isn't it? Banks have cash. Besides, there must be merchants and ranchers who deposit their money there."

Ned nodded, and he began to tell her what he knew about the bank. He'd been in Jasper a time or two, although not lately, but he guessed the town itself was doing well enough. After all, the railroad went through it. When he finished, Emma was silent for a time, then she said that nobody would suspect a man and woman of robbing a bank. Ned reined in his horse and stared at her. "A woman'd get scared," he said.

And Emma replied, "I didn't get scared with a runaway team, did I? If you are of a mind, I am determined to join you."

"I wouldn't take a woman as a partner," Ned said.

"And would you take a man you know less well than me?"

Ned thought that over and repeated, "I wouldn't take a woman."

"I thought you wanted to buy a ranch, and I believe I may be the means for you to do so. Or am I mistaken?"

She was not, Ned decided. He mulled over her suggestion for a long time before he told her grudgingly that it might work. And by the time they reached The Chili Queen, they had put together a plan. It had almost fallen apart, however, when they disagreed on what percentage of the take Emma should get. Ned thought he was generous to offer a third, but she demanded half. Finally, they settled on forty percent, and Ned had added, "We'll split fifty-fifty if we ever pull a second job together." It was a joke, but Emma had nodded seriously.

Ned wasn't sure that in the end, he would go through

with it, or Emma either. And maybe they would have called it off, but then they saw how much Addie opposed it. That made Ned more determined, and Emma seemed to be more resolved, too. Ned didn't understand women much. He'd have thought Addie and Emma would have been of one mind. Instead, they seemed to pull him in different directions.

"I'll hold you to account if anything happens," Addie had warned. Ned was about to say he wouldn't let anything happen to his partner. Then he realized that Addie was not speaking to him, but to Emma.

Once the sun rose in the sky, the day turned hot. Emma removed the blanket, then her cape and, in a few minutes, the jacket. After a while, she unbuttoned the top button of her blouse and rolled up her sleeves. Finally, she put on a droopy sunbonnet. "Do I look like a homesteader?" she asked. The night before, she had inquired of Addie if she could borrow a dress that would be suitable for a farm wife, but Addie had scoffed and said the women at The Chili Queen didn't have such. Ned said what she wore wouldn't matter because farm women in New Mexico put on their best clothes to go to town. Besides, he'd never seen Emma wear a dress that anyone would notice, although he didn't say as much. The sunbonnet gave the right touch, however. Only a farm wife would wear it with a silk dress. Besides, it hid Emma's face, not that anyone would notice that, either.

Ned didn't mind the sun. He enjoyed looking over the prairie where clouds made shadow patches on the gold-brown vegetation. Spring was his favorite time of year on the Great Plains, when the wildflowers bloomed, sprinkling brightness like colored glass through the green of the new grasses. But late summer was pretty, too, when the grass dried to the color of wheat, with clumps of purple wild asters. Ned pointed to a streak of them, and Emma smiled.

"I don't believe I ever saw a flower I didn't like," she said, then frowned as if recalling something.

"Looks like there's one you don't like," Ned said.

"Lilies. I never liked lilies. They always remind me of the dead." She shivered, and Ned raised his eyebrow, but Emma didn't explain, so Ned didn't ask who'd died. Perhaps Emma was thinking about her father—or her mother; Emma had never mentioned her. Or maybe there was something deep in Emma, some dark secret that terrorized her in the night. Addie was like that. Ned was sure there were things Addie hadn't told him; he knew her life had been dark. He doubted that life had been excessively bad for Emma.

Ned himself was remarkably free of conflict. The only part of his past he regretted was losing touch with his sisters, Alice, and the older one, Lizzie. If he ever settled down, he might write them and tell them where he was. He didn't even know if they had survived the war, and that was more than twenty years before. Alice's husband had been a Union volunteer; Ned wondered if he had made it through the war. Lizzie's husband had too high an opinion of himself, and Ned didn't care much about him. Ned had other sisters and brothers, too, and he was curious to know if his parents were still alive. He wondered about all of them, and sometimes he thought he'd like to go back to Ft. Madison and find out if they were still there. He wouldn't have to see them, just check into a hotel under another name and inquire about the Keelers. He'd never been sorry he'd run off. In fact, he had few regrets at all about his life. Ned had killed a few men—three to be exact. He was sorry, but it couldn't be helped, so he didn't dwell on it. The world was a better place without all of them.

One thing was sure. If he had stayed at home, he'd never have met Addie. He had no regrets about her. Ned had known many women, but he had loved Addie best of all. Ned didn't care much for clinging women, and he'd liked Addie right well from the first time he saw her. They'd had an understanding that they were both free as frogs. Addie'd made it clear she didn't want to settle down. The Chili Queen was hers to run, and she didn't care for any interference from Ned. If he was looking for a wife, she'd told him, he best move along and not waste his time. Did he want to settle down? Well, he hadn't back then, but recently, he'd thought about it once or twice. Probably it was the ranch that made him consider a wife and a family. Every now and then a picture flitted through his mind of a house, a baby in a cradle, a rocker with a woman bent over her sewing in the quiet of the evening. Ned couldn't picture Addie in that rocker. And lately, things had been unhandy between them. Addie had gotten crabbed, and Ned had grown a little dissatisfied with her. He was reluctant to move along, however. Ned didn't like making decisions.

After a while, Emma reached into her bag and took out her piecing. It was an oddly homey thing, sitting next to her while she stitched. Ned remembered how his sisters went to quilting in the afternoon, after their chores were done. Sometimes, he sat with them, laughing and joking while he mended a harness or whittled a cog his father needed for a piece of machinery. Ned had always been good with his hands. On the farm, there'd been much work to do, and Ned hadn't minded it. But then his father drove him too much, like a horse that was rode hard and not rubbed down.

Ned wondered when he'd become so lazy. Maybe it was Addie. She wouldn't let him do anything around The Chili Queen, so he'd given up offering. Whenever he said he'd nail up a board that had come loose or rehang a door that didn't fit, Addie told him not to bother himself. So after a time Ned didn't. And sometimes he missed the pleasure of working with his hands, fixing a thing that was broken or shaping something new. He thought it might be nice to do things for a woman, to have one need him.

"My sisters sewed," he said, glancing at the patchwork in Emma's lap.

"Most women do," Emma replied.

"I mean, they were good. In school, I couldn't get the hang of geometry, so my sister Lizzie explained it to me with her quilting pieces. They're all squares and triangles."

"I never knew a man who noticed," Emma said, looking up at him. The sun hit her square in the face, and she squinted. Despite the dark shadow the bonnet cast on Emma's face, Ned could see the lines around her eyes. There were lines at the corners of her mouth, too. Ned wondered how old she was, whether she were too old to have children. Then he wondered why he'd thought about that.

"My folks always said that idle hands are the devil's plaything," he remarked, as Emma took a few tiny stitches on her needle.

"I believe the devil has played with me already," she replied.

For their nooning, they found a place at the edge of a streambed, where it cut deep into the earth. Half a dozen giant cottonwoods lined one side of the bank, the only trees visible. The prairie was a mottled brown, and on the horizon a herd of antelope bounded along on slender legs. "They are so graceful, they seem to be sailing in the air," Emma observed. Ned was thinking the same thing, and it gladdened him that Emma enjoyed the prairie. He unhitched the horses and let them drink from the trickle of water that flowed through the dirt, then hobbled them and set them to graze. Emma took a basket from the wagon and set out a loaf of dry bread, hard cheese, and some pickles on a napkin. "Welcome must have decided we should eat like poor farmers," she said, nodding at the meager meal.

"Welcome ought to hush up with her complaining. She's not the boss of us," Ned replied. "If she weren't such a worker, Addie would toss her out, she's that ornery." He took out his knife and cut the bread into chunks, then hacked off pieces of the cheese. "We'll have us a good supper at the hotel tonight."

"I don't mind sleeping in the wagon. We wouldn't want

to draw attention to ourselves by spending money for a hotel," Emma said.

"Oh, it's not such a fancy one, although the dining room is nice enough. Besides, the hotel's part of my plan. It's got a back door that opens direct on the bank. The two buildings aren't more than a dozen steps apart. That bank's such easy pickings, I'm surprised nobody's taken it before. We'll just go down the stairs, out the door, into the bank, then back to the hotel when we're done. Like I told Addie, it's as easy as honey."

"Nothing's as easy as honey," Emma told him. Her voice was so harsh that Ned glanced up at her. Emma broke off a crumb of bread and put it into her mouth. "Just when you think a thing's that easy, a bee comes along—a whole swarm of bees—and you get stung." She seemed to be talking more to herself than to Ned. She stood up. "I believe I'll walk about until you are ready to commence. My limbs are knotted up."

"Take your time. The horses have to rest, and I don't mind a nap," Ned told her. "You look at that watch of yours, and if I'm not awake in an hour, you shake me." He put his hat over his face, and in a minute or two, he was asleep.

When she woke him, Emma already had packed away the lunch things and hitched the horses to the wagon.

Jasper was more respectable than Nalgitas. It had fewer saloons, and two church steeples rose above the cabins and clapboard houses. In the twilight, Jasper looked soft and homey—and more prosperous than Nalgitas, too. The depot was twice the size of the one at Nalgitas and so new that it hadn't yet been painted. The JASPER sign leaned against the wall facing the tracks. Prosperity meant that there would be more people in the bank than Ned had figured on. And the bank might have installed a whale of a safe, too. But good times also meant money in the bank. That part of it pleased Ned, and he reached for Emma's hand. Her skin wasn't rough, as he'd imagined, but as soft as Addie's. Addie didn't work at card games anymore, but she still kept her hands supple.

Like Nalgitas, Jasper had been cut out of the prairie. The main street was half a dozen blocks long, lined with brick buildings and a sprinkling of stone structures. Awnings shaded the entrances to stores, and trees had been planted along the streets, which gave the town a finished look. Ned pointed out the Union Hotel, a two-story red brick building with a double door in front, as they drove past it, telling Emma they'd leave the horses and wagon at the livery, then walk to the hotel. The train had just arrived, and there was no reason to let the hotel clerk know they'd driven to Jasper in a wagon. Of course, if anyone asked—if the sheriff got suspicious and inquired, for instance—he'd find out easy enough. But it would take a few minutes, and sometimes that made all the difference between a successful robbery and getting caught. Emma agreed that made sense.

They parked the wagon beside the stable, and Ned made arrangements for the horses. Then he picked up their bags and carried them down the board sidewalk. Emma, walking beside him, was as drab as the farmers and shopkeepers they passed. Nobody made note of her. Ned himself, dressed in worn pants, his shirt soiled and stained with sweat from the day's drive in the sun, blended in, too. Ned didn't care much for disguises. A few days' growth of beard, a little dirt on his face, his hair slicked down, and he was no longer a handsome young man, but just a saddle tramp. People had a hard time describing him. Even Addie barely recognized his face in a wanted poster.

"We need a room," Ned told the desk clerk, looking down at the guest register. Ned's eyes were one thing he couldn't change, and he didn't want the clerk to notice they were green.

"Two rooms, brother," Emma spoke up.

"What?" Ned stammered. For an instant, he didn't understand what Emma was talking about. The desk clerk smirked.

Then Emma hissed in a voice so low that only the two men heard her. "I have told you we are civilized people, and I will sleep in my own room. You are too cheap for your own good. If I have come all this way to keep house for you, I insist you obey the laws of propriety. Two rooms, sir. Do you have them?" Emma looked the clerk in the face. "Have I said something to amuse you?"

The smile faded from the clerk's face, and he looked down at the register. "Oh, no, ma'am. We got aplenty of rooms. Yes we do. You want side by side?"

"I want mine upstairs, in the back, where I will not be bothered by the noise. The farthest back, please. My brother can speak for himself."

"You can put me across from her," Ned said. He was so tickled at Emma that he wanted to laugh, but instead, he rubbed his eyes and looked away from the clerk as if he were embarrassed.

"You want to sign," the clerk said.

They had forgotten to talk about a name to use. Ned reached for the register and pronounced the name as he wrote it: "William Smith."

He set down the pen, and the clerk turned to Emma. "What's your name?"

"Miss Smith," she replied in such a way that the clerk did not inquire about her given name.

The man gave Ned two keys, and Ned picked up the bags, leading the way upstairs. The rooms were at the end of a long hall, on either side of the back stairs. Ned unlocked both doors and let Emma choose her room. Then he set down her bag and grinned. "By zam, Emma! I couldn't have done that better myself. You're a plain natural actress."

Emma blushed. "It just came to me."

"For that, I'll buy you the best supper in Jasper. You let me put my things in the other room, and let's go."

"I need to wash and put on a fresh dress. Call for me in an hour," Emma told him.

An hour was a long time, and Ned was dry enough from the drive to spit cotton. So he went down to a saloon that was off the hotel lobby. Just one of the four tables was occupied, and a single man stood at one end of the bar. He looked like a lot of old bums who stood with their bellies to the bar, telling of the money they had spent the night before, but no go, and the bartender did not seem inclined to give him a free drink. Ned was in no mood for a conversation with a man who intended to go to work getting intoxicated and would accomplish it with Ned's money, if he could, so Ned went to the other end of the bar and ordered rye. He hadn't even tasted it when the desk clerk stepped up next to him, and nodded at the bartender for his own glass of whiskey.

"You expecting to settle at Jasper, Mr. Smith?" the clerk asked.

Ned shrugged. "Hereabouts."

"I don't guess your sister's too pleased about it."

Ned looked down at his drink. "My sister's not pleased about much of anything."

"Sorry to hear it." The clerk didn't sound the least bit sorry.

"I'm not saying she isn't a good woman. She is. Yes sir, she is, but she is hard-pressed to find something to her liking. She sees herself a higher authority on most things." Ned let out a sigh. Playacting came naturally to him. Still, he was cautious, wondering why the clerk was so friendly.

"Here to buy supplies? You a farmer, are you?"

Ned nodded.

"Where'd you come from?"

Ned stiffened then. It wasn't good manners in New Mexico or anywhere else he knew of to inquire too much about a stranger—wasn't smart, either. "Someplace where they don't ask so many questions." He spoke in an even voice, but the clerk took his meaning.

There was a pause while the man cleared his throat, then said, "I expect it'll be a long winter."

"Might be." Ned finished his drink and considered another but decided against it.

"If I was you, I'd find myself a little something to think about those winter nights."

Ned relaxed. The clerk was a shill for a whorehouse. "What would that be?" he asked.

The clerk gave a nervous laugh. "Well, seeing as how you're a husky young fellow, you might want to get your wick dipped. I guess you catch my meaning." He glanced over at Ned.

Ned examined his empty glass and didn't reply.

"No disrespect meant," the clerk said, setting down his own glass and turning away.

"What was it you were suggesting?" Ned asked.

The clerk grinned and tried to catch Ned's eye in the mirror in front of them, but Ned was looking away. "We have a real fine establishment called Elsie Mae's. It's on Maiden Lane, just down from the depot. You can't miss it. 'Elsie Mae's' is written on the front window in gold. Classy it is. Clean." The clerk shook his head to emphasize what he'd said, then added, "First-class. You be sure to say Lemuel sent you."

"You got only one hookhouse in this town, Lemuel?" Ned asked. He winked at the clerk in the mirror then. The bar was so dark that the man couldn't see the color of Ned's eyes, even if they'd been bright red.

"You got only one hookhouse where you come from?" Lemuel shot back.

Ned didn't answer.

"There's the French Brewery, only you'd best stay away from it. Girls there are rough as a cob. But maybe that's your preference."

"Either place, you get your cut, right?"

The clerk shrugged.

Ned didn't want to give the man a reason to dislike

him—or to remember him any more than necessary—so he said pleasantly, "If I was to go to one or the other, I'd say you sent me."

The front door of the hotel opened, and a man with a star pinned to his vest walked through the lobby to the saloon, coming up on the other side of the clerk. "Lemuel," he said by way of greeting, but he was looking at Ned. The two men got up from their table and left. The man at the other end of the bar looked at his drink, but Ned knew he was listening.

"Sheriff," Lemuel replied.

"Sheriff Tate," he said, introducing himself to Ned. The man was short and so fat he could hardly tote himself. He had a florid face and eyes as close together as an earthworm's.

"Sheriff," Ned said.

"This here's Mr. Smith," Lemuel said.

The sheriff squinted his wormy eyes at Ned, as if he were trying to place him. "Nice name, Smith," he said. "You been to Jasper before?"

"He's new," Lemuel replied for Ned.

"You look familiar."

"I look like everybody's brother," Ned told him.

The sheriff studied Ned. "Yeah, I guess that's it. What's your business in Jasper, Mr. Smith?" The bartender filled a glass and set it down in front of the sheriff.

The clerk answered again. "Oh, he's a farmer. I've been telling him about our finer establishments." The clerk raised an eyebrow at the sheriff, who didn't respond. "He checked in with his sister. She walks like a chicken in high oats," he said in a manner uncouth.

"Say!" Ned protested, although he was glad for the remark since it caused the sheriff to lose interest in him.

The lobby door opened again, and a man entered and walked to the desk, looking around. The clerk licked the edge of his glass and left.

Ned was ready to leave, too, but he didn't want the sheriff to think he was anxious to get away. He motioned for the bartender to fill his glass and thought about buying a drink for the sheriff, but that might make the man suspicious. Farmers didn't go around buying liquor for people. "Here's to you," Ned said.

"And right back at you," the sheriff replied, although he didn't raise his glass.

Ned tried to think of something a farmer might ask. "You got a doctor here? My sister has female complaints."

The sheriff shifted as if he were uncomfortable. "Yeah, we got one, but he ain't worth a gob of spit. I'd say stay away from him, unless you want to kill her. I myself suffer from piles and the bowel complaint, and every potion he gives me makes it worse. I can't sit a horse worth nothing. Can't sit down at all sometimes." He launched into his symptoms, while Ned grunted in sympathy from time to time. "I'm pretty sorry right now," the sheriff finished up.

"I best tell her to doctor herself then," Ned said. He pointed his thumb toward the desk clerk. "He told me about Elsie Mae's."

"I expect he did. It's all right. But I'd stay away from the French Brewery, if I was you. I guess he told you that, too."

"Yes sir, he did."

There was a commotion outside, and the sheriff glanced toward the door and winced. "It ain't such a bad job, as long as I don't have to deal with no outlaws or ride no horse." He sighed, and squinted at Ned as if he were trying again to place him. Then he shrugged and walked stiff-legged out of the room, calling over his shoulder, "Luck to you, Mr. Smith."

Ned had finished only half his whiskey. He picked up his glass, decided he didn't want the drink, and set it back down, slapping some money on the bar. Then Ned thought better of it. A farmer wouldn't be so generous. He spread out the coins and pocketed two. Then he went upstairs and knocked on Emma's door. She emerged into the dark hall, a shawl over her shoulders, and followed Ned back down the stairs.

The dining room was fancier than the rest of the hotel. A chandelier with candles and crystal drops hung in the center of the large room, which had been painted a dark green, with gold designs on the walls near the ceiling. The floor was striped with alternating boards of ash and walnut. The tables were covered with white cloths and set with white china and candles instead of kerosene lamps. Ned led the way to the most secluded table in the room, and started to sit down. Then something reminded him of the manners he'd been taught long before, and he pulled out one of the little caned chairs for Emma. She sat down gracefully, and before seating himself, Ned looked around to see if he recognized anyone. He didn't. It was late, only four of the tables were occupied, and Emma was the only woman in the room.

She had removed her shawl and set it on an empty chair next to her. Ned started to sit down, then stopped as he stared at Emma. She didn't have on enough clothes to keep a cat warm. She wore a black silk dress that was pulled in tight at her slim waist and cut so low in front that Ned got an admirable view of her breasts. The two frills on the top of her dress not only failed to hide Emma's bosom, but called attention to it. Nestled in the center of the top frill was a brooch with a lady painted on it. The little portrait stuck up high enough to cover about a quarter-inch of Emma's cleavage. Her breasts were smooth, not pitted and dimpled like Addie's. The candle-light gave them a silvery white sheen that reminded Ned of the quicksilver the chemists had used in the mills in What Cheer to extract gold from ore. Emma cleared her throat, and Ned, embarrassed at having been caught, raised his eyes. Emma seemed amused as she stared at him. Ned stared back. A peculiar sensation stole over his feelings as he took in Emma's face and hair. Instead of being braided or tied in a knot, her hair was twisted on the back of her head into a fashionable series of loops and coils. The flickering light turned her hair a glossy black, with streaks of white, like feathers, shimmering through it. The style showed off Emma's high cheekbones and made her eyes larger. She was not beautiful in the ripe, delicious way that Addie had been when Ned first met her. Instead, Emma was striking—elegant, Ned thought. His gaze shifted from Emma's face to her body again. It was lean and firm. He could almost see her bones. Emma was meat while Addie was potatoes. Ned searched for a word to describe her, then remembered what the desk clerk had said about Elsie Mae's. Emma had class. She was clean, too.

Ned leaned forward and took Emma's hand. "You sure don't look like a . . . a . . ." He'd started to say whore, then realized that while Addie would have considered that high praise, Emma might not take it as a compliment. For the first time in his life, Ned was awkward around a woman, and finished, "like a farmer from Kansas." It was not excessively fine praise.

If Emma guessed what he'd been about to say, she didn't let on. She dipped her head as though she'd just been paid an excellent compliment, and her eyes sparkled.

Ned wondered what to say next, but the truth was that in the past twenty years, he hadn't spent much time with women who weren't whores. He asked himself what he'd say to his sisters, but that didn't help, because what he felt for Emma just then wasn't in the least what a man would feel for his sisters. He gave her the sleepy-eyed grin that never failed to stir Addie and said the only thing that came to mind. "The gravy's first-rate here."

"What?" Emma asked.

"They use cream. Not milk. That's the secret."

"Cream," Emma repeated, looking at Ned as if the secret of the gravy were every bit as fascinating as being told she didn't look like a farmer.

"Maybe you coming from a farm, you wouldn't think about that, but in New Mexico, there aren't so many cows. Cream is hard to come by."

"Cream," Emma said solemnly.

Ned nodded.

"Is that why you want to buy a ranch in Colorado, so

that you can have cream?"

Ned laughed. "Oh, those are beef cattle. Milking one of them, why, you might as well try shaking hands with a rattlesnake." Suddenly, Ned knew that never in his life had he sounded like such a fool as he did at that moment. Ever since he'd met Emma, he'd felt superior to her, showing off as he initiated her into the world of crime. Now she was the worldly one, poised, aloof, mysterious even. He'd been right when he said she didn't bring to mind a Kansas farm woman. In fact, Ned would bet that Emma's life on a farm was not the whole piece of cloth. She had acquired sophistication somewhere else. He wondered if she had gone to an eastern school.

Emma watched him, as if she were enjoying his discomfort. She licked her lips and leaned forward. "What do they serve here besides gravy?" she asked.

Ned chuckled. One of the reasons people found him so good-natured was that he could laugh at himself. "Why would you want anything but gravy?" he asked. "I don't expect there's room inside that dress for a muchness of anything else. My, you do look so pretty and fine." Ned felt like a fly around a pitcher of molasses.

But he grew more confident as he saw that the remark flustered Emma. "Is the dress too daring? I had planned to be married in it, and I thought it was a shame to waste it." She reached for her shawl, but Ned shook his head, and she left the shawl on the back of the chair. Emma chuckled. "I do believe Mr. Withers did me a favor in bringing me to New Mexico and discarding me. Why, if I'd married him, I would be cooking supper in an open hearth just now instead of eating in a fine hotel." She paused and added, "The woman is my mother."

Ned raised his eyes. He had been staring at her bosom again, just above the brooch. He was relieved when a waiter arrived to take their order. He took a deep breath and collected himself so much that he referred to Emma as his sister.

After the waiter left, Emma straightened the silverware in front of her. Then she aligned the salt shaker with the sugar bowl. "You are right about our staying in this hotel. Before you called for me, I availed myself of the opportunity to look about. It appears that we are the only two occupants of the second floor. Since the trains have already arrived from both east and west, I doubt that others will be checking in. A guest with a room on the first floor might use the back door, of course, but there is a jog in the hall there, preventing anyone from seeing the door until he reaches it. I believe we can go and come without being seen. It is an ideal setup."

Ned cocked his head. "How would you know what makes an ideal setup?"

Emma considered him a moment. Then she leaned forward and said brusquely, "I have cast my lot with you and propose to know everything I can about our undertaking. I did not think you would want a partner who was ignorant. Or did you bring me here for some other purpose?"

"If I'd had some other purpose in mind, I'd have stayed at The Chili Queen," he replied in the same tone.

"Quite right," Emma said. "Now, shall we get down to the fine points of it?"

The waiter interrupted, setting down plates in front of them. Emma picked up her fork and considered the boiled mackerel she'd ordered, but she didn't eat. Ned, on the other hand, took several bites of his dinner before he said anything. "There aren't any fine points. If you plan things out too much, you don't make allowance for anything going wrong. We go to the bank in the morning, when it's busy, and change a bill. That'll just give me a chance to see how things lay out, how many people they got working there, whether the safe's open. That's all." Ned forked half of an enchilada into his mouth and swallowed. "Noon. My guess is noon's the best time to take it. We'll wait till the banker goes to dinner. That'll leave one clerk, two at most."

Ned stopped talking as the waiter took away his plate. "Sister, you've eaten hardly a bite," he said sharply.

"It doesn't suit me," Emma replied, sitting back so that the waiter could remove her plate, too. "Except for the gravy, of course." Ned saw the corners of her mouth turn up.

Ned asked for coffee and dessert for the two of them. "Anything but vinegar pie. I am heartily sick of vinegar pie." He glanced at Emma. "Begging your pardon, sister."

The waiter returned with the coffee and two dishes. "Indian pudding," he said, putting the desserts on the table.

"What's that?" Emma asked.

"Cornmeal and molasses," he replied.

Emma made a face. "Oh, brother, I do not believe I could eat such a mixture."

"Well, you could try," Ned said. When the waiter turned away, Ned told Emma, "There's not a person who's met you here who would consider you to be anything but an ill-tempered spinster."

"A heavy clog, a good nuisance," Emma elaborated. "You have complimented me, to be sure," she added wryly.

"It is meant to be a compliment. Whoever would suspect us of being anything but what we pretend to be? I believe every man here gives me his sympathy that I go to farming with such a woman."

Emma did not appear to be altogether pleased, and she looked at Ned for a long time. Then she picked up her spoon and tasted the pudding. She looked at the dessert without comment, but she took another bite. "Be careful. There are raisins."

Ned gave her a questioning look.

"You said you didn't like them, never did. Or am I wrong?"

"You have a good memory."

"I rarely forget a thing. Tell me about your ranch," she said.

"It's at Telluride in Colorado. It's just a ranch," Ned replied. But it wasn't just a ranch. Ever since he'd first seen it, Ned had dreamed about the property night and morning. Ned wanted to tell her about the ranch. And as he looked into Emma's eyes, he knew she was not just making conversation; she wanted to hear about it. Emma's hand toyed with her brooch, and she looked at him with luminous eyes, her mouth half-open. As he stared at her, Ned knew he had the heart disease. He set down his spoon and pushed aside his dish, although Indian pudding was an especial favorite of his. He leaned as close to Emma as he could and began to describe the high mountain valleys that made up the ranch. In the spring, when he had first seen the place, its meadows were a bright green, the translucent green of a glass bottle. The mountains surrounding the fields were sharp, like drawings of the Alps in a picture book, and snow stayed year-round in the deep crevices near the peaks. A stream ran through the meadows, a stream that didn't dry up in late summer like the ones in New Mexico. Ned knew, because he had been there two weeks before. He paused to gulp his coffee, then he looked at Emma shyly.

"Go on," she encouraged.

"There's a house with a veranda big enough for two rocking chairs. So I guess there'd be a family to go with it, maybe a little girl with a face like that." He nodded at the brooch and felt himself flush.

Emma gave him a sliver of a smile, but she was silent, and Ned was sorry he'd said that. After all, it was Addie he should be thinking about taking to the ranch. But at that moment, Ned knew he was finished with Addie. He flushed as he realized that it was Emma he saw sitting in the rocker beside him on the porch.

Emma looked into his eyes as he talked, staring dreamily and murmuring, "I should like to live in such a spot, with a child, a little girl." Then suddenly, something he didn't understand came over her face, and she turned hard. "Well, like you say, for want of money, it will never be yours. Ever," Emma told him. "You are likely to see it no more." She paused and as though she had read his thoughts, she added, "And I am not one who would take to ranching."

The words were were as cold as the water that bubbled

in the stream. Ned had told Addie he was looking at a ranch, but Emma was the only person he'd confided in about his dreams for it, and she had just told him he was a fool.

"Maybe I'll get enough tomorrow to make up for it."

Emma snorted and reached for her shawl. "So you are just like the graveyard; you will take anything. I wonder now if there is much money in the bank. Jasper does not appear to be such a rich town as I thought." She stood up and wrapped the shawl around herself. Ned smoldered as he set down a dollar and four bits for the suppers, then followed Emma out of the dining room. He saw her to the door of her room, then without bidding her good night, he crossed the hall to his own room.

But he thought better of it and turned and went down the stairs and outside, heading for Maiden Lane. He reached Elsie Mae's. The gold lettering on the window was edged in black, and he thought Addie ought to paint something like that on the window of The Chili Queen. Thinking about Addie made him uneasy. He did not want to be with a woman who reminded him of Addie. But being in need of female companionship, he continued along Maiden Lane. He turned in at a bit house, where he paid a quarter for two shots of whiskey and got tight very quick. He lost ten dollars in a game of seven-up. Then feeling blue and a great deal sorry for himself, Ned asked directions to the French Brewery.

FIVE

Emma looked older than dirt when Ned called for her

in the morning. The night before, on the way to the French Brewery, he had gotten tight as a boot on bellywash at Cockney Jack's Saloon. Then he'd called at the French Brewery, where he'd engaged a big blonde named Carmel for three dollars—a dollar more than Addie's girls charged—stripped her to the bare pelt, but did not get much in the way of satisfaction. Afterward, he'd smoked a twenty-five-cent cigar, then went back to the hotel and washed his feet and went to bed.

The breakfast of pig's feet and Oregon apples had improved neither his stomach nor his mood. He had not bothered with a shave, telling himself a fresh shave would only make him stand out among the farmers and saddle tramps, but the truth was, he couldn't endure the sound of the blade scraping across his skin. The only thing that pleasured him was the memory of Emma across the table from him the night previous, her face shining like quartz in the candlelight. But now as he looked at her, he wondered if his bleary eyes had distorted her image. She was indeed a sorry sight.

Emma stood before him dressed in her traveling costume—the black dress and the sunbonnet of the day before, both still dusty from the trip. Like her clothes, her face seemed to have a layer of something dusty on it, and her skin was dull. Ned sorely could not believe she was the same woman he had found so enchanting just twelve hours earlier.

She must have guessed Ned's disappointment, because she asked, "Did you think I would wear my wedding dress to shop for sacks of flour?"

Ned grunted. She was right of course. He did not want

even a sparkle in her eye to draw attention. Still, he had not gotten her out of his mind since he had delivered her to her door after supper. He expected some spark of recognition on her part to show that she, too, had a few warm memories of their dinner, even if it had ended badly. He was not used to women who remembered him indifferently, so Ned waited, giving Emma a chance to remark on that evening, but she closed her door and brushed past him without another word. He followed her down the stairs and out the door, then caught up as she crossed the street.

"Other way. The general store is in that direction," he said.

"I thought you would want to check out the bank first. It wouldn't be wise to cash our bill too close to noon, when somebody might remember we had just been there, would it?"

Ned would have thought of that if he hadn't been hung over, and he blamed Emma for his state. He grunted, as he set off in the direction of the bank, ahead of her, taking long strides so that she had to hurry to catch up with him. He turned into the side street and reached the bank before she did, pausing at the door for her before he preceded her inside. Half a dozen people waited in line for a teller, and they looked exactly like Ned and Emma.

The banker was seated at a desk behind a railing, and he glanced at the two newcomers, sizing them up. Ned touched his hat in deference, obscuring his face as he did so, but the banker returned to his paperwork without acknowledging either of them. He had already dismissed them as likely prospects and would be hard-pressed to bring them to mind ever again, Ned knew, and that was just what he wanted. He and Emma waited their turn at the teller's cage, where the clerk, taking his cue from the banker, made them wait a minute while he finished counting money. Then he looked up, raising an eyebrow instead of speaking.

Ned cleared his throat, as if he were embarrassed to be there. "Think we could get change for this?" He shoved a bill under a metal grate.

The teller picked it up and examined it. Then without asking what change Ned wanted, he counted out several coins.

"Obliged," Ned muttered. He studied the bank as if he'd never seen such a grand establishment, while Emma glanced behind the counter and moved around to stare at the safe. Neither the clerk nor the banker paid attention to them, and after they had taken in everything, Ned and Emma left. By the time they reached the main street, Ned's mood, along with his head, had improved considerably. "It *is* as easy as honey," he told Emma. "The safe's wide open. There's money in the till. We could have taken it right then if there hadn't been any customers, but it'll be better if the banker's not around. The teller won't risk his neck. All we have to do is make sure he's alone."

"The safe is open, and there appears to be plenty of money in the teller's drawer. The buildings on either side are boarded up, and the front door is visible only from the back of the hotel. It looks almost too easy," Emma replied. When Ned frowned, she added quickly, "But how would I know?"

"Yes," Ned agreed. "How would you know?"

"Will he leave the safe open all day?"

"He's a big man, and Addie says he's lazy. I don't suppose he likes to heft himself off that chair more than he has to. We'll just have to hope he leaves it open when he goes to dinner."

They walked abreast now as they made their way down the boardwalk to a sign that said SPILLMAN & GOTTSCHALK, GENERAL MERCHANDISE. Like the bank, the store was crowded, which was fine with Ned, because he was in no hurry. Emma, a shopping list in her hand, lost herself among the other women as she studied the patent medicines and fancy groceries—the oysters and herring and imported peppermint candies—in their bright tins, placed at eye level to tempt shoppers. Ned watched her finger a bolt of cloth that lay on the counter, carefully straightening the fabric when she was finished and tucking under the raw edge. She looked up and stared longingly at a yellow-and-white spotted coffeepot sitting among the tin cups and queensware plates that were stacked on a shelf. When she reached the back of the store, she took in the shoes and slippers, the gents' furnishings, and the corsets and hosiery along the back wall. Emma let out a snort of disdain when she saw the glass case with a display of fans, some made of feathers, others of folded paper painted with exotic scenes.

Ned himself wandered along the other side of the room, picking up a whip and testing it against his hand. He passed the dog collars and window shades, the lamps and brass fittings, then stopped to examine a hoe that was leaning next to the cold stove.

"Lookit here, sister. Here is a fine hoe," he called.

Emma sent him a hard look. "We have a hoe," she replied. "Before we throw away good money on another, we must wait and see if we can make a crop in this god-forsaken land."

Two rawboned women dressed remarkably like Emma stopped to look her over and nod in agreement. "New Mexico is the awfulest sight I ever did see. It's wore me out good," one remarked. "Bless God," muttered the other.

A man who looked as if he'd worn out six or seven bodies with the same face regarded the women, then glanced at Ned with sympathy and said, "Farming out here's harder than pushing a wheelbarrow with rope handles."

"I guess it beats making shoes in a factory," Ned told him. "Her," Ned lowered his voice, "I thought she would jump at the sun with happiness to have her own house. But she has got in meanness since she arrived."

"You new?" the man asked.

Ned nodded. "How long you been here?"

"Since way back when hell wasn't no bigger than Jasper." He turned his back to the women and said in a low voice, "That's just wind stuff they're saying. They like it better than they let on. You snook a look at your woman days when the rains come down and the prairie's green, and you'll see I'm right. They like it well enough after a rain."

"You mean it rains here?" Ned asked.

"Sure, a regular toad strangler—every five years." The man laughed and clamped Ned on the shoulder. Ned wondered what it would be like if he really were a farmer, talking with men like this one about crops and the weather, complaining about the land and the women. Then he remembered he hated farming.

The man began to ask Ned about his place, but just then, the clerk called the farmer by name, and he went to the counter. His wife came up alongside him and began reading off the foodstuffs on her list.

When the couple was finished, the clerk nodded at Ned and Emma.

"We already got most of what we need. We'll be buying just a few rations," Emma told him. "I'd be wanting a gallon of molasses, saleratus, a bottle of vanilla. What do you charge for brown sugar?" Emma and Ned had decided earlier that they would purchase items that Addie or Welcome could use.

"Fifty cents the pound."

"Then I expect you can keep it. I'm not a fool to throw away my money." With the stub of a pencil lying on the counter, Emma crossed the item off her list. After she had ordered Arbuckle's Coffee at twelve cents a pound and a pound box of Stickney & Poors cinnamon for two bits, Emma picked up a package of sweet mignonette seeds and asked the price. When the clerk told her ten cents, Emma returned the package to its box and said she would write home and get the seeds for the price of a stamp. She bought two wool blankets, bartering the clerk down from $2.00 each to $3.50 for the pair. Then she asked for a round tin box of Maillard's Caprices, explaining to Ned that the purchase was not extravagant since once the candy was gone, she could use the copper-colored container to store her pins. Finally, she pointed to a bolt of yellow cloth, and the clerk used a ladder to reach it. He spread it out in front of Emma, who ran her hand over the fabric, which was sprigged with red and blue flowers.

"I expect you'd like a piece of that for your quilt," Ned spoke up.

"I always fancied yellow," Emma said.

"Well, you get it then."

Emma ordered a quarter-yard. The clerk measured it out, giving her a fraction of an inch more.

Ned glanced around the store, then spotted the yellow coffeepot he'd seen Emma admire. "That up there. We'll take it, too," he said, pointing, "and a couple of tin cups."

Emma frowned. "We surely cannot afford it."

"It's yellow. You said you like yellow, and I'm treating you to it. Now don't complain." Ned wasn't sure a coffeepot was a good present to give Emma, but as a dirt farmer, he couldn't very well spend money for a necklace or a silk dress.

"Why, brother, I believe you've gone soft in the head."

As the clerk totaled their purchases, Emma eyed the fancy foodstuffs and said, "I guess it wouldn't rob us to buy a tin of oysters for you and a bottle of peaches. 'Twill remind us of home." She pointed to the cans. Ned added some crackers and sardines and a small shovel, then paid and told the clerk to store the order until after dinner, when they would pick it up.

Since it was still only midmorning, Ned and Emma strolled along the boardwalk, peering into the stores. After Nalgitas's handful of meager businesses, Ned found Jasper rich and tempting, with blocks of fine establishments—two more hotels, restaurants and saloons, and stores. He and Emma passed a butcher shop with lard pails sitting in the window and hams and breakfast bacon hanging from hooks inside. Flies covered a beef carcass that was laid across a counter, and Emma made a face, but Ned only laughed. "I've eaten many pieces of beef that were worse," he said.

Emma paused in front of a jewelry store to admire the brooches and rings in their little boxes. "I always cared best for rubies," she said, leaning closer to a ring in the center of the display. She strolled on and stopped at a millinery, studying the hats and gloves and bottles of perfume in the window. She cocked her head at one hat and lowered her voice to a whisper. "If bank robbing does not suit me, I believe I might open up a hat shop here, no matter what Addie says."

Ned, who did not know about such things, moved along to a photographer's studio. "I guess we don't care to get our pictures took," he told Emma.

"The sheriff might like it if we did," she replied.

As he laughed, Ned looked down the boardwalk to a saloon where two men had just emerged, and he stiffened. "Turn back," he ordered in a low voice. Without a word, Emma did as she was told, at the same time adjusting the bonnet to cover more of her face. Ned slouched a little as he looked at the props in the photographer's window.

The two men sauntered down the boardwalk toward them, and as they reached the photographer's studio, the smaller man swerved and bumped Ned's elbow. "Hey, Jesse," he said softly, "look who I just run into."

Jesse, a giant of a man with long black hair that hung around his swarthy face, smiled at Ned, showing a mouthful of broken teeth. "We used to have a friend that looked like you. We don't see him no more, do we, Earlie?"

Ned shrugged and smiled back. "Folks get busy."

"We heard about that," Earlie said. "We heard you got real lucky."

"I heard you were dried up and dead, one of you anyway," Ned told them.

Earlie smirked, showing even teeth under a blond mustache. He was a head shorter than Jesse and had a pretty look to him. "Yeah, I did, too. But I didn't hear 'bout you throwing no funeral."

"I was in mourning," Ned replied. "You just get in?"

"Yesterday. We went to the cockfighting pit, but we were too late to see the fun," Jesse replied, scratching his face, which was pockmarked with scars from black measles. "You going to introduce us?" Jesse tried to get a good look at Emma. Her back was still turned to them.

"Naw," Ned laughed. "Why would my sister want to meet a couple of saddle bums?"

Emma turned around nonetheless. Her face, shaded by the sunbonnet, seemed even darker and older than before.

The men lost interest. "I guess she's your sister, after all," Jesse said. "She is poorly thin and old."

"She's ageable, all right. Maybe she's your mother," Earlie added.

"Hey!" Ned said. It was the second time since he'd arrived in Jasper that he'd defended Emma.

"Oh, don't mind Earlie. He fell down drunk last night, and somebody stepped on his nose." Earlie scowled while Jesse laughed at him, then leaned against the window of the photography studio and sized up Ned. "You gone to farming, have you?" he asked.

Ned looked away as he nodded.

"How come you done that?" Jesse asked.

"I'll say it real slow so's you can catch it. I never knew anybody who got old robbing people. Everybody's got to settle down."

"Not us," Earlie said.

Suddenly, Ned caught sight of Sheriff Tate coming out of a cigar store across the street. He jerked his head in the sheriff's direction, and Jesse and Earlie exchanged glances. "Come on, Jess, let's ride. Be seeing you," Earlie told Ned, and without another word, the two faded into a group of men who were walking past.

Ned took Emma's arm and hurried her along in the opposite direction, toward the hotel. He walked as quickly as he could without drawing attention. Emma seemed to sense the urgency and did not question him about the two men until they had collected their keys from the desk clerk and reached her room. Ned closed and locked the door, then went to the window and moved the curtain a little to peer out at the street. Neither of the men was in view. He let out a sigh of relief.

"Who are they?" Emma asked.

"The Minder brothers," Ned replied, straightening the curtain and moving to the side of the window. He did not care to stand where he could be seen. Emma had removed the sunbonnet, and he thought he saw her flinch. "Heard of them?"

"No. As least, I don't think so."

"Earlie and Black Jesse Minder. I heard they were

killed. I wish they had been. I guess they're still alive because the devil didn't want them, and the Lord wouldn't have them." He pulled out a chair, set it just out of view from anyone looking up from the street, and straddled it. "Black Jesse is braggedy-talking and ugly from ignorance, but Earlie is the big toad in the puddle. And he is purely evil." Ned lifted the corner of the curtain and looked out the window again. "I rode with the Minders once, but I quit them. I wouldn't join up with them again if it would turn me to gold."

"They're bank robbers?" Emma asked.

"No, they're not smart enough. Mostly they rob and kill people they meet up with."

"Highwaymen then."

Ned put his chin on the top of the chair and stared straight at Emma. "If you want to put a fancy name to it, you can call them that. I call them vagabonds, scoundrels—murderers. They kill even when they don't have to. They like it." Ned shook his head back and forth a couple of times, trying to rid himself of a memory.

"What is it?" Emma asked. She had seated herself on the bed and leaned forward.

"You don't want to hear it," Ned said, rubbing his hands over his face. The hangover was gone, replaced by a feeling of unease about the Minders.

Emma continued to stare at him, until Ned looked up and shook his head at her. "You wouldn't want to know," he repeated.

"Yes, I would. When we agreed to rob this bank, I considered it to be something of a prank, but since last night, I have been weighing the seriousness of it. If you are mixed up with two killers who are here, perhaps we should reconsider. At the very least, I should like to know your connection with them."

Ned considered her words then nodded glumly. "Sometime back, I met up with Earlie and Black Jesse in Taos and kept company with them. We pulled a couple of jobs, nothing big. They seemed all right at first, not too bright, but most outlaws aren't very smart." Ned glanced up at Emma and grinned. "Some are."

She smiled a little.

"I didn't see right off that they were a pair of hard cases. But later, we robbed a man, and Earlie shot him. He didn't have to because the man had already given us his money. Earlie did it for pleasure. I was afraid they would shoot me, too, so I got to thinking then that I'd go off by myself. But I hadn't figured out how to leave them." Ned nodded to himself, recalling the dilemma. "Then one day, we were on our way down from Colorado. We saw two barefoot, redheaded boys on a horse, one in front of the other, riding it bareback. Twins or thereabouts because they looked just alike. They couldn't have been more than eight or ten years old. They were singing when we rode by them on the trail, and they waved at us, happy as hogs in a wallow. When we got past a little ways, Earlie bet Black Jesse ten dollars he could get them both with a single bullet. He used a rifle. The bullet went clear through one into the other. They fell off the horse and lay still, and Earlie and Jesse rode back to see were they both dead. They argued about it some. Jesse said one was still moving when they got there, but Earlie said he died in a few minutes, so that counted."

Emma's face turned to such sadness that for a moment, Ned thought she might cry. He sorely felt like crying himself. Recounting the story had unnerved him. "It's been some years. I never told anybody," he said. "I believed the safest thing to do was disappear and never see them again. That's what I did. I never saw them until today."

"Why didn't you stop them from killing the boys?" Emma asked.

The curtain swayed a little in the breeze, and Ned jumped. Then he settled back down in the chair, looking dejected as he stared at the floor. He didn't say anything, and Emma leaned forward and asked again, "Why?"

Ned let out his breath. He leaned back until he was balancing the chair on two legs. "I thought they were joking at first. By the time I realized Earlie meant it, Black Jesse had pulled a gun on me. He'd have killed me if I'd made a move. So I thought maybe I could talk them out of it. I said, 'You got better things to waste your bullets on.' Earlie smiled like he agreed with me, and I thought he'd forget about it. But all of a sudden, he turned and shot the boys. I should have tried to stop him, hit his horse maybe."

Emma thought that over. Then she reached out and touched Ned's arm. He was startled and looked up at her. "Sometimes we have to choose between two things that are evil. He'd have shot the boys anyway—and you, too. You'd have been throwing your life away for nothing."

"Black Jesse laughed at me later, saying he'd only been bluffing, but I knew he would shoot me up like lacework. Still, I should have thought of something."

"You're not partly God. You couldn't have done anything for them if you were dead, could you?" Emma asked.

Ned stared at the pattern on the bedroom wall made by the sun going through the lace curtain. One of the designs looked like a pickle, and he had an urge to trace it on the wall with his finger, but he stayed in the chair, thinking over what Emma had said. "It has occupied my mind ever since. I've looked at it a hundred ways to Sunday and never figured out what I could have done different."

"You can't do it different. It's a lesson of life. You learned from it, and next time . . ." She grew quiet, and Ned thought she was done, but then, she said quietly, "I myself have learned from evil." Ned wanted to ask what evil she had encountered on a Kansas farm, but Emma seemed to shake off whatever she had been thinking. She stood up and went to the window and looked through the curtain. She moved closer and put her eye to a hole in the lace and stared through it. "I believe those are the two men we have been talking about," she said.

Ned moved the curtain an inch and looked out. The Minder brothers were riding under their window. He could see their bedrolls tied behind their saddles. After the two men passed the hotel, Ned pressed his face against the glass and watched until he could no longer see them. "I guess they're leaving, just like they said," he told Emma. He grinned, and Emma smiled back. Ned left the window and went up close to her, taking her chin in his hand. "Maybe you haven't thought serious enough about this. You can still say no."

"There won't be any shooting, will there?"

Ned shook his head. "I'll tell you what. If anybody's

inside the bank besides the teller, we won't go in. The teller won't risk his life for somebody else's money, but the banker might. If he gets back before we have a chance to pull the job, we'll call it off."

"That would please Welcome."

"What's she got to do with it?"

"I was only making an observation." Then Emma said, "I agree with your terms."

"You sure?"

"Yes."

Ned reached over and touched her cheek with the back of his fingers then abruptly pulled away his hand and said brusquely, "I'll go change my clothes and come back in ten minutes."

"I'll be ready."

She was. When Ned entered Emma's room without knocking, she was dressed in men's pants and shirt, a handkerchief knotted around her neck and a worn hat on her head that covered her hair. Ned had given her the hat, but Emma had gotten the rest of the outfit on her own. She looked like a young man, and although they would cover their faces when they went into the bank, Emma nonetheless had rubbed something on her chin that made her look as if she had a few days' growth of beard. Ned took a gun out of his pocket and handed it to her, but Emma declined it.

"I've brought a revolver with me," she said. "After all, I might have needed protection from Mr. Withers."

"You sure are a steady one," Ned told her, rubbing his hand over the stubble on his face. "Shoot, I don't guess I ever met anybody so cool, even a man." He felt nervous, as he always did before a job, and wondered if it showed.

They made their way down the stairs and out the back door of the hotel. Through the glass window of the bank, Ned could see that the banker's chair was empty. But someone was talking to the clerk. "By zam," he muttered. He took out the makings of a cigarette, sprinkling tobacco on a paper and licking it. Before he could put away the fixings, Emma took the tobacco bag and papers from him and made her own. Ned stared at her so long that Emma, amused, reached into her pocket for a match, which she struck on her pants' leg, and lit her cigarette. Then she held the match for Ned. "I never saw a lady smoke a cigarette before," he said, inhaling.

"Addie smokes."

Ned was about to reply that Addie was not a lady, but thought better of it. The cigarette relaxed him. He and Emma would draw no more attention than any other pair of men who had stopped for a smoke.

Ned strained his neck to peer inside the bank, but it was dark, and all he could see was a black figure with his back to the window. "Hurry up," he muttered as he finished his cigarette and threw the butt into the dirt. He didn't want a second cigarette, but taking out the makings gave him something to do, so he rolled another. As he used his teeth to pull the string on the tobacco bag tight, he glanced at the bank again. There was movement inside. "He's leaving," he muttered to Emma, who had sat down on the step and was leaning forward with her arms on her knees, her back to the bank. Ned dropped the cigarette and broke it apart with his foot, then stuffed the bag into his shirt pocket. He squinted to see what was going on. *"They're* leaving. There are two of them. Must be farmers asking for a loan. Maybe they got treated better than us."

Of a sudden, the door of the bank was jerked open, and two men hurried out. Emma jumped up, but before she and Ned could retreat into the hotel, the Minder brothers rushed out of the bank and stopped in front of them.

Earlie narrowed his eyes at the two, then smirked. "That teller in there, he's color-blind. He can't tell his money from mine." Earlie raised the gun so that it was pointed at Ned. But Ned was more concerned with the knife in Earlie's belt, which was big and covered with blood.

Black Jesse grabbed Earlie's arm. "You whack him down outside here, and somebody'll hear it. Come on."

Earlie thought that over for a few seconds. "I guess it's your lucky day, Ned boy." Black Jesse started down the street, but Earlie held the gun on Ned a few seconds longer, then he pointed it at Emma. "Was you going to the bank?" he asked. "They ain't got no money left."

"Is he dead?" Emma asked.

Earlie shrugged. "He makes sounds like a calf that's got its throat cut." Earlie laughed, then turned and ran after his brother, and the two turned the corner. In a few seconds, Ned heard horses galloping away.

Ned grabbed Emma's arm and tried to pull her inside the hotel, but she resisted. "That teller, he may be dying. We ought to help."

"And get hanged for something the Minders did? How are we going to explain what we're doing out here and why you're dressed like a man?"

"We can't let him die. I can't let a man die, not one who doesn't deserve it."

Ned thought that over. The teller bothered him, too.

"Give me your hat," Emma said, reaching up and untying his neckerchief. "I'll change clothes. You go upstairs with me, then come down the front steps and say you heard yelling at the bank."

Ned wished he'd thought it through that way. He turned and led the way upstairs, but just as they got to Emma's room, they heard a commotion on the street. Someone yelled, and then there were footsteps. Emma collapsed onto her bed with a sigh of relief. She looked ashy, as she put her hands to her face and seemed to shrink into herself. "I believe I am very foolish," she said.

Ned sat beside her and put his arm around her. "It's done with."

"We could have been the ones who injured that man. We might have shot him."

"We weren't," Ned replied. "You can't fret about what didn't happen."

"We must leave."

Ned wanted to hold her longer, but Emma was right. It was dangerous to stay. They changed their clothes and picked up their bags, and in a few minutes, they were in the lobby, where the desk clerk told them the bank had been robbed. "Two men. They knifed poor old Stingy Dan, the teller. He scratched out 'Minder' in blood on the floor, but myself, I heard one of the Minders was dead. My guess is it was a Minder paired up with Ned Partner. He hangs out not far from here. But a pair of old ladies could have robbed Stingy Dan. Hell, your sister here could have pulled it off." He cocked his head at Emma and ran his tongue over his teeth.

Emma appeared only mildly annoyed. "Well, then, if farming does not work out, we shall have a new way to earn our livelihood." Then she raised an eyebrow at the clerk. "I for one should prefer robbing hotels that over-charge."

Ned paid four dollars for the two rooms, and he and Emma walked to the livery stable, where they collected the horses and wagons. They stopped to pick up the box of rations they had bought at Spillman & Gottschalk, for the grocery clerk would think it strange if the purchases were left behind. Then Ned took a north road out of town instead of heading east to Nalgitas. The Minders were likely to go southwest toward Santa Fe, where they were known to have kin. So the posse would go that way, too, Ned explained to Emma. But if the fool desk clerk con-vinced the sheriff that Ned Partner had robbed the bank, the posse would ride east toward Nalgitas. So the two of them were better off going straight north, then circling east in the morning.

Ned wished he'd bought a whip at the store to hurry the horses. He slapped the reins over their backs, and they ran like the devil for a minute or two, then exhausted them-selves and settled back into their slow plod, and nothing would arouse them. From time to time, Ned turned around to see whether anyone was behind them, but there was no sign of the sheriff. After an hour or two, he relaxed. Without thinking, he slapped Emma's knee and exclaimed, "I guess we got away with it."

Emma stared at him a moment before turning away. "With what?"

Ned felt silly. She was right, of course. They hadn't

gotten away with anything. They had only gotten away. It had been a foolhardy adventure. Even if they hadn't pulled off the robbery, they could have been arrested. He wouldn't like it on his conscience that he was responsible for Emma winding up in prison. Hell, he wouldn't like it to be on his conscience that he was in prison. He'd seen how upset Emma was when she heard the teller was knifed. What if Ned had shot the man? Would Emma have insisted they go for a doctor? And what if Emma had shot him? She'd have been as useless then as jelly in the sun. Maybe they were damn-fool lucky that they'd gotten away.

He slapped the horses with the reins again, out of frustration, really, since it still did no good. He glanced at Emma, who was staring out across the plains. A wind had picked up since they left Jasper, moving the prairie grasses like waves on the Mississippi. The wind was hot, but it felt good. It calmed him, and after a while Ned's good humor returned. He smiled to himself when he realized that he and Emma would have to camp somewhere that night. Their plan had been to return to Nalgitas the way they'd come, driving all night. But going north, as they were, there was no way they could reach Nalgitas. They would have to spend the night together.

"We will have to find an encampment this evening," Emma said, as if reading his thoughts. Then she laughed. "It is a good thing we bought those blankets and the provisions. Why, we even have a coffeepot and cups."

"Are you sorry we did this?" Ned asked. "I wasn't very smart, I guess."

"No, you are smart enough. I will hand you that."

Emma shrugged. "But neither you nor I thought it through, and it will cost us. You will get something back for these horses, but we are out the price of the hotel and what we purchased at the store. If you will let me know the amount, I will reimburse you half when I get my money from John."

"You don't have to do that."

"Perhaps I will give you forty percent then, as you agreed to pay me only that amount from the proceeds."

"But I intended to give you half all along," Ned said, then laughed. "I believe you could make your living running a bank, not robbing one."

They rode through the afternoon, not talking much. From time to time, Ned turned to look behind them. Emma did, too, but the road was deserted. Ned had convinced himself they were alone on the prairie and was thinking about a campsite when Emma touched his arm. "Behind us there is dust," she said.

Ned turned and judging from the dirt that was stirred up, he knew there was more than one rider. He urged the team forward, then gave up, knowing his horses couldn't outrun a cow, let alone men on horseback. Whoever it was would catch up in a few minutes. He removed his gun from the holster and placed it on the wagon seat between them, while Emma put her own gun beside her, under her skirt. Then she reached for her sewing basket. When the posse caught up with them, Emma was stitching.

The sheriff shifted painfully in his saddle as he stopped beside the wagon. "You folks seen anybody?" he asked.

"Not since we left Jasper," Ned replied.

"Bank got robbed. We're looking for two men."

"We heard about that. The hotel clerk told us," Ned said.

"He also told us the teller was hurt," Emma said, putting her sewing in her lap and leaning forward. "Is he all right?"

"He died out. He said the Minder brothers done it. They're as mean as they come. There wasn't any need to smash Stingy Dan—God rest his soul—since he gave them the money." The sheriff touched his hat again. "If it is the Minders, you folks best be on the lookout. There ain't ever no knowing what they'll do."

"What makes you think they came this way?" Ned asked.

The sheriff jerked his thumb at one of the three deputies who accompanied him. "Wattie here says two men left out right after the robbery, heading this way. Could have been anybody, but we got to go in some direction, and this is as good as any. The information's pretty scattering. Wattie says it could have been Ned Partner, too. He used to raise old scratch out this way, but I ain't heard of him in a while."

"Are there no honest people in this country?" Emma asked tartly.

"Only yourselves, I reckon," the sheriff said in way of a joke. "Say, you wouldn't have buttermilk on you, would you? This is agitation work, and I sure would like a glass of buttermilk."

"I would like one myself. I could drink buttermilk all day," Ned told him, although he hated the stuff.

The sheriff seemed in no hurry to move along. Then Ned remembered the man's pains and knew he sorely did hurt and would want an excuse to sit longer. So Ned said,

"I guess we'd best hurry along home. We wouldn't want to meet whoever did the deed."

"Where was you farming?" the sheriff asked.

Ned swallowed. "The Johnson place," he said.

The sheriff cocked his head and thought a moment, then nodded. Ned knew he'd never heard of anybody named Johnson but didn't want to admit it.

"We are not buggy riding. If you have no further need of us, we must be on our way," Emma said.

Ned rolled his eyes to show that Emma was an exasperation. The sheriff touched his hat to her and muttered, "Ma'am." Then he led the posse past the wagon and rode off.

"Sheriff Tate is meek as a sheep and dumb as a calf," Ned observed, as he urged the horses down the road the posse had taken. "Still, I don't like the idea of my name festering in his mind."

"Out here, we're as plain to see as an elephant in a watch pocket," Emma told him. "Perhaps we should leave the wagon behind and ride the horses."

Ned had thought the same thing, although he did not know how much faster they would go riding bareback on a pair of old plugs. Perhaps they could acquire horses at a farm, but he doubted it. Then he remembered a man he'd once ridden with who'd gone to farming. He had a place not far away and was known to accommodate his old friends. Ned told Emma to climb back in the wagon and put on her shirt and pants. She did so without a question, and when she was dressed, Ned asked her to make two bedrolls out of the blankets, wrapping up inside them as much of the rations and anything else she wanted as two horses could carry. While Emma picked through their things, Ned turned the wagon off the road onto a trail that wound through a gully. He stopped at a protected spot and said Emma should wait there for him with the bedrolls. Taking a shovel from the wagon, he asked her to bury any clothes she hadn't wrapped in the blankets, while he went on alone to see about horses. He didn't want his friend to know he was with a woman. Ned promised to be back in an hour. He clicked his tongue at the team and took off as fast as they could go, before Emma could ask what he'd do if his friend wasn't there or couldn't spare the stock.

But the man was at home, happy to provide Ned with two horses and saddles, although he drove a hard bargain. Ned had to give him the team and wagon along with the provisions left in it and pay him fifty dollars. Ned didn't have time to argue, however. As he told Emma later, it was root, hog, or die, and he was lucky to get the horses at any price.

The sky had turned crimson by the time Ned returned to Emma, who was waiting next to a mound of dirt covered by rocks. The shovel stuck out of one of two fat bedrolls, lying next to Emma's portmanteau. As he fitted the bag's handle over his own saddle horn, Ned explained that there was a canyon to the west where they would camp. He picked up a bedroll and said they couldn't have made it with the wagon, for the trail into the depths was suitable only for horses. He wished the light would last longer, but he thought he could find it in the dark. The ride would be a hard one, Ned said, glancing at Emma to see if she was up to it.

Emma only nodded, as she finished securing the second

bedroll. Ned was impressed at the expert way she fastened it to her saddle, and for an instant, he wondered where she had learned such a thing. That wasn't something a farm girl would know, but it didn't matter, and the thought left his mind. He mounted and galloped off, Emma behind him.

They crossed the main road and angled west across the prairie, to avoid the posse if it returned. Ned would be hard-pressed to explain to the sheriff why he and his sister had abandoned their wagon and were mounted on horses, and why Emma was dressed like a man. There was no trail, and they rode through the long dried grass until it was dark. If they had to, they could make a campsite on the prairie, Ned supposed, although he wouldn't feel comfortably safe about it. But Ned was good at remembering trails, and he spotted a rock formation that looked familiar and led Emma to it. He dismounted, and leading his horse, he looked for a cut between two rocks that marked the entrance into the depths. It took nearly thirty minutes, but at last, he found the spot and told Emma they would reach the bottom in an hour or so.

He looked at her face to gauge how tired she was, but by then, it was too dark for him to make out her features. Emma seemed to know what he was thinking, however, and she said, "I will make it."

As he mounted his horse and led the way, Ned felt a drop of rain on his hand, then another. "By zam! It hasn't rained in five years, and we get it tonight. It'll be slow going."

"But the rain will cover our tracks," Emma replied. "No one can follow us."

The canyon wall was no shelter against the storm, and the going was miserable. The trail that hugged the side of the cliff was steep, and Ned feared the moisture would wash it out, so he went slowly. After a while, the rain turned into hail that seemed as big as guinea hen eggs. Ned hoped it wouldn't make the horses skittish and considered waiting for the hail to stop. But the horses were just as likely to panic while standing still, so Ned kept on. As they descended into the canyon in the heavy dark, the hail turned to a steady drizzle. Once, Ned's horse stumbled, and Ned pulled him up tight, sweating a little despite the rain that made the night as cold as November. On one side of the trail was a sharp drop-off, and if the horse lost his footing, both he and Ned would fall hundreds of feet onto the canyon floor. He wondered what Emma would do if he disappeared over the edge. Behind him, Emma's horse dislodged a stone that rolled past him and fell so far into the canyon that he didn't hear it land. Then he heard Emma cry out and turned quickly, but he couldn't see her in the blackness.

"A branch hit me," she called.

Ned wondered if he should dismount and lead his horse, but he wasn't sure there was even room to do that. Besides, the trail was slick, and the horse was surer footed than he was. So he kept going, letting the horse feel the way. After a long time, there was a flash that showed they had reached a wide place on the trail. Ned waited for Emma to come up beside him. "You going to make it?" he asked her.

"You will not find me wanting," she replied. "But I wish I had bought a heavy coat. I would find it a more agreeable companion than the rain."

Ned could think of a number of more agreeable companions, but he didn't mention them. "Not much farther now," he told her, although he knew they had come only a little way down the trail.

He led off into the darkness again, staying as close to the rock wall as possible, Emma behind him. The rain didn't let up, but after a while, the wind no longer penetrated the canyon. Another flash of lightning lit up the trail, illuminating the drop-off beside them. Ned wondered if Emma was afraid of heights. There was nothing he could do about it if she was, so he didn't ask.

Ned judged it was nearly midnight when the trail finally leveled off, then widened. It had taken them four, maybe five hours to make the descent. He stopped his horse and waited for Emma, who was farther behind than he'd thought. But in a few minutes, she stopped beside him, breathing heavily.

"Done?" she asked.

"A little farther. There's an adobe somewhere down here. It's better shelter than a tree."

"Can you find it?"

Her voice shook, and Ned knew she was shivering and tired, but she didn't complain. He was tempted to leave her there and look for the shack, but he wasn't sure he could find his way back to her. So he said they would search together. But after half an hour of looking, Emma begged Ned to camp where they were. He picked a spot under a rock overhang, and they unsaddled the horses. Since it was too wet to make a fire, they wrapped themselves in their blankets, then Ned opened the sardines that

Emma had stuffed into one of the bedrolls, and they ate them with damp crackers. Ned stashed their other things, pleased that Emma had brought along the coffeepot and a pound of coffee. She would wake to the smell of camp coffee. Ned told her as much, as he opened the lid of the pot and braced it against a rock where it would catch the rainwater. He wished they had bought sausages and pork ribs so they could have a decent breakfast. "Do you think a shovel would work as a frying pan?" he asked Emma. She didn't reply, and Ned looked closely at her, but he had talked her to sleep. He gently pulled the blanket up to Emma's chin, then studied her shape in the darkness before he lay down a few feet away from her and fell into a deep sleep.

As it turned out, Emma wasn't awakened by the smell of coffee, but by the toe of a boot pressed against her. So was Ned, although the boot toe gave him a sharp kick. He awakened in an instant, and his first thought was that the posse had followed them into the canyon. But as he slowly raised his head, he was overcome by a feeling of revulsion, even before he recognized Earlie's sly face. Earlie was drunk and stinking very bad, and he held a gun in his hand. It was pointed at Ned.

"We don't see you for maybe four, five years. Now we see you twice in one day," Black Jesse told him.

Ned did not correct him to say it had been twice in two days. Instead, he glanced at Emma, who was lying on her side. Her eyelids flickered, and he knew she was only pretending to be in a very sound sleep. Black Jesse prodded her with his toe, and said, "Hello, the house." Emma sat up. If she was frightened, she did not show it. In fact, she covered a yawn with her hand.

"Me and Earlie stayed up there, in that little house. You remember it, Ned boy? It's big enough to room us all. You could have slept there, too, out of the rain," Black Jesse said.

Ned remembered the house, of course, and with a sickening feeling, he remembered, too, how he knew about it. He and the Minder brothers had camped there.

"We finished up our whiskey and was just wondering what to have for breakfast, and we seen your horse tracks," Black Jesse continued. "But you can't tell from the trail of a snake if it's coming or going, so we sneaked up, and here you are."

"We haven't much, but you're welcome to it," Emma said. She pulled on her boots and reached into the pile of provisions, but Earlie stepped on her hand. Emma winced but said nothing.

"I guess I'll take your guns first," Earlie said. He picked up Ned's gun, which was next to his saddle, and Black Jesse kicked aside Emma's blankets and found hers. Earlie continued to hold his gun on Ned, while Black Jesse built a fire. Moving slowly and deliberately, Emma found the coffee beans and spread a handful of them onto a rock, then smashed them with a stone, and dumped the grounds into the pot of rainwater. She made a fire and set the pot on the flames. Then she laid out the two tin cups she had bought in Jasper and the canned goods and told the Minders to help themselves. Emma was so calm that Ned wondered whether she realized the danger they were in.

He reached for one of the cans, but Earlie cocked his gun, pointing it at Ned's head. "Us first."

Ned grinned at him, and crossed his legs, leaning back against his saddle. "I guess I'm not hungry."

Earlie slid his eyes to Emma. Ned didn't like the look, and he started to say something to divert Earlie's attention, but Earlie cut him off. "I guess I'm not hungry, neither." He licked his lips. Emma glanced at him, then lowered her eyes, and Ned thought she trembled a little. "You aren't really Ned's sister?" Earlie asked her.

"My name is Emma," she replied. She had gotten up, and she stood beside the fire then. Her arms were crossed protectively in front of her chest. But her feet were a little apart, as if she were ready to spring. Ned hoped she wouldn't until he figured something out. It would be almost impossible for the two of them, without guns, to take the Minders. He hoped Emma wouldn't panic.

Earlie continued to stare at Emma, a little leer on his lips. "No, I guess I ain't so hungry just yet."

Emma sent Ned a helpless look, and Ned glanced around for some kind of weapon, but Earlie was too smart for him. He kicked a stone out of Ned's reach.

"Come here," Earlie told Emma.

She stayed where she was.

Earlie's voice grew hard. "Do what I say. You don't think you're too good for me, do you?"

Emma shook her head. "No," she said in a tiny voice. She seemed unable to move.

Suddenly, Earlie reached out and gripped her, yanking her so hard that she cried out in pain. Ned half-rose, but Earlie pointed the gun at him. "If you move again, I'll kill you—her, too," he said, and Ned knew he would. But he couldn't let Earlie take Emma. He knew what the man could do.

"Come on to Nalgitas. I'll get you all the girls you want," Ned said easily. "Young ones. They know how to take care of a man."

"Maybe—when I'm done here," Earlie replied.

Ned moved his legs a little, ready to spring at Earlie. He would likely get killed then, and that would leave Emma on her own. She turned her head to Ned and mouthed the words, "Two evils."

At first, Ned didn't know what she meant. Then he remembered what she had told him after he'd related the story of the Minders and the redheaded boys. She'd said that sometimes a person had to choose between two evil things. Maybe she had come to the same conclusion Ned had, that he ought not to get killed right away, that maybe in a minute, he could come up with a way to rescue her. Ned thought that what Earlie would do was a terrible thing, but it was not as bad as both of them getting killed. And Ned was sure that if the Minders killed him, they would kill Emma, too. Still, he couldn't let Earlie ravish her. "Don't do it," Ned said in a low voice.

Earlie only laughed. "If he moves, you kill him, Jesse. You get your turn next," Earlie said, as he dragged Emma away. "Now, come on peaceable. You can't think of any way you'd better like to have it." With one last look at Ned, Emma went with Earlie.

"Stop him. I'll make it worth your while," Ned told Jesse in a low voice.

But Jesse only grinned at him and raised his gun a little

higher. "Earlie's made funny," he explained. "He don't like nobody to watch. I hope he don't cut her. They're no good to me after he cuts 'em." Jesse shook his head. "Maybe she won't mind. Some women, the worse you treat them, the better they like you." He frowned, then added, "Earlie's some worse than when you knew him."

Earlie and Emma had disappeared behind an outcropping of rocks. Ned heard a scuffle, and Emma's faint voice pleading, "No, please," then a slap.

Black Jesse didn't pay attention. He reached for one of the cups and threw it at Ned. "I'd like some coffee right well."

Ned swallowed hard to control his voice. "I'd like it right well myself. Any objections?"

Jesse thought it over. "I don't expect Earlie would mind."

Ned was deliberate and slow, just as Emma had been when she'd made the coffee, so as not to alarm Jesse. He set one of the cups beside him, then used his shirttail to lift the coffeepot from the fire. "Let's see if it's done," he said, opening the lid and raising the pot so that he could peer inside.

At that moment, there was a scream of terror, an inhuman high-pitched sound that hung in the air. For an instant, Ned thought that Earlie and Emma had been attacked by a panther, but in his gut he knew the scream was Emma's. The sound was so piercing that it startled Black Jesse, who half-rose and turned toward the noise. Ned saw his chance and flung the coffee into Black Jesse's face. Jesse dropped his gun as he put his hands to his burned flesh. Instead of going for the weapon, Ned picked up a huge rock with both hands and brought it down on Jesse's head. Jesse didn't yell. He made a single noise that sounded like "Whoomp." Made strong with madness, Ned hit him again—and again, until the top of Jesse's head was smashed in, and blood and gore covered his face. Jesse fell forward, his arm in the fire.

Ned didn't look to see if Jesse was dead; he knew he was. He grabbed the man's gun and started after Earlie and Emma. He moved stealthfully, not knowing if Earlie had heard the sound of the rock against Jesse's skull. It would be safer to circle around and catch Earlie from the other side, but Ned knew there wasn't time. He hoped he wasn't too late and he rushed forward—and found himself looking down the barrel of Earlie's gun. Beyond was a body on the ground.

Ned didn't stop to think. He would die, but Earlie would die, too. He raised his gun, hoping he could get off a shot before Earlie killed him, when Emma's voice pierced through the fog of his mind. "Ned!" she cried, and he looked up to see that he was facing Emma, their guns pointed at each other. As if she had exhausted her control in that single word, Emma dropped the weapon, just as her legs gave out. Ned caught her as she fell, and he lowered her to the ground.

"He's dead," Emma told him.

"Black Jesse, too," Ned told her. "I smashed his head."

"I stabbed Earlie. I stabbed a man to death," Emma told him.

"He wasn't a man. He was an animal." Ned put his arms around Emma and held her, not asking her what had happened but waiting for Emma to tell him.

She didn't cry then. Instead, she went limp. Ned cradled her for a long time, rocking back and forth with her, until she roused herself and said, "I had a knife in my boot. He didn't expect it. When he turned away, I stabbed him in the back. Did you hear him?"

"I thought that was you."

Emma shook her head against Ned's chest. "I must have killed him the first time, but I kept stabbing and stabbing. I couldn't stop."

For the first time, Ned saw the blood on her shirt. The shirt was ripped, too, and he asked, "Did he—?"

"No," Emma replied. "No. He only tore my clothes."

After a few minutes, Ned lifted Emma to her feet. "I'll have to bury the bodies so no one will find them. I ought to bury them in a ditch like dogs, but there aren't any ditches," he told her. "You sit by the fire." He led her back to their camp and wrapped a blanket around her, then built up the flames, although it was already hot in the canyon. Then he went back for Earlie's body. While Emma huddled beside the fire, crying silently, Ned dug a grave in the soft mud. Before he buried the two men, he found their horses and went through the saddlebags, pulling out a canvas sack filled with money. He dumped the loot beside Emma, then threw the bag and saddles into the grave. He removed the bridles from the horses and dropped the bridles in, too. At last, he dragged the two bodies to the grave and buried them facedown. Ned shoveled in the dirt and smoothed the mound, covering it with rocks and broken branches.

It was almost noon when he finished and sat down beside Emma. "The horses are better than ours, but someone might recognize them," Ned said. "The saddles, bridles, I don't want them. But the money, well, I guess we deserve it."

"What?" Emma asked, and Ned realized she hadn't even seen the money bag he'd put down beside her.

He reached over and opened it, extracting the money and counting it quickly. "Over thirteen hundred dollars," he said. Then he went back through the money, dividing it into two piles, and put one in her lap. "Fifty-fifty," he said. Emma just stared at him, so he tucked the money into her saddlebag. He put his share into his coat pocket, then threw the bag into the fire.

"We ought to get out of here," he told her after a few minutes. "Can you sit a horse?"

Emma nodded.

"If we ride hard, we can make it to Nalgitas tonight. But we don't have to. We can camp again, if you want to."

"No," she told him. "We must get back."

While Ned saddled their horses, Emma went through their things and took out a blouse. She stripped off her torn shirt, ripped it into pieces, and flung them about. She found a depression in a boulder where rainwater had collected and washed the blood off her face and arms, then put on the blouse. By the time she returned to Ned, the horses were saddled, the bedrolls secured. Ned had even tidied up the campsite so that anyone coming across it would not know they had been there.

Emma let Ned help her mount, and he stood beside her a moment, his hand on her leg. "We won't tell anybody about this," he said. "If Addie asks, and she will, we'll say the Minders got to the bank first, that we saw them."

"How will we explain the money?"

"We won't tell anybody about that, either. There's no way Addie will know, and who is there for you to tell?"

Emma thought that over. "I would rather endure their ridicule at our failure than have to relive this morning for them."

"Earlie and Black Jesse were common dogs. Perdition is too good for them. We had no choice. Remember that. There was no choice." Ned looked up at her for a long time, while Emma stared down at him.

"No choice," she repeated.

He started toward his horse, then turned and went back to Emma, reaching up for her hand. "I don't like this life much anymore. When I buy that ranch . . . Well, do you think you'd like to live on a ranch?" Ned hadn't meant to blurt that out, but he felt joy on the way when he said it. His green eyes crinkled as he smiled. "With what you get from your brother, we could put our money together. I guess you know what I'm asking."

Emma touched her hand to her mouth in surprise. There was a cut on her lip, and her cheek was bruised, probably where Earlie had struck her, and her eyes were red, but Ned thought she was beautiful. He was glad he had asked her to marry him.

"I don't know what to answer," Emma said at last. "I can't think about that now."

He'd surprised her, Ned thought. Well, by zam, he'd surprised himself. He should have waited until they were out of this place and the Minders were far behind. It hadn't been the right time. But he wasn't discouraged. He mounted his horse, then he leaned over and kissed Emma on the mouth.

When he pulled away, Emma gave him a grave look. "I cannot make plans now. I must wait until after the business with John is done." She had a look on her face of great sadness.

SIX

It was nearly midnight when Ned and Emma rode up to The Chili Queen. They unsaddled their horses in the barn, then Ned walked Emma to the back door of the parlor house. Through the window, in the dim glow of a kerosene light on the kitchen table, he could see Addie and Welcome. He'd thought Addie would be working still, but it must have been a slow night. Ned didn't care to go inside, but he couldn't let Emma face the two women alone. They would pester her with questions, and she might break down and tell them what had happened. That would only cause problems for him and pain for her. So he followed Emma into the kitchen.

"La!" Addie said when her eyes lit upon Ned and Emma. "Lookit who's here." She was a little tight. "We had a few less than a hundred customers, so we were obliged to shut up early."

Ned grinned at her. "We rode like hell to get back. I guess you were worried."

Addie picked up a glass and drank, spilling a little down the front of her dress. "Not me. I didn't worry." She brushed the drops into the fabric.

"Well, I evermore bejesus did. I thought one of them must have got killed, him or she," Welcome said to Addie.

Welcome was full of liquor, too, and Emma eyed her curiously. "Somebody hurt you," she said to Emma, looking at her closely. It was a statement, not a question.

"I got bucked off a horse," Emma replied curtly. "I didn't get killed."

"Naw," Ned said. "Neither one of us got killed, didn't even come close." He might as well get the telling over with. "Somebody robbed the bank before we did. We had to go north so's nobody'd suspicion us." Then Ned told the story he and Emma had made up. "We camped out on the prairie. The wagon broke down, and we left it behind. Then we traded in the team on a couple of horses. When we woke up, one of the horses had got loose of his hobbles, and we spent the morning looking for him. It was a damn long ride home, and I am purely sore," he finished.

Addie didn't seem interested. She glanced at Welcome as if the two shared some secret. Then she waved her hand at Ned, dismissing his story. She'd been on the drink for a long time, or she'd have lit into him for abandoning her wagon.

"You got a letter," Addie told Emma, nodding at an envelope propped up against the lamp. Ned looked from Addie to Emma to Welcome, who glowered at him. Addie might have forgiven him for going to Jasper with Emma, but Welcome had not. Ned didn't know why Welcome got so agitated about him. There was something uncommon strange about her, but he couldn't say what it was. Maybe she was just anxious to get her $250.

Ned reached for the letter, but Addie snatched it up and handed it to Emma. The letter was enclosed in a real envelope, whose flap was wrinkled. It had been steamed open, then glued shut with a lumpy paste. Emma examined the flap but didn't say anything about it. "The letter's from John," she said, examining the writing on the front. She slipped into a chair. "Did he send the money?" She looked at Ned, who thought it would be a fine thing if they got both the bank loot and the money from John on the same day.

Addie shrugged. "How would we know? We've been waiting for you to get back to find out." She winked at Welcome.

Emma slit open the envelope with her finger and took out a folded sheet. She peered into the envelope, but it contained only a note. Emma read it to herself. She closed her eyes for a moment—Ned couldn't tell if it was from fatigue or disappointment. She opened them and muttered, "My brother's coming here." She went to the cupboard for a glass, then sat down again and poured herself a healthy slug of whiskey.

"What?" Ned asked.

"He doubtless feels your husband is not to be trusted, and neither are you," Addie said. "That's what he says, at any rate."

"Yes, that is precisely what he says. I should have known it would not be so simple to cheat him. It is John's earnest request to meet and examine my husband." Emma took a drink of whiskey.

"It ain't your lucky day, oh no," Welcome said, fingering a scar on her arm. Ned hadn't noticed the lacerations before, and he stared at them, wondering what Welcome had done to deserve them. She sent him a hard look as she rolled down her sleeves, then turned to Emma and commanded, "Read that letter out loud."

Emma set the paper on the table and flattened it with her hand. Ned could see that some of the ink had run, probably from the steam Addie had used to open the envelope. Emma leaned over the paper, her hands against her forehead, and read the letter to them without stopping:

"*Sister*

"*It is a remarkable peculiarity that you have found an investment you believe is to my advantage, so soon after your marriage. But having heard much of opportunity in the West and the backwardness of those living there in taking advantage of it, I have determined to see for myself whether I should put my money with you. I am not such a fool as to send you the money without proper investigation. But if after meeting Mr. Withers, I am convinced he is to be trusted, I will agree to your terms. I will arrive in Nalgitas on Friday next, the same afternoon train you took. Meet me.*

"*Your Brother*

"*John Roby*"

"Why, he writes a real pretty letter," Addie chuckled.

"Jolly enough to make a parson dance," Welcome agreed, and the two of them broke into laughter. Ned wondered how long they'd been drinking.

Emma finished the whiskey, then crossed her arms on the table and put her head down. "I will get on the train tomorrow and go away. When I am settled and have a position, I shall send you money to pay for my keep, Addie." She sounded weary, and her words were muffled.

Ned sucked in his breath, but it was Addie who spoke. "Why ever would you do that?"

"Because I do not care to face my own brother and tell

him I am a swindler." Emma rose. "I am very tired, and I must pack my things."

Addie waved her arm. "Oh, sit on back down. Me and Welcome already figured it out. Ned can pretend to be your husband. It was Welcome's idea."

Ned thought it was a good idea and said as much.

But Emma didn't think so. Instead of sitting down again, she held onto the back of the chair and looked at the others. "I don't believe that would work. John is too smart."

Ned shook off his weariness. His plans—Emma, the ranch—depended on the money. She didn't seem to realize that. "It's a swell idea. Why, it's no big thing to convince him we're married," he said a little desperately. "Either way, he'll know you're a swindler. So you might as well leave Nalgitas with his money as without it."

Emma closed her eyes, and Ned wondered if she would fall asleep standing there. He was surprised that, tired as she was, she had drunk the whiskey. It would have made him pass out. Then Emma waved her hand. "I am excessively tired. I cannot think clearly. Let me decide in the morning."

"You got nothing to lose to try it," Addie told her. But Emma put up her hand and turned around.

After Emma closed the bedroom door, Addie reached for the bottle on the table and poured whiskey into her glass and then into Welcome's. She didn't offer Ned a drink. She didn't even look up as he turned and went out the door. When Ned glanced back through the window, Addie and Welcome were bent over the table, Addie's curls almost touching Welcome's head rag, and he heard

Addie mimic Emma's words: "I am excessively tired myself. If she doesn't decide in the morning, we'll decide for her."

Welcome was arguing with Emma out near the clothesline when Ned emerged from the barn the next day, and his first thought was that Emma had made the decision to leave Nalgitas before her brother arrived. Sadness swept over him, for it meant that Emma was leaving him, too. Then he realized that Welcome was talking about him.

"You got no business out with that man on them moon-shining nights," Welcome said. "You have forgotten way back yonder things?" Ned didn't understand what Welcome meant by that and was curious to hear more, but Welcome heard his footsteps and whirled around.

"What are you blowing about?' Ned asked her.

Welcome sniffed. "Miss Addie is full of misery with worry over you."

"No such a thing," Ned replied. Addie didn't worry about his work any more than he worried about hers. But maybe Welcome wasn't referring to robbing banks. Addie and Welcome might have guessed his feelings for Emma. Ned hoped not. Addie would know soon enough—and he didn't care about Welcome, of course—but it was best that neither one of them found out until after Emma had gotten the money from her brother. He didn't want any more complications.

Ned considered how he would tell Addie, but he knew there was no right way. The two of them had had a good run of it, and their time together was longer than either of them had ever been with anyone else. But they'd both known it would end sometime. They'd made it clear in the beginning that they wouldn't make claims on each other. Addie'd never pestered him to marry her; that was why things had been so easy between them. Ned hadn't changed his mind about their getting married, and he believed Addie had not, either. He was fond of Addie and didn't want to hurt her. But it was best to put off telling her how things stood between them for as long as he could.

Welcome sent Ned a disapproving look. He ignored her and turned to Emma and grinned. "So are you going to marry me?"

Emma's eyes grew wide, and she clasped her hands in front of her, and Ned could have smacked himself. Emma was thinking about his real proposal. What he was asking her now was whether she'd agree to let Ned pretend to be her husband. "Just for the day," he added quickly. "Just until your brother leaves."

"Maybe her brother won't think you're good enough for her," Welcome interjected.

"I'm good enough for anybody," Ned protested.

Emma ignored Welcome. "I have studied on it and don't see that there is anything to lose. The only chance I have to get the money is to have a husband. It is a good plan. Besides, I will enjoy John's surprise when he discovers that I have married such a handsome man."

Ned flushed and moved into the shade of the barn and hunkered down. "I believe you know that somewhere along the road I came over, I learned a little playacting. I won't let you down."

Emma peered into the shadows at him with a smile that

told Ned she knew he would not. "John's coming is a great drawback. He will be wary of your motives, but I do not believe he will question that you are my husband. John thinks himself a fine judge of character, so we must concentrate on his good impression of you."

"Then it's settled," Ned said.

Emma nodded. "I shall have to convince John that he cannot see the land, that to let the seller know we have taken in a partner would be to put the deal in jeopardy. John may agree to it since sometimes he is so greedy that he does not always use good sense."

Welcome had been listening closely, looking from Ned to Emma. Now she turned to Emma. "It sounds to me like you got more at work here than cheating a man of his money." The two turned to her. "Oh, the money matters. It matters most. But money gets spent, and bimeby, it'll be gone. What lasts, what you'll remember in your certain later time, is you cheated your brother to his face." Welcome laughed a deep, guttural laugh. "Myself, I never felt sad or glad about what I done." She shut her mouth, as if she'd said too much.

"What did you do that you feel so right about it?" Ned asked.

Welcome clapped her hands together. "Oh, I ain't fractious. I just done what I had to. I worked for the end of tribulation and the end of beatings and shoes that fit my feet."

"Well, you'll get enough to buy any shoes you want," Ned said, thinking over what Welcome had told them. She was right in saying that for Emma, the money was only part of the reason she was fleecing her brother. There was something else to it, more than she had said. Perhaps she would tell him sometime. Ned turned from Welcome to Emma. He watched as Emma reached out and patted the black woman's arm, but Welcome pulled away. "Drop no tears for me," she said.

Emma's nervousness increased as John's arrival drew near. Ned wondered how she could have been so calm in planning the bank robbery but so edgy at meeting her own brother. Maybe it was the memory of the Minder boys that made her act as if she had the jimjams. Now that they were back in Nalgitas, Emma had not brought up the events of that morning in the canyon. Once, Ned had asked her if she was all right, but she had looked through him and not replied. If she wanted to talk about it, he thought, she'd bring it up. Maybe if they didn't talk about it, she'd forget it. When he studied on it, Ned decided that Emma's agitation had to do with her brother, and it picked up on Friday, before his arrival. Ned wondered what it was about John Roby that aggravated Emma so. Addie had said that he was a mean man, the kind of mean that would make them all feel good about cheating him. Perhaps Emma feared him, was afraid of what he'd do when he found out she'd taken advantage of him. Maybe she'd begun to feel guilty about stealing money from her own brother, but somehow, Ned didn't think so. Emma didn't seem to have much of a conscience. That was an odd thing.

Emma could hardly stand still as she and Ned waited on the platform for the train. Ned himself felt easy. This was as simple a job as he'd ever pulled. And a comfortably safe one, too. John Roby wasn't likely such a damn fool as to kill a fellow for pretending to be married to his sister. Besides, farmers didn't carry guns.

The day was hot enough to melt Ned out of the broadcloth suit that he had put on to impress John. He sat down on a bench in the shade, while Emma paced back and forth on the platform. Beads of sweat stood out on her brow, although Ned didn't know if they were from the heat, the exercise, or her nerves. She hadn't perspired like that riding in the hot sun to Jasper. Half a dozen times Emma came over to him and asked why the train was late. Now she perched for a minute on the edge of the bench beside him and leaned forward to peer down the tracks.

Ned tried to calm her. "You thought any more about what I asked you?"

"About what?" Emma asked, distracted. Then she stopped fidgeting and turned to look at him. "Oh," she said, "your ranch." She took a deep breath, but before she could say more, there was the sound of a train whistle far off, and Emma jumped up. She looked relieved, although Ned didn't know if it was because she wouldn't have to answer his question just then or that the waiting for her brother was almost over. He preferred the latter explanation, and, indeed, by the time the train pulled to a stop at the depot, Emma seemed like a different woman, much calmer.

Five passengers got off the train. Then Emma gasped, and Ned turned to look at a wiry, beady-eyed man, disliking him at once. But he was not John Roby, because Emma touched Ned's arm and started toward a black-haired man who was an inch or two taller than Ned and powerfully built. Ned was surprised that Emma's brother was so uncommonly fine-looking. He had expected an evil countenance, but John Roby had pleasing features. His was the sort of face that would attract a woman, Ned thought. But that didn't mean anything. Earlie Minder had been handsome, too.

John took Emma's hands and looked at her a minute. Then Emma pulled away and said, "John, I should like you to be acquainted with my husband, Walter Withers." Ned thought the word "husband" stuck in her throat, but John didn't seem to notice. He turned and sized up Ned, starting at Ned's face and moving slowly down his body. When he reached Ned's feet, his eyes started back up again until they reached Ned's extended arm, and he took Ned's hand. The handshake was firm, but something in John Roby's eyes chilled Ned. They were vacant, like the eyes of a gunfighter.

"He is called Ned," Emma told John.

The way the two of them treated each other was indeed stilted, Ned thought. There were no pleasantries. Neither inquired about the other's health or made small talk. They just stood there, until the other passengers disappeared and the conductor called, "All aboard."

"Well, I guess you might be wanting a drink. Nalgitas has more saloons than good women," Ned said, in an effort to ease the tension.

"I do not discuss business in saloons, and I am here to talk business," John replied, then turned to Emma. "Sister, has marriage caused you to frequent such places?"

Ned was tempted to retort that Emma regularly got as full as a goose, but he held his tongue and let Emma reply.

"There is no need to say such a thing to me. I have brought you a business proposition. I believe I deserve your respect for it." If they spoke like that to each other in front of a third person, Ned wondered, how poisonous was their conversation when they were alone?

John set down his bag and stepped off the platform and scooped up a handful of dirt, smelling it, then letting it sift through his fingers. Ned had seen farmers do that. He'd done it himself when he was a boy. "Not much good for crops," John said.

"No, but fine for ranching," Ned told him.

"I don't know about ranching," John said.

"I do, enough to know the property in question is a fine investment. I would buy it myself, if I had the money."

"So you say," John told him. "I should like to see it for myself."

"What good would that do? You already said you don't know about ranching," Emma spoke up.

"Besides, like Emma wrote you, we can't show it to you. You'll have to trust us. If you don't, the deal is off."

"I don't trust *you* worth a buckfart," John retorted. "I don't know you."

"You know me," Emma told him. "You know I have a head for investment. Father said so, and you have said it yourself. And Ned is a fine rancher. He has built up his ranch"—Emma stopped for a minute and smiled at Ned coyly—"*our* ranch, from nothing."

John studied Ned so long that Ned grew uncomfortable and looked away. "You come from money?" John asked.

"I come from Iowa," Ned replied.

"Fought for the North, did you?" John's face tightened,

and Ned wondered if the man's hardness came from something that had happened to him in the war. Emma'd never said that her brother had gone for a soldier.

"I tried to join up as a drummer boy in Iowa, but my father stopped me. So I ran away and went west instead," Ned said.

"That would have been more than twenty years ago. What have you done since?" John asked.

Ned wondered what John would say if he told him he'd spent the time robbing banks. But instead, he replied, "I worked as a cowboy in Texas, then up in Colorado some. For a long time, I wasted my money on liquor, on women." Ned could make himself blush at will, although he couldn't recall ever having done so for a man. "Then I decided I'd best change my ways if I didn't want to end up a saddle bum. So I saved up, and five years ago, I bought my land. It prospers."

"You drink?"

"Some. Not so much."

John nodded. "A religious man, are you?"

Ned wasn't sure how to answer—Emma hadn't said whether John was a churchgoing man—so he decided to be truthful. "Not that anyone would notice. But I endeavor to treat a fellow as good as I can—no reason not to. There's Catholic preaching here once a month. I can't say that I go in for it, for I'm not a papist." Then, inspired, Ned added, "The priest married me and Emma. He's the only man of the cloth who comes to Nalgitas, and I thought my wife would want a preacher doing the honors, even though he's not of her persuasion. It seemed proper." He winked at Emma, who flushed.

As Emma looked down at her hands, John glanced at her, waiting a moment for her to look up, but she didn't. So he changed the subject. "What's this about gold discoveries?" he asked.

Ned took off his hat and scratched his head. "There is activity. I myself have not seen it, so I don't know the truth of it. The price asked for the land is a fair one, more than fair, without the minerals. I am inclined to dismiss the gold talk, as I do not rely on another man's say-so." Emma smiled at him, and Ned knew he had said the right thing. From what Emma had told him, Ned did not believe John would dismiss the mineral possibilities at all.

The wind picked up, stirring the dust, and John sat down on the edge of the platform and pressed the heels of his hands against his eyes. He seemed very tired and a little distracted. Emma quickly sat down next to him and began to massage his neck, and Ned was surprised that with the rancor between them, Emma was so solicitous of her brother. "You have had a headache come on," she said. "We will get you to the hotel at once and see if they can make a raw potato poultice to put on your eye. Ned and I are staying in a boardinghouse, but as there is no additional room there, we have made arrangements for you elsewhere." She turned to Ned. "John suffers from sick headaches. Bright sun makes them worse. He must have darkness." Then she mouthed, "The war."

Ned didn't care much about John's headaches, and he hoped they wouldn't stop John from handing over the money. Then he thought the headaches might be a good thing, clouding the man's judgment. "We haven't got much time. We best transact our business right away," Ned said.

The pain on John's face was obvious when he looked up at Ned. "Yes, I will do it then," he said.

"Give me your money now. We have to pay in cash," Ned said. "I will take care of it while Emma tends to you."

Pressing his hands to his eyes again, John rocked back and forth a minute. Then he stood up and faced Ned. "I would see your money first."

"What?" Ned asked.

"Your five thousand seven hundred fifty. If we are each to put up half, I would see the money first."

"I don't have it on my person," Ned stammered. "You wouldn't expect me to carry it with me, would you?"

"I would."

Emma looked at Ned with alarm, then said to John, "He has it. I can assure you of that. I have seen the money myself." She put her hand on John's arm.

Staring at Ned with eyes that were the pale blue of ice on a river and brushing off Emma's hand, John took a step forward and asked, "Do you take me for a fool?"

Behind John, Emma looked frantic. "We will show it to you later, John. Ned and I will take the morning train to Jasper, where we will complete the transaction. The seller has a fondness for me and says he likes to deal with me. Give me the money now, and I will add it to Ned's, and we will show you the whole in the morning."

"I guess I'll give you my money in the morning then."

Emma took a deep breath that calmed her some. "Oh, no," Emma said. "We would not want to show bystanders what is in our pocketbooks. If you give me the money now, I will pack it securely, so there will be no chance of

Ned and me being robbed."

"I am not concerned about what happens to you on the train," John said in a voice as cold as his eyes. "I am concerned about myself being robbed before you get on the train."

"By your own sister?" Emma's voice was as hard as John's.

"By a man I met just today. I have agreed to go partners with him. It is too much to expect me to hand over my money to him. In the morning, after I have counted his greenbacks—and he has counted mine—your husband and I will both give the money to you. Then you alone will take the train, since, as you say, the seller likes to deal with you. Ned and I will stay here, until you complete the transaction and return. If your husband goes with you, then he will have the advantage of me." When he finished speaking, John shuddered with pain and clapped a hand against his right eye. Then he picked up his bag and asked them for directions to the hotel. "I propose we meet here a few minutes prior to the arrival of the train. If you are not here, then I'll take the next train for Kansas." Without a word of good-bye, John started off along the road into town, walking past The Chili Queen without giving it a glance.

As John disappeared, Ned sat down on the platform. "Whew!" he said. "I never met anybody I disliked so quick."

Emma slumped down beside him, tucking her skirt around her, for the wind was fierce. "It was a foolish idea. I should have known John wouldn't be tricked so easily. If there were a train leaving right now, I would board it, no matter where it was going."

Ned looked at her in surprise. "You're giving up?"

"What else is there to do?"

Ned didn't answer. Instead, he leaned forward, his hands clasped between his knees. "What if your brother goes around town asking questions?"

"Oh, he won't do that," Emma said quickly. "He is too private. Besides, the pain will keep him confined until morning. He will try the raw potato on his eye, mustard plasters on his wrists and neck, and hot footbaths. Then he must take to his bed and lie in darkness. He eats and drinks little when he has these attacks, and sometimes the pain is so great, he cannot even talk. Besides, he would not inquire about us for fear someone would laugh at him. More than anything in the world, John hates being made a fool of; that is another reason why our scheme would have worked." Emma stood up and adjusted her bonnet. "Perhaps Addie will be kind enough to allow me to stay with her just one more day, so that I will not have to face my brother. When we do not show up in the morning, John will take the train home."

"After all we've planned, you're giving up?" Ned asked.

Emma touched his arm and said gently, "Perhaps John was not clear enough. We cannot get the money until we show him fifty-seven fifty of our own. Unless we can rob a bank of that amount between now and tomorrow morning, we are done for."

As Ned leaned forward to stare at the ground and think the thing through, Emma suddenly took his hand and squeezed it. "We were foolish to count on the money," she said, "although it pleasured me to dream about what we would do with it." She smiled at him. "It will warm me in the years to come to think I might have been by your side."

Ned took a deep breath and exhaled. "What if I had the money? What if I could come up with all of it? If I had that ranch, you'd come with me, wouldn't you?" He blushed, but not on purpose this time. "Would you marry me?"

For a long time, Emma stared off into the distance. The hills far to the west had turned blue under the afternoon sky. Emma took off her bonnet and used it to swish the air back and forth in front of her face.

"I never took a chance like this on anybody before," Ned said when she didn't answer. "I want the ranch so much I'd kill anybody who took it away from me—even your brother. And I'm asking you to share that ranch with me"—Ned glanced at her slyly—"after we visit a preacher, that is."

Emma turned to him, studying Ned's face and replying in a solemn voice, "This had best wait until later."

Ned gripped her arm. "No, I ask for your answer now."

Emma looked confused. "What does it matter?"

"This business with your brother depends on it. I must have your answer."

Emma looked away and thought it over. Then she sighed and said, "Yes, I believe if we could buy a ranch together, I would go with you." She gave a sad smile. "I thank you for asking. I hope you will remember that I care for you and that you will forgive me one day."

Ned thought that was an odd thing for Emma to say, but

he was suddenly too excited to think about it. "Well, by zam! I have the money. I do. It's hidden in the barn at The Chili Queen, more than five thousand dollars. I got it in a robbery, and that with what we took from the Minders is more than enough." As Ned grinned at Emma and gripped her hand, he felt joy come over him. He had proposed, and she had accepted. And they would live forever on a ranch in the Colorado mountains. He pulled her to him and kissed her, lightly and sweetly. Emma kissed him back, then pulled away and looked around. But no one was in sight. Emma leaned forward and kissed him again.

On the way back to The Chili Queen, Ned talked through his plan with Emma, chuckling that in trying to protect himself, John had given the two of them the perfect opportunity to leave Nalgitas with the money. He and John would give Emma their cash at the station the next morning. Emma would get on the train to Jasper, just as John had ordered. But instead of waiting in Nalgitas for her to return, Ned would ride to Jasper and join her, just as soon as he could get away from John. Since the train did not go directly to Jasper but first turned north to What Cheer, Ned might even get to Jasper in time to meet the train. John wouldn't expect Emma to return until the following day and it would take another day for him to follow her as far as Jasper, so they would have two days' start on him, and they probably wouldn't even need it. John would assume they had taken the train farther west. He'd never suspect they had gone on horseback to Colorado. "You pack only what you can carry on the train, since it isn't likely Addie would be in a mood to send along your trunk," Ned told her.

"Will you tell Addie?" Emma asked, as they turned into The Chili Queen, slowing their steps so as to finish their conversation before they reached the door.

"Later. When it's done. Before I leave," Ned replied. He didn't want Addie spoiling things. Besides, he had a presentiment that Addie already knew about his feelings for Emma.

Addie was not in the kitchen when Ned and Emma went inside, and for that, Ned was grateful. The two hookers were in the parlor, and Ned could hear laughter, then Addie's loud voice. Emma seemed preoccupied, but that was to be expected. After all, she was about to rob her brother, then marry Ned Partner. It was almost too much for any woman. She told Ned she must get her things together and went into the bedroom and closed the door. Ned had to pack, too. He started for the barn but ran into Welcome.

"You got my money?" She grinned.

"Tomorrow," he told her sharply. "We'll get it at the station, and I will damn soon give you your amount."

"Don't be so biggity-acting," Welcome told him. "I earned it as much as you, which is to say not at all."

"Without me, there wouldn't be any money."

Welcome dismissed him with a wave. "You sound like a white man preaching." She passed him and went on into the house.

Ned continued to the barn and unlocked the door to the little room where he slept. He would have to decide what to take with him—Addie wasn't likely to ship his trunk, either—but that wouldn't be a problem. Even after four years at The Chili Queen, he didn't have much. He opened his trunk and took out a photograph of his family and studied it. Once he and Emma were settled, he'd write his sister Alice, tell her where he was, maybe invite her to Colorado. He smiled at that. After more than twenty years on his own, he would have a family again. By zam, he might even have his own family! Until he'd met Emma, Ned never had thought about such a thing. He wondered if Emma was a bearing woman. She had said she was more than thirty-five this good year, and that ought to be young enough. His mother had had children—pupped, as his father put it—into her forties and maybe longer; he hadn't stayed around to find out. It would be nice to have a son, maybe two. But if Emma couldn't, well, then, it didn't matter.

Ned rolled his clothes and the picture inside two blankets, then secured the roll with straps so that he could tie it behind his saddle. He filled his saddlebags with the other things he wanted to take, leaving room for provisions. When he had returned the rest of his belongings to the trunk, Ned reached behind a board and drew out a leather bag, loosened the drawstrings, and dumped the money onto his bunk. He added the cash from the bank job in Jasper. Then he counted it, first making five piles of $1,000 each, another of $750. He stuffed the remaining money—almost $500—into his pocket. He placed the $5,750 in the bag and returned it to the hiding place.

By the time Ned had finished his preparations, the sun had gone down, and he was hungry. He went to The Chili Queen, where Welcome had left a pan of tamales and two plates, and he sat in the dark and ate quite hearty. He wondered if he should take a plate of food to Emma. Then he saw the empty whiskey bottle on the floor. Maybe she had decided to have a shot for supper instead. The door to the bedroom was closed, and while he was tempted to knock, Ned didn't want to awaken Emma. They had a difficult day ahead, and she might already be in her bedclothes. The idea made Ned smile. He rolled a cigarette and smoked it, listening to the sounds coming from the front of the house. A woman shrieked, then laughed, and there was a loud guffaw. He thought he heard Addie's voice and the click of glasses. Addie ought to buy a piano and hire a professor. Ned would tell her so. Then he realized he would not see her in the morning, might not ever see her again. Ned wondered if he'd miss the easy life he had had at The Chili Queen, but he knew he wouldn't—not when he was going to live in Colorado with Emma.

He rolled another cigarette and went to the window to look out at the night. The stars were bright, and there was a half-moon. That was good, since the next night, he and Emma would be riding until late. He saw something move near the shack where Welcome lived and narrowed his eyes to make out what it was—probably a dog, maybe a coyote. Then he saw Welcome emerge from the shadows and start down the road into town, moving quickly, taking long strides. Where was she going in such a hurry? Ned wondered. But he forgot about Welcome as he himself stepped outside. He breathed in the air, which was scented with sage, tossed the cigarette into the dirt, and made his way to the barn. Ned Partner felt tip-top.

When he got up the next morning, he still felt good, especially for one who hadn't slept much and dreamed dreadful solemn dreams when he did. He blamed the Minders and hoped that Emma had slept better.

Ned went into The Chili Queen, sorry when he got there to find that Addie was up, too, and waiting for him. More likely, she hadn't yet gone to bed, since she was bedecked with fine feathers and gewgaws. Welcome was at the stove fixing a breakfast of eggs and mutton ribs.

"Welcome says you don't have the money yet," Addie complained. She looked a little blue.

"Oh, it's coming," Ned told her. "Emma's brother said he'd give it to us at the depot. Emma's going to take it to Jasper. We told him we had to sign the papers there."

Welcome set a plate in front of Addie, who shoved it over to Ned and leaned forward, her pillowy bosom resting on the table. "Are you going with her?" Addie asked.

Ned shook his head as he reached for the plate.

"You trust her to take that money all by herself?" Addie asked.

Ned glanced toward the bedroom, but the door was closed. "Her brother won't let me. I trust her. I'll ride out and meet her in Jasper and bring back our share. Why, if something goes wrong, I'll pay you myself."

Addie sniffed, then signaled for Welcome to bring her another plate. "I stayed up till I don't know how late, then went to bed sober. I guess I got an appetite after all." Then she turned to Ned. "That man's going to hand over his money just like that?"

The door to the bedroom opened then, and Emma stepped out, wearing her traveling costume. She looked as if she had not slept much, either. She must have been listening on the other side of the door, because she said, "Ned will have to show his own money. Do you remember that I wrote John that Ned would put up half?" she asked. "Well, John wants proof. Ned says he has the amount hidden away."

Ned was sorry Emma had brought that up, and he glanced at Addie, who frowned and stared into the cup of coffee in front of her. Suddenly, she brightened. "I believe I would like to see that, too," she said and turned to Welcome. "Wouldn't you like to see it?"

Welcome glanced at Addie, then at Emma. Instead of replying, she asked Emma if she wanted breakfast. Emma shook her head no. "What would we be doing at the station 'cept interfere?" Welcome asked Addie.

"I guess we'll see about that, as well," Addie replied. "Yes, we'll see what we see."

Ned felt uneasy. This was his main chance, and Addie getting mixed up in it threatened to spoil it. So he told her straight out to stay away. Emma, too, protested, saying Addie and Welcome would make John suspicious. Besides, Emma added, John might remember Addie, since he'd seen her when Emma had boarded the train in Kansas. John was good at remembering faces, she said. Even Welcome remarked that Addie might jeopardize the black woman's $250.

But Addie waved her hand, dismissing the objections and saying the three of them did not rule her. She had a right to go to the train station if she wanted to. Besides, she would dress herself as plain as Emma, and even last night's customers wouldn't recognize her. No matter what Ned and Emma and Welcome said, Addie was adamant. So Ned did the only thing he could think of: He made Addie part of the plan. Actually, it was Emma's idea. They would tell John that Addie ran the boarding-house where they stayed and had overheard them talk about taking five thousand dollars to the station. She insisted on going along—no matter that they said they didn't want her to—to make sure they weren't robbed. They'd say she was a little crazy and were afraid she would talk if they didn't humor her.

Addie went into the bedroom then, calling for Welcome to bring her a pitcher of hot water. Welcome took in the teakettle and filled the bowl, shutting the door as she left. Addie was in the bedroom so long that Ned had to bang on the door and threaten to leave without her. At that, Addie emerged, looking every bit as plain as Emma. She wore a two-piece dress of drab cotton that was cut big in front and made her look dumpy. A sunbonnet covered her brassy hair, and she carried a purse as ugly as a picnic hamper. Addie had been right: A customer from last night wouldn't have given her a second look. Ned himself would pass her on the street without recognizing her.

John was waiting on the bench outside the depot when Ned, carrying Emma's heavy portmanteau, and the three women arrived. John stood up and looked from Ned and Emma to Addie and Welcome, and it was clear he was not pleased. "Who are they?" he inquired.

"Good morning, John," Emma said. "I hope your headache has abated."

"Enough," he said.

"John's headaches leave him sore-headed the next day.

He can take little else but brandy and sugar. Have you eaten?"

"I ate bread and honey and sucked eggs." John waved his hand, dismissing the talk of his health. "Will you make me ask you a second time who these women are?"

Emma said meekly, "This is Mrs. French, who runs the boardinghouse where we stay, and her hired woman, Welcome."

Addie regarded John coyly—she couldn't help it; that was her nature, Ned knew—while Welcome beamed. Ned noticed she had put on a clean apron.

Ned started to explain about Addie and Welcome, but Emma raised a hand. She drew John aside and spoke to him earnestly. When she was finished, John scowled at the two women, but Emma said something about how it wouldn't make any difference. So after giving Addie and Welcome a harsh look, John all but ignored them.

"I brought the money," Ned told him, speaking in a low voice, although the four of them were the only ones on the platform. He drew out the bag he had removed that morning from the hiding place. At the same time, John took a wallet from his coat pocket and handed it to Ned. Both men turned aside to count each other's money, while Emma looked nervously from one to the other.

"It is there," John said.

"Did you think I would cheat my wife's own brother?" Ned asked. His own nervousness had disappeared, as it always did once he began a job. "What kind of man steals from his own kin?"

John didn't reply. He took his wallet from Ned and handed it to Emma, along with Ned's money bag. Emma started to put them into her purse, but Addie, watching her closely, frowned. She started to say something, then shut her mouth, but she couldn't stay quiet. "I do not mean to interfere, but you are asking to get robbed, carrying money like that in a purse," she told Emma. "There's all kinds of pickpockets that ride the cars. I myself had twenty dollars stole from me on this very train. You must wrap it up safe and tie it to yourself."

"What?" Emma asked.

Addie took a large black silk handkerchief from her pocket and handed it to Emma, who removed the money and folded it inside the scarf. The result was sloppy, and Addie took the money from her and wrapped the scarf around it, tying the corners into tight knots. Then she removed a long silk scarf from around her neck and told Emma to raise her arms. "I'll fasten this package of skin-plasters to your person," she said. Addie pulled up the bottom of her own shirtwaist and placed the money next to her stomach to show what she meant. She motioned for Emma to put up her arms again so that she could tie the bundle to her corset. As she placed the money against Emma's stomach, Addie caught Ned watching and cleared her throat. "She is a lady, even if she is your 'wife,'" Addie said, and Ned felt embarrassed. John must have, too, for both men glanced away.

Addie tied the bundle of money in place with the second scarf, but the silk was slippery, and she was not satisfied. So she went through her reticule and took out a carpetbag purse made like an envelope. She emptied out her own coins and a handkerchief, then put the bundle inside and fastened the lock. She tied the rough purse to Emma, winding the long scarf around Emma's body twice and fastening it into such a tight knot that Emma would have to slit the silk with a knife to remove the purse. Emma was safe from pickpockets, all right. But that hadn't been Addie's only purpose in fastening the money to Emma. Ned was sorely sure that Addie wanted Emma to have an uncomfortable trip; the rough purse surely would bruise Emma's ribs. But Ned did not believe that Emma would mind. She had been through so much already that a little chafing wouldn't bother her. Thinking about what she and Ned were going to do with the money was enough to ease the discomfort.

"You look only a little fat," Addie said, her smile belying the unkind words. "Have a nice trip, my dear." Addie suddenly stood on her toes and kissed Emma's cheek. "On your return, I'll treat you to a custard pie."

The train arrived then, on time. John produced a one-way ticket to Jasper, telling Emma she and Ned could pay the return fare, and the five of them walked to the cars. Emma said she would return the next day.

"You be careful, honey," Ned said, suddenly remembering that he was Emma's husband. He wondered if he should kiss her good-bye, but when he saw John glaring at him and Addie paying particular attention, he decided not to. Emma got on the car alone and found a seat, leaning out the window to wave as the train began to roll forward.

When it was almost out of sight, John turned to Ned and said, "I am in need of laudanum for my head. Is there a chemist in this place?"

"Oh, I'll show you," Welcome spoke up. "I got to go to

the market myself."

Ned tried not to show his pleasure at John's illness. He had thought Emma's brother would trail him about all day, but if he had to take opium for his pain, he would likely want to bed down again. That meant Ned could leave for Jasper at once. "I have work to do. If I finish, I'll call on you when the sun goes down and see if you want to stretch your legs, maybe get a dinner of codfish and crackers," he said, then smiled to himself. Sundown would not catch Ned within miles of Nalgitas.

When John didn't reply, Ned said, "Or if you don't feel like getting up, I'll ask Mrs. French here to send Welcome with a bowl of broth."

"I'll tend to myself," John said. "I'll meet you here at train-time tomorrow. We will talk about the cattle when Emma gets back—just the three of us." He sent a hard look at Addie, as if to say she was not expected. "Hurry along," he told Welcome.

"We'll give the ground fits with our feets," she replied, and the two walked quickly into town.

Ned and Addie followed at a slower pace, walking along in silence. "I'll be leaving now," Ned said when they reached The Chili Queen.

Addie stepped onto the front step and took off her sunbonnet. "Are you coming back, Ned?"

"Why, sure thing. Why wouldn't I?" Ned grinned at her.

"I mean it," Addie said. There was a catch in her voice.

Ned moved a little closer. With Addie on the step, the two of them were the same height, and he looked directly into her eyes, which were wet. Something decent in Ned told him Addie deserved the truth. He looked away. "No.

I reckon I won't be seeing you again."

"It's like I figured, then," Addie said, and then her voice broke.

Ned hoped she wouldn't give him any knotty talk, and he said quickly, "We had some good times, Addie, the best times I ever had. And I loved you plenty and am grateful for it. But we agreed at the beginning it wasn't for keeps, and any idea I ever had otherwise, I gave it up a long time ago. You told me you didn't want anything permanent." He looked up at her. "I'll be sending you your money. You can trust me on that."

Addie nodded and looked at him a long time, while tears ran down her plump cheeks. She started to speak but thought better of it and abruptly turned and went inside, shutting the door behind her. Ned stared at it, knowing he and Addie had just closed the door on four good years. But he wasn't tempted to open it. He'd be fair, more than fair. He'd send her $250 for Welcome and $500 for herself, twice the amount Addie expected.

"Good-bye, Addie," Ned said softly, then turned and hurried to the barn. He collected his blanket roll and saddlebags, went into the kitchen long enough to take some provisions. Then he saddled the horse, mounted, and rode west, never once looking back over his shoulder at The Chili Queen.

Ned reached Jasper before the train did. The train was late, most likely due to a breakdown, or maybe the engine had hit a cow, the agent explained. The man seemed inclined to talk, but Ned was preoccupied and turned away. He wondered if he should find a preacher in Jasper but decided that was not a good idea. Getting married would take precious time. Besides, somebody might remember that when he and Emma had been there only a few days before, she was his sister. Perhaps, since they were getting married, Emma would be willing to share his blanket when they camped on the prairie that night, but if she said no, that was all right. After all, she would be his wife. He didn't mind so much that she would want to wait.

Ned thought about buying supplies but decided against that, too, since someone in Spillman & Gottschalk might recognize him. He'd taken enough food from The Chili Queen to last until they reached Taos. Ned went to the livery stable and looked at the horses for sale, liked two of them but thought Emma should choose her own mount. Then he walked along the street looking for a saloon. He was about to go inside when he realized he didn't want to smell like a brewery when he met Emma, so he wandered into a gents' furnishing shop and paid $2.50 for a hat. Then as he walked past the jewelry store, he remembered that Emma had admired something in the display.

Ned listened for the train whistle, and not hearing it, he went inside and said he would take the ruby ring in the window. He didn't even ask the price. After all, he had five hundred dollars in his pocket, and Emma would be arriving soon with more than ten thousand dollars. He paid and went back to the station to wait. When the train pulled in thirty minutes later, Ned stood in the center of the platform, grinning, his new hat in one hand, his other hand in his pocket, clutching the little ring box. He almost wished then that he had looked for a parson so that he could surprise Emma right then with her wedding ring. He had never been so happy in his life.

Ned fairly danced with anticipation as the conductor jumped off the train and set down the step. A large woman in brown got off, taking her time, followed by a man dressed in a linen suit. The conductor glanced inside the car, then looked at his watch and started off to the station house.

"Wait a minute," Ned said. "You got another passenger."

"Nope," the conductor said. "That's all that's getting off at Jasper."

Ned shook his head. "I'm meeting somebody. I know she's on this train."

"She must have missed it then."

"I guess you better check again, sir. I saw her get on at Nalgitas," Ned said. He did not wish to be rude, but the conductor, his eyes red, appeared to be on a bust.

"Oh, that one." The conductor shook his head. "She got off at What Cheer. We had to make a special stop, since the train don't normally stop there. First time in three, maybe four months that we done it. Her ticket said Jasper. I told her there weren't nobody living in What Cheer. But she said she knew where she was going and got sharp with me. It don't matter to me if she has to sit there all night." He scratched his ear. "Maybe somebody's meeting her. I asked, but she didn't say."

Ned frowned at the conductor, too stubborn to let himself believe the man was not mistaken. "That must have been somebody else. I'm looking for a woman in a black dress, tall, black hair. She carried a red carpetbag with her."

"That's the one. I guess if you was to meet her, you ought to be there, or she ought to be here." The conductor laughed and walked down the tracks.

"She got off at What Cheer?" Ned called after him.

"That's what I said, didn't I?" the conductor answered over his shoulder.

Ned took a few steps forward then sprang onto the train. Emma had fallen asleep. She hadn't slept well the night before, and they would laugh that she had almost slept through the stop. The train had only two passenger cars, and Ned searched both of them, but Emma was not on board. He stepped down off the train and stood staring east along the tracks. No, he told himself. He and Emma were going to get married. They had agreed to buy a ranch. He had given her his money. It was a mistake. Maybe Emma had misunderstood. Maybe she had thought Ned would meet her in What Cheer, after all. That was it.

But it wasn't. Slowly, Ned realized there had been a mistake all right. But it was his mistake. He did not know how or why, but Emma had suckered him. He stood on the platform a moment, too stunned to move. Then he took a step forward, and another, then broke into a run for the livery stable. After going hard all day, his own horse was used up. He'd have to trade it in on a fresh one for the ride to What Cheer. Talking fast, Ned negotiated a deal, paying more than he should for a good horse, but what did that matter when everything he had in the world was at stake? By sunset, when the train pulled out, headed west, Ned was already riding northeast, toward What Cheer.

Ned raged throughout the night. For the first few hours,

he rode with wrath, pushing the horse as hard as he could. Then a little reason returned. The horse, while not much to look at, was tough, hardy, and surefooted, and would be good for several days, but Ned would have to conserve its strength. Besides, there was no hurry to reach What Cheer. Emma would be gone, and finding her trail at night would be as hard as filling up a water barrel with a thimble. He'd have to wait until daylight.

So he slowed his pace and curbed his anger enough to study on Emma. What she had done was clever—brilliant in fact. She was no amateur, that was for sure. She was a professional, a swindler manufactured in hell. But why had she picked him? Why go all the way to Nalgitas to rob him when she could target someone with far more money? It didn't make sense. And who was she? Ned didn't know of any brother-and-sister teams. Maybe she and John had come from the East.

Although he could have found his way to What Cheer in the dark, Ned was grateful for the stars. And he was glad the sky was so different from the night sky when he and Emma had ridden into the dark canyon. Thinking about that time made Ned grimace. He was tempted to hurry the horse, but he was in control of himself now, so instead, he reined in the animal and dismounted for a few minutes, to let them both rest.

It was well past midnight when Ned reached What Cheer, maybe later, although he was not sure because he didn't have a watch. Ned unsaddled the horse and hobbled it, then spread his blankets on the grass beside the old depot. As he lay down, he spotted a red bag shoved under the platform and pulled it out. It was Emma's portmanteau, and inside were the black dress, the hat, crumpled up, and the yellow coffeepot he had bought her. The speckled pot had been his gift to Emma, and she had left it there to taunt him. Perhaps he'd take it with him and give it back to her. Ned smiled grimly at the idea and put the pot beside his saddlebags. He wished he had stopped long enough to buy a bottle of rye so that he could get beastly drunk, but perhaps it was just as well he hadn't, as he did not want to be tight all the next day.

He covered himself with a blanket and went to sleep, wondering just who Emma was. A swarm of buffalo gnats aroused Ned at dawn with a furious assault, and he awoke, covered with bites, to know himself a fool. As the previous day's events washed over him, Ned tried to think who Emma might be. Most of the women he knew who worked the other side of the law were prostitutes. There were female cardsharps, too. Addie had been one. Maybe Emma was a bank robber. There was no reason a woman couldn't rob a bank, as Emma had proved. But Emma wasn't really a robber. She was a bunco artist. Something stirred in the back of Ned's mind. He'd heard of a woman in Colorado who fleeced men. Ned thought hard, forcing himself to remember her name—Emma something. That wasn't quite right; maybe it was Em. He rolled the name over in his mind—Em, Em-ma, Ma. Then the name came back to him: Ma—Ma Sarpy.

He sat upright, scratching at a bite on his arm until he drew blood, and tried to recall what he'd heard about her. Not much. Someone had mentioned a month or two before that she'd been caught and put into jail up around Breckenridge, and he'd wondered then what kind of punishment the law would give an old lady. He'd assumed she was old because she was called "Ma." Her targets were usually men who were crooked enough to hide in a snake's shadow. She seemed to be getting even for something, and folks kind of admired Ma Sarpy. But Ned had never put much stock in the idea that she was anything but a clever sharper whose victims were either scofflaws or men too embarrassed to report the crimes to the authorities. And Ma Sarpy usually kept the stakes low enough so that her victims shrugged off the loss instead of pursuing her. Maybe in the beginning she had sought to right some wrong, but now she was just another thief.

Did she have a brother? He'd never heard of one. Ned smacked his forehead with his hand. Why, he couldn't reason any better than a sheep. John Roby wasn't Emma's brother. He was her lover, maybe her husband. And for a reason Ned couldn't say, that made him killing mad.

emma

SEVEN

Emma watched the train until it was out of sight, then

she stripped off the dress and threw it down onto the platform. She tried to untie the purse that Addie had strapped to her chest, but the knots held, so Emma decided to leave the bundle where it was. Addie's way was as good as any to carry the money. She unlaced the corset and tugged it off, leaving the money bundle fastened against her chemise. Then she put on riding pants and slipped on a shirt but left it open, because the air was very hot. She'd fasten it over the bundle later. After she had put on her boots, Emma removed the other contents from her bag— a coat, the framed picture of John, her mother's brooch, her watch, a book of poetry, a coat, her riding gloves, her piecework and sewing kit, the man's watch she always carried. And there was the coffeepot. Emma was not much for sentiment, and she wondered what had possessed her to put it into the bag, instead of leaving it behind at The Chili Queen. John would wonder, too, and he might tease her, and Emma didn't want that. So she shoved the coffeepot back into the satchel, along with the dress and corset, and pushed the bag under the platform where it would rot away. She laid the other things in a neat row beside her.

Welcome had packed a dinner, and Addie spread out the contents on the linen napkin that it was wrapped in. She wasn't hungry, and the idea of food did not appeal to her, but she had a hard ride ahead, and they would not want to waste time stopping to eat, so she chewed on a chicken sandwich, then gnawed an apple, putting aside the spice cake for later. Welcome knew spice cake was her favorite and had baked it just for her. Welcome had been thoughtful, making the two weeks at The Chili Queen easier than they might have been, although Emma had felt Welcome hovering over her like an uneasy spirit, even when she slept. Addie and Ned had been kind, too, and that brought to Emma's heart a feeling of sadness at her mean deceit. She didn't feel right about this job, not about robbing people who had been good to her. Addie was not the cruel woman that Emma had expected her to be. And Ned—he had been more than good to her; he had offered her a home and his hand in marriage. She had not wanted that, had not even seen it coming. And she had not wanted to hurt him, but there was no way she could have called off the job. Thinking about Ned and the ranch, where they might have made a home had circumstances been different, made her sad.

It was not safe for her heart to dwell too much on home, so she turned her thoughts to the ride ahead. She tossed the apple core as far away as she could and stood up. Since she would be spending the rest of the day and part of the night on a horse, it would be a good idea to exercise her legs while she waited.

She walked down the deserted street of What Cheer, pausing to look into the saloon, then stopping at the house where she and Ned had tied their horses. Ned had picked a blossom for her that day, a red wildflower, and she looked around for one like it to fasten to her shirt. She stopped herself then. This would not do. Ned had awakened something long dead in her. He had brought her joy that she hadn't known for a long time, and thoughts of him made her heart ache. Emma thought of his lazy eyes, how they turned green in the bright shining light from the sun, his hair and the way it was blown into curls by the wind, Ned's hands, which were firm and shaped like Tom's. Emma had almost forgotten about Tom's hands. Tom was a part of her life such a long time ago, before she met John, of course. She must put Ned into a compartment of her mind and lock it up, just as she had Tom. Her life before was shut away, and except for the dreams, which she could not control, she did not let herself call it up very often. In a few days, she would forget about Ned. He was no more important than any of the others whom she and John had cheated. Still, the others had been bad men. They had deserved what they got. Ned was different. She hadn't known that. But it couldn't be helped now. Her loyalty was to John, and loyalty, Emma had decided long ago, was more important than love. Without John, Emma likely would be dead—or worse: She might not be dead. She might still be that vengeful creature hovering between life and death that she had been when John found her. Sometimes it seemed as if she had lived as long as people twice her age.

With a start, she wondered if Addie felt that way sometimes. She remembered Addie shivering as she looked out the train window at the hardscrabble farm. While she had been sure she would dislike Addie—although she did not despise madams, as John did—Emma found herself impressed that, whatever her background and her reasons for turning out, Addie had a high opinion of herself and her profession. Ned told her that Addie was arrested for prostitution in San Antonio once and brought before a judge. Instead of declaring there had been a mistake, Addie had announced, "I am indeed a soiled dove, and if it is against the law, why did you yourself visit me Saturday night, your honor?" Under different circumstances, Addie could have been her friend.

Emma did not want to think about what she had done to Addie—or what Addie would do to her if she had the chance—so she shook the thoughts from her head, and she hurried back to the station. The sun shone out pretty hot, and she had worked herself up so that she panted like a sheep on a summer day. She looked south where the grass was burned yellow and the ground parched up, to see if she could catch a glimpse of John. But it was too early for him to arrive. She knew both John and Ned wanted to get away from each other, so one of them would think up an excuse, and they would hurry off in opposite directions. She and John had planned that he would slip away while Ned remained in Nalgitas until the train returned the next day. They didn't know until the last minute that Ned planned to meet her in Jasper. That would give them less of a head start, and Emma was anxious to be gone. She was fidgety, had been since the letter from John arrived and she knew she and John and Ned would be together. She had worried she might make a mistake, spoil things, or worse, Ned might figure out what was going on and John would be in danger. She would not forgive herself for that.

She sat down in the shade of the depot beside her things and thought it would be nice to take a nap. When she hadn't been able to sleep last night at The Chili Queen, she'd gone into the kitchen in the dark, hoping to make tea. Then she'd been afraid that if she built up the fire in the stove, she would wake Addie or one of the girls, or that Welcome would see the light and want to know what was wrong. She could not abide Welcome's questions and dark eyes peering into her soul, so Emma had gone out onto the back porch, where she sat for an hour or two.

Now, she rested her head against the depot wall, smelling the sage and listening to the *scat* sound of bugs that flew past her. Some creature made a rustling noise in the long grass, and she wondered if there were rattle-snakes about. But snakes weren't what she feared. She feared Ned. If he caught up with them, he would have no pity for her. Emma forced herself to turn her mind away from him again and picked up her sewing, but her fingers were damp, and they made her needle sticky. It squeaked as it went through the fabric. Besides, the little square of yellow that she was working came from the fabric Ned had bought her in Jasper. She set aside her piecing and looked out over the prairie, shading her eyes as she stared at the sun-washed grass. The heat made Emma sluggish, and despite her nervousness, she rested her head against the depot wall and fell asleep.

When she awoke, feeling a little refreshed, she tried to think how long she had slept. But her watch had stopped, and she hadn't wound Tom's watch since she left Georgetown, for fear Addie would hear the ticking in her purse and become curious. She opened it and read the inscription: *Tom. Forever. Apr. 20, 1868. Em.* The time-piece was gold and expensive, and it hadn't been used much—farmers didn't carry around valuable jewelry in their jeans pockets. Of course, she should have left it home, but she could not bring herself to part with it.

Emma set it beside the other things lined up next to her, straightened the book, and refolded her sewing. John teased her about her compulsion for tidiness, but their success was due in no small part to Emma's orderliness and attention to the smallest detail. The symmetry of her articles pleased her. It wouldn't take any time at all to store the possessions in her saddlebags and tie the coat behind her saddle.

Emma found the spice cake and ate it, neatly folding the napkin and placing it in the bag under the platform. She picked up the sewing again, examined her tiny stitches, then removed a raveling thread on one side of the block. It was cooler in the shade of the depot, and Emma thought stitching would calm her nerves. So she put her needle into the fabric, taking six, seven, eight stitches. As she pulled the thread through the material, she glanced up, and saw a rider moving through the rabbit brush, whose leaves were almost white in the sunlight. She secured the needle in the quilt block and stood, raising her arm to wave, but caution caused her to put it back down. What if the rider were not John? He might be a cowboy or a prospector—or even Ned. What if something had gone wrong and Ned was coming after her? The thought gave her a moment of terror, but she calmed herself. Ned would be on his way to Jasper. He would not know yet that she had gotten off the train at What Cheer. Still, she quickly collected her things and bundled them up in the coat, excepting the gun, which she secured in her belt. Then she slipped into the depot and buttoned her shirt as she peered out the window.

The horseman was out of sight. Emma checked the gun, wondering what she would do if the rider turned out to be Ned. She moved along the wall of the depot, the gun in her hand, and looked through a place where the board siding had broken away. The rider was clear now. She recognized him and rushed outside and waved the bundle. John astride a fine black horse and leading a second mount rode straight to her. He dismounted onto the platform and clasped Emma in his arms. Then he held her a little away and looked at her and said, "My God, it is you. I scarce believed that drab woman at the station was my Emmie. Oh, it has been dreadful lonesome these two weeks."

"I've missed you, too," Emma said, putting her head against his shoulder. And she had. She felt warm and safe against him, just like always.

John looked at her, well pleased. "When we are home, you can put on your crimson velvet, and I shall take you to the Frenchman's for a meal cooked in the right style. This has been an ordeal for you, and we will have a big time." He turned his attention to the second horse then. "You'll like him. One thing I'll say for Charley is he sure knows his horseflesh. He said Ned Partner tried to buy them a few days ago, but Charley beat him to it." John chuckled.

"We'll talk about it later. We must be gone. We have a big day's journey, and it is already late," Emma said. She unrolled the coat and stuffed her things into the saddlebags. John tied the coat to the saddle of her horse.

"You think he'll follow then?"

"Of course," Emma said. "Wouldn't you, if someone relieved you of five thousand seven hundred and fifty dollars and made you out to be a natural idiot?" She had not meant to sound so sharp and smiled at John to take away the sting of her words.

"We did that, didn't we?" John held the horse while she mounted, then handed her the reins. "He will be grossly insulted and blame Addie, then take his leave of her, and that is what Charley wanted. And we have his money; that is what we wanted."

"Yes, but Ned will also go to hell and back to get that money. He will be rash, reckless, and foolhardy in his pursuit of us," Emma warned, as John mounted and led the way north. "If he kills us, he will be easy in the heart about it."

John turned in the saddle to study Emma. "Were you in danger, then?"

The words were as much a question as a statement. "No. At least, I don't think so," Emma said.

"Well, you're safe now."

But she was not, Emma knew. Even with John beside her, she was not safe. She kicked her horse and rode on ahead of him.

The two of them rode until twilight, enduring the dust and discomfort without complaining. John wanted to stop then, but Emma urged him on, through the sunset, although her head ached from riding in the bright sun without a hat and she was greatly fatigued.

"We have a full day on him. He won't leave until morning," John told her.

Emma knew that John was weak, as he always was after one of his headaches. Still, she urged him to go on. "You don't know him. Ned has lost altogether everything he had." She shook her head a little to rid herself of the feeling of sadness that had come over her heart at those words. Ned had lost more than money, but, of course, she didn't tell that to John. "Our best hope is that the train will depart Jasper before he arrives, and believing I am there, he will take the time to search the town for me. When he doesn't find me, he will think that I did not get off the train but went on, cheating both of you. I should have told you to keep him in Nalgitas longer."

"It's too late to worry about that. Even if the worst happens and he gets there before the train, he will be riding a spent horse."

"He could buy one in Jasper."

"And take any nag that is available, just as he did in Nalgitas." John shot her a look. "Yes, I heard about the two of you going to Jasper. You knew I would. But that is your business. Besides, if I had to spend more than one day in Nalgitas, I, too, would find a way to get out."

Emma looked out at the rabbit brush, whose blooms made blotches of yellow as far as she could see. When she did not reply, John continued, "And you have said he is not such a good horseman as we are. Even if he finds a fine horse and rides tremendous hard and reaches What Cheer tonight, he won't be able to pick up the trail in the dark." Their own horses were good, and they knew where to acquire fresh ones if they needed them. "Besides," John continued, "Charley says Ned Partner has scrambled eggs for brains."

"No, he does not," Emma retorted, wondering why she felt it necessary to defend Ned. "He is easygoing, and for that reason, some believe him to be stupid, but I am not of that opinion. In fact, I was afraid he would see through the whole thing. He does now, of course."

"Do you think he will figure out who you are?" John asked, when they stopped to water and rest the horses.

Emma shrugged. "Addie has heard of me. She brought up my name once. On the train, she sought to frighten me about blacklegs and told me some were women. She mentioned several whose names I believe she made up, as they sounded like prostitutes. Then she said Ma Sarpy was in the jail in Breckenridge."

John's ice blue eyes were mirthful. "Then I believe we must avoid Breckenridge at all costs. They did not mention Georgetown?"

Emma shook her head. "We should be safe at home. I am anxious to be there."

John thought that over as they mounted the horses again. "Nonetheless, we should be prudent and consider turning west at Pueblo and going through Leadville. If Ned does follow us as far as Pueblo, he'll figure we're headed for Denver. Who would believe we'd leave the main road to go through the mountains? Does he connect you with Denver?"

Emma didn't know. She couldn't recall mentioning Denver to him—nor Leadville and certainly not Georgetown. She did not like the idea of taking the mountain route because it meant extra days in the saddle. But she knew John was right, although she shuddered at the idea, for the tiredness already had seeped into her bones.

John turned and studied her. "Can you make it?"

Ned had asked her the same thing, and she gave the same reply. "You will not find me wanting."

When they came across a coulee with a trickle of water

for the horses, John called a halt for the night, although Emma was willing to ride on. She felt exposed on the prairie, under a bright moon the color of butter, and refused to let John build a fire. Since the night was bright, Emma was afraid that Ned, following behind, would see the smoke. So they ate a cold supper, then rolled up in the blankets John had brought, to sleep away the day's fatigue.

Sometime after midnight, Emma was shaken awake. At first, she thought that Ned had found them, and she cursed herself for not insisting they keep a watch. But it was John who had awakened her, saying she had muttered loudly in her sleep, then had cried out.

"Nightmares?" he asked, holding her so tightly that she could not move.

"Yes," Emma whispered, as the dream flooded back over her. The dreams that once made her afraid to fall asleep at night had become less frequent over the years, but they still came, usually just after she and John had finished a job. The excitement, the little wave of terror, the letdown when it was over brought them on.

"I'll sit with you," John said, but Emma told him no. She wanted him to keep his arms around her and make her feel safe, but he was exhausted after the headache and the events of the day. One of them should get some sleep, and she knew she would not be that one. Besides, she never slept much. John reached for his saddlebags and took out a bottle of whiskey and handed it to Emma. "Maybe this will help, but be careful. You don't want to get full when we have a long ride tomorrow."

There was a time when liquor had been the only thing

that helped. Emma uncorked the bottle and took a sip, but she found the whiskey excessively bitter, and she gave the bottle back to John.

"They deserved it, Addie and Ned. All the others, too," John said, lying on his back and looking up at the stars.

"The others, perhaps, but not Ned and Addie. We were wrong about them. They aren't so bad—not like Charley said. Addie, I think even you might have liked her." Suddenly Emma leaned forward and said, "John, we killed the Minder brothers, Ned and I did. I stabbed Earlie, and Ned shot Black Jesse. They were as evil as everybody said they were, horrid men devoid of morality. Earlie was just like Yank Markham. We buried them where nobody will ever find them, buried them facedown. I wish they had buried Yank that way, facing toward hell."

Emma hadn't been sure that she would tell John about the Minders, but now that she had started, she told him everything, how she and Ned were ready to rob the bank at Jasper and how the Minders had gotten there first. She told him of riding into the canyon in the rain to get away from the sheriff and camping and waking up to find the Minders standing over them. Earlie had forced her to go with him, she said, and when he turned away, she stabbed him over and over again, just the way she would have stabbed Yank Markham. In fact, she wasn't sure but what she thought it was Yank she was killing. Emma didn't cry as she talked; her voice was steady. It was almost as if she were telling about something that had happened to another woman. Not until she was finished did Emma realize John had wrapped his blanket around her shoulders and was caressing her back and arms. "I was glad we did it, John, glad we killed them. Ned told me a story about two boys the Minders murdered. They were vile men, and they deserved to die. They'll never hurt anyone again. I'm glad they're gone."

Emma paused, then she began to shake. "But Earlie . . . looking into his eyes when he started for me, it brought it all back about Yank and the others, details I'd forgotten. It was raining when we rode into the canyon. There was thunder. It always makes me shudder—because of Cora Nellie. She was afraid of it. There was thunder the night before Yank came, and we took Cora Nellie into bed with us to calm her."

"I know," John said, and his steady voice calmed her. He rocked back and forth with Emma in his arms. He stayed with her like that, holding her and murmuring that she was safe, until Emma told him she was all right and that he should go sleep. She would check on the horses and sit under the stars a little longer, until she was sleepy.

"I don't suppose you will ever be free of that terrible rough time," John said.

Emma didn't answer, and they both knew she never would. After a while, John went to sleep, but not Emma. Wrapped in a blanket, she sat in the dark and let the dread of that time wash over her, as if it had all happened that very day. In reality, the day had been eight years before.

Emma was nineteen when she married Tom Sarpy. She met him the morning he arrived in Galena, Illinois, seeking his fortune. He had fought in the Union army under Ulysses S. Grant and decided that the town that claimed the general ought to be as good a place as any for a man to get a start. Emma was hanging up sheets in the back of the boardinghouse where she cooked and cleaned and did the washing. She appraised Tom from the corner of her eye as he climbed the hillside and stopped at the boardinghouse.

"Sir," she mumbled, for her mouth was full of clothespins that stuck out like buck teeth.

Tom cocked his head a little and grinned at her. "You got a room, do you?" he asked. Afterward, he told her he wasn't looking for a place to stay at all, since he had little money, and he husbanded it. But inquiring about a room was the only way he could think of to strike up a conversation with Emma. He found her mightily attractive.

Emma took the clothespins from her mouth and nodded, a little afraid her voice would betray her if she talked, for she was already wondering if it were possible to fall in love at first sight. She took Tom inside the boardinghouse and showed him accommodations on the second floor, directly below her own attic room. Emma had lived in the boardinghouse since she was sixteen, when her father died from grief. Her mother had passed on two years before that, and Emma's father never recovered. Her parents had been cultured people, her mother from a family in New Jersey, where she had attended a finishing school, just as Emma told Addie. Emma was raised in the sunshine of childhood to take pleasure in poetry, to stitch a pretty seam, to speak with refinement. Her father was a prosperous farmer, but things had gone awry after Emma's mother's death, and in place of the substantial estate her parents had expected to leave their only child, Emma inherited debts. So instead of attending a college, as her parents had planned, Emma quit secondary school to work in the boardinghouse. She had had proposals of marriage—back then, she had been quite pretty, tall, with black hair and strong features—but no one caught her fancy until Tom Sarpy came whistling up the steep road to the boardinghouse.

"You'll have to stay a month. That's the rule," Emma said, when she was sure her voice was steady. There was no rule to that effect, but Emma had such a feeling just then about Tom Sarpy that she could not bear for him to leave before they got to know each other.

Later, Tom admitted, "I would have stayed a year if you'd asked me to." But as it turned out, a month was long enough, and when it was up, they were wed—a marriage of true love. It developed in a homey way, for Tom had little money to spend on courting. He helped Emma in the kitchen, talking as he shelled peas and stoned raisins. He chopped wood while she rubbed sheets and shirts on a scrubboard. When Emma's day was done, the two of them walked past the prosperous cottages and gaudy mansions of Galena and out along the river or sat on the porch, Emma's piecework in her lap.

"I have never known a woman to be so direct spoken," Tom told her one evening, as they stopped to rest from their walk, in front of a brick mansion with white trim that dripped from the eaves like icicles. He did not care for a simpering woman, he said. "You are good-natured in accepting the hardship that's befalled you." He plunged ahead without thinking. "I need a wife who isn't afraid of hard work, and you would suit me finely." He blushed furiously at that, for it wasn't the proposal he had intended.

Nor was it the proposal Emma wanted. She looked away, studied the mansard roof of the great house where the dying rays of the sun lit up the pattern of diamonds made by the multicolored shingles. She was disappointed, although she would have accepted any offer of marriage from Tom, for he had stirred her heart to a froth. He was cheerful and lighthearted, and he made friends with everyone. Emma admired those qualities since she herself was dour at times, and she was wary of people. But she longed for more than Tom's telling her she was a worker and that they were suitably matched. She wanted words of love and undying devotion, silly though they might be. Emma was practical, oh, yes, but in her heart, there was romance. She had dreamed of being swept off her feet by a boy who would hand her a bouquet of roses as he knelt on one knee, begging for her hand.

Tom seemed to sense that. Suddenly, he grabbed her hands in his and looked earnestly into her eyes. "You are the truest girl I've ever met, and I love you more than life itself. Why, if you don't agree to marry me, I shall leave this minute for the western gold fields, and you will have to clean out my room and throw my things onto the rubbish heap." Then despite the dusty street and two women watching from the pergola in the yard, Tom dropped to his knees, a mournful look on his face.

It was a bit of foolishness that Emma cherished for the rest of her life. And right then, she leaned over and kissed Tom on the mouth and told him, "Why, I will follow you anywhere, and I would prefer to do it as your wife—" she whispered devilishly, "although it is not absolutely necessary." Then she blushed furiously, and Tom knew it was absolutely necessary.

The two of them tried to buy land in the splendid-looking farming country of rolling hills around Galena, but what was available was too costly, and neither of them had money—Emma barely had enough to pay for the gold watch she gave Tom as a wedding present. Besides, they were adventurous, and so not long after they were married, they decided to check out for themselves the new agricultural El Dorado in the West. They piled their few belongings into a wagon and left Galena for a Colorado homestead, settling near the rough little town of Mingo.

The farm was as cheerless a prospect as anyone could imagine, hardly the first-rate land to cultivate they had hoped for, but they got by, and neither Tom nor Emma ever regretted moving to Colorado. The two of them were indeed well suited. Emma worked beside Tom in the fields, planting and harvesting, and he built her as nice a house as he could make from strips of sod he dug from the plains. He even installed a glass window. They made friends with other homesteaders, and they attended the little church the settlers had started. Emma had a fine voice and a flair for drama, and she acted in the theatricals and tableaux vivants that passed for culture in Mingo.

Two years after Tom and Emma married, Cora Nellie was born. She was early and small, and her parents knew before she was very old that Cora Nellie would always have the sweet, simple mind of a child.

When that became clear, Emma fretted. "I have failed you," Emma told Tom.

Tom shushed her. "Cora Nellie is God's perfect child,

for she will never know the evils of the world," he said. And Emma believed him.

The two of them hoped for other children, someone to take care of Cora Nellie after they were gone, but that had not happened. And so they considered the little girl their lucky piece.

As if to make up for her simple mind, Cora Nellie grew into an exceptionally pleasing child in looks, with coal black hair, white skin, and eyes the color of Emma's—the color of the prairie sky. "She looks like my doll baby," Lorena Spenser, a neighbor girl, told Emma, and indeed, the little girl was as pretty and as delicate as a china doll.

Cora Nellie was seven when Yank Markham rode into the Sarpy barnyard with three other men. Mingo was a lawless place, attracting desperadoes and malcontents, and Yank wasn't the first man of unsavory character to stop at the Sarpy farm to ask for a meal or a fresh horse. But Tom welcomed everyone most heartily, ready to share whatever was on hand, and the little family was never molested.

Emma, too, was friendly to wayfarers, but she didn't like the looks of Yank and his companions. She was glad Tom was in the barn that day instead of working the fields. He emerged with his disarming smile, holding out his hand to Yank and saying, " 'Light, stranger, and take a drink. There's a dipper for yourself there by the well, and a trough yonder for your horses. My wife has been frying doughnuts. I guess this is your lucky day."

"Guess 'tis," Yank replied, dismounting.

Emma, who was at the well, called, "Come along, Cora Nellie," for she didn't like the way one of the men stared at the little girl. But as Cora Nellie passed the man, he reached down and grabbed her arm. "Hello there, girlie," he said.

Cora Nellie was not afraid. She had not known cruelty in her life, and she smiled up at the stranger. But Tom was alarmed. "Hold on there," he called, starting for the man.

Without warning, Yank pulled a gun and shot Tom in the leg. Tom fell to the ground, looking up at Yank more in surprise than fear. Then Yank shot Tom in the shoulder, and the awfulness of what was happening seemed to hit him.

"Emma," Tom cried, "I—"

Yank did not let him finish. Grinning, he shot again, shattering the top of Tom's head with a bullet. Emma heard Cora Nellie scream—or maybe it was her own screams she heard; she was never quite sure. She rushed to grab the little girl from the outlaw and run with her to the house. If she could get inside the soddie and bolt the door, she would fire at the men from the window. She could use a gun. But Yank caught her hair and wrapped his hand in it, and the second outlaw dismounted, gripping Cora Nellie in such a way that Emma knew he had pulled the little child's arm from its socket. In a single movement, he ripped the little girl's dress and drawers from her and threw her onto the ground.

Cora Nellie began to cry and talk in her gibberish. The man stopped unbottoning his pants long enough to turn to his companions and remark, "Why, she's as dumb as a jackass rabbit. Be quiet, little dummy, and pretend I'm your pawpaw." He reached over and smacked Cora Nellie across the mouth to shut her up. Then he dropped down on top of her.

Yank twisted Emma's arm behind her back and taunted her. "He likes the little ones. Not me. I go for the ladies like you." Emma kicked Yank very bad, so he held her head between his huge, rough hands and forced her to watch as the man raped Cora Nellie. Emma never could erase the sight from her mind, remembering every detail of that time. The grain in the fields was full and yellow, and the roof of the sod house was green with weeds that had sprung up after the moisture. The ground was muddy from the night's storm, and Cora Nellie's pale yellow dress lay in the barnyard, covered with grime, like trampled yellow tulips. There was mud on the little girl's face and hair, too. As she wrenched her head free to plead with Yank, Emma could see the bits of tobacco that clung to his beard and the filthy red bandana around his neck. Yank breathed through his mouth, and Emma remembered the rotten teeth behind the thick lips, and the fetid breath. There was the scent of stinkweed, too, and some flower— lilies, she thought, although she'd never planted lilies and couldn't have said what their smell was. Maybe there had been lilies at the service afterward.

"Stop him. Please stop. You may take what you want, but leave her alone. She's only a pitiful child," Emma begged.

"I expect we could take most anything we want without your say," he laughed.

Cora Nellie screamed then, as her eyes rolled back into her head until only the whites showed. She went limp as the outlaw covered her with his large body. Then finished, he slowly stood up and stepped on Cora Nellie's mouth.

Emma thought she could hear the little girl's bones crack. He kicked her until she lay facedown in the mud and smothered. Then he looked at Emma with yellow wolf-eyes and said, "I guess I done full justice to her."

The men watched until Cora Nellie stopped moving. Then they commenced with Emma. Yank was first. "Show me your tater hole," he told her, moisture running down his face from the corners of her mouth. When she did not move, Yank pulled at her skirt so hard that she fell to the ground.

After Yank was done, Emma was bleeding, and her arm was broken. The others followed, even the man who had just raped and murdered Cora Nellie, and when it was over, Emma was unconscious. The men probably thought she was dead, so they did not shoot her. Instead, they ransacked the house and ate the doughnuts. Then as they rode off, one set fire to the barn.

A neighbor, an early settler and old Indian fighter named Ben Bondurant, saw the smoke and went to investigate. When he found Emma lying in the mud, he thought she was dead, but then, he rolled her over, and she moaned, so he took her to a nearby homestead. He had never seen a woman "so strewed with mutilation. A white man beats an Indian any day for pure evil," Bondurant said, as he carried Emma into the house of her neighbors, the Spensers.

"We'll get them. We've dealt with evil before," Mr. Spenser said darkly, but Emma begged him not to organize a posse, telling him Yank and his gang were too far away by then to be caught. The real reason she did not want them to go was that her neighbors were farmers, not killers, and if they caught up with Yank Markham, they could be murdered themselves. So Emma's friends buried Tom and Cora Nellie. Then the men tended the Sarpy farm; the women cared for Emma.

She recovered in body but not in the heart. She had accepted the deaths of her parents, but the loss of her husband and daughter—she had never expected that. She tried religion, but it didn't help. The idea of revenge did, however, and she sold the homestead to the Spensers. Then she went to Denver, because it was said that Yank frequented that city. She found work singing and acting a little at the Palace, a gambling hall, which seemed the most likely place to encounter Yank or one of his men. She didn't know the others' names, but she would recognize them, each one of them. And when she did, she would kill them. At night, after the nightmares came, she planned ways to prolong their agony, telling them why they would die, but in truth, she knew she would not do that for fear something would go wrong and they would get away. The minute she spotted one of the men, she would take a gun and shoot him. And if she were hanged forthwith, what did it matter? She had such lowness of spirits that she would be glad for death.

Yank never came into the Palace, but a year or two after Emma arrived in Denver, Yank was arrested for killing a man in a saloon, tried, and sentenced to die. Emma attended the hanging. As Yank walked past her on the way to the gallows, Emma spit at him. "Filth!" she cried.

Yank stopped and looked at her curiously. He narrowed his eyes as if trying to place her then muttered, "I'd take you, whore, but I ain't got the time just now." And she knew the man who had murdered her husband and daughter, who had destroyed her life, did not even recognize her. Watching Yank die brought her some relief, but not enough. Three other men had not paid for killing Tom and Cora Nellie.

Some time later, John Roby found Emma in grief. He'd come into the Palace and seen her perform, and he was curious about why a woman with such obvious breeding worked there. "It would be my pleasure to buy you a drink," he said one day, as she sat by herself at a table in the Palace. Drinking with customers was part of Emma's job; the girls made a profit from every glass of whiskey sold. But Emma did not seek out men, did not want to drink with them. She preferred to drink alone, and she drank a great deal.

She gestured to a chair, and John sat down. "You may buy me a whiskey if you will do the talking," she replied.

"A bargain," John told her. He bought her whiskey that night and the next and many nights after that. And one evening they sat and drank and drank and sat, and when the bottle was empty, Emma blurted out the story of Tom and Cora Nellie. After Emma was finished, John took her hand and held it, and Emma, looking up at him, thought she saw tears in his eyes.

"They wait for you where the dead wait for the living," he said, and that comforted her. They became lovers after that.

John was a complicated man. "I am as cold as a dog's nose," he told her. He was, but not where Emma was concerned. His treatment of her was always loving, and he sometimes surprised her with his kindly acts toward others. Emma wondered if they atoned for something in his past. Once, for instance, they were walking late at night when they saw three mule skinners tormenting a Negro. Two held his arms while the third struck him with a whip. The man's shirt was in shreds and his back bloody. The men frightened Emma, and she thought the black man must have done something terrible. But in reality, he had only failed to step off the boardwalk into the mud to let the ruffians pass, and that had enraged them. Several men who had stopped to watch muttered about the injustice, but only John went to the black man's aid. He grabbed the whip from the bullies and struck the man and his companions with it, and they ran off. Then she and John took the injured man to a chemist and purchased a salve for his wounds. Later John convinced the proprietor of the Palace to give the man a job as an entertainer.

If John would risk his safety so easily for a stranger, what would he not do for her, Emma wondered, and that made her feel truly safe for the first time since Tom died. In the years following, Emma had grown to like John dearly, although it was not the deep, abiding love she had shared with Tom. The feeling she had for John was as much gratitude as love. Emma had been wearied out in body and mind when she met John, tired of loneliness. John had returned to her a certain pleasure in living. And Emma repaid him by calming the demons in John's life.

"I was married once, too, in Cairo, where I had a dry goods business. It was very prosperous," he said one evening, not long after he had saved the life of the Negro. They were dining at Charpiot's restaurant. John liked her to dress up so that he could take her to fine places.

"We had no children, so I thought it my duty to answer the call for volunteers. I then took as partner a banker, who would oversee the business." His eyes went pale in the gaslight. "I stayed until the end of the war. When I was mustered out, I went home to find my partner had sold the store only a few weeks before and run off with my wife. I was wretched in the extreme and thought to take my life."

John stayed in Cairo for a year or two, hoping his wife would return, he continued. Then he received word that his wife and the banker had gone to the Colorado gold country. John followed them as far as Breckenridge, then lost track of them. Having learned cards in the army, John was good enough to support himself as a gambler, and gambling let him move from camp to camp, for, like Emma, he was consumed with revenge.

John stopped talking then, and a look of such sorrow as she had never seen in a man came over John's face. Emma reached out and touched his hand. She sensed he had not told the story to anyone, and she knew that it was excessively painful for him to recall.

John gripped Emma's hand so hard that he hurt her, but she did not pull away. "It was years later, and I had despaired of finding her," he continued. "I was playing poker in one of the Tiger Alley hellholes, in Leadville. A woman approached me. I thought she was a beggar, so old and emaciated was she. Then she spoke my name."

"Your wife," Emma said.

John nodded, unable to speak. He dug his fingernails into Emma's hand, but she did not flinch. "She was dying of tuberculosis," he said at last. "The banker had gone through the money and placed her with a madam in Still-born Alley, who forced her into despicable acts. When she sickened, that evil woman threw her out, to live on charity." John took a moment to control his anger, then explained that he had nursed her until she died. "I forgave her, for I still loved her. And I promised myself I would avenge her," John said. Now Emma knew why there was a rage that burned white hot in John Roby. He'd never turned his anger on Emma, for he had a true softness for her, but she had seen him direct it at others. She had seen how his eyes grew pale whenever he recognized the pro-prietor of a house of joy.

"I have an abiding hatred for both madams and bankers," John explained later that evening, as they sat in the Palace, following Emma's performance. She nodded in agreement. She didn't care for them herself. Emma had no use for women who made their living off other women's bodies, and she despised the pompous, well-satisfied bankers who frequented the Palace, one in partic-ular. A prostitute whose fancy man had given her a sum of money to hide for him had entrusted it to the banker. A week later, when she asked for it, the banker denied that he had received so much as a half-cent from her. The fancy man beat the woman nearly to death.

"It's too bad someone can't trick him out of money—and get revenge for her," Emma said.

"Maybe someone can," John told her.

That was the beginning of their partnership. The next time the banker was at the Palace, Emma asked him for a loan of two hundred dollars. She pointed to John and said he had on him stock in the Mineral King that he had been trying to sell the night before. "He has been drunk since then and does not know that the mine has announced a rich discovery this very day, tripling the price of the stock." Emma parted her lips and smiled at the banker. "If you will loan me the two hundred dollars, I will buy the stock and repay you with an extra hundred." The banker refused Emma the loan, and as soon as she left, he went to John and bought the shares himself, just as John and Emma knew he would.

But the stock had not gone up threefold in value, for the officers of the mining company had not revealed a discovery. Instead, they had announced that the ore was played out, and the stock was worthless. The banker had no recourse. After all, he had taken Emma's information and used it for his own advantage. And to complain, he would have to admit he had tried to cheat John.

The two hundred dollars John and Emma cleared, minus the few dollars they paid for the Mineral King shares, wasn't much, but it made them realize they had a talent for defrauding others. The bunco schemes required all their abilities—intelligence, coolness, acting skills, and detachment, for both of them could be as unsentimental as mathematics—and it allowed them to satisfy their demons. Emma needed someone to keep her from the lonely hours. John's dark side required that others pay for the hurt done to him. And he seemed to need a woman to protect, as he had been unable to protect his wife.

Both John and Emma were tired of the gambling-hall life, and they were glad to find something as lucrative as the bunco game. It let them spend a few weeks a year working, and the rest of their time was their own. They were good partners, each perfectly understanding the other, and Emma thought their relationship endured as much from their ability to work together as their affection for each other. John was as intensely loyal to her, Emma knew, as she was to him.

The two thought up their jobs themselves. They could have made more money robbing banks or stagecoaches, but holdups didn't appeal to them. They liked the excitement and the challenge of using their victims' own greed to cheat them. At times, they employed confederates, although they generally avoided anyone who came to them to avenge some wrong. Charley Pea was different. Emma had known him in Mingo, where he was the blacksmith. He had helped bury Tom, had worked the Sarpy fields for her after Tom died. She encountered Charley again in Denver, and he explained that Addie had told people in Nalgitas that his wife, Mayme, was a prostitute. "She didn't need to say that. It wasn't her right," Charley told Emma fiercely.

Mayme, who was four months pregnant, brooded on the wrong, he continued, and when Mayme miscarried, Charley blamed Addie. Mayme hadn't gotten pregnant again, and Charley wondered if he would ever have a son. He blamed Addie for that, too, and the blame had turned into hatred. "Addie French is worthless as fungus," he told Emma.

Emma owed a debt to Charley, so she presented the idea to John, emphasizing the fact that Addie was a madam, a woman John would despise immediately. Besides, the challenge was ideal for John and Emma. The bunco would be complicated and dangerous, and the two of them liked that. So they agreed to trick Ned Partner out of the money he had taken in a bank robbery. Charley believed that Ned would be so angry at the loss that he'd blame Addie and quit Nalgitas. Charley would get even, and John and Emma would keep the money.

The plan was a simple one, although it almost died aborning, for Emma and John did not know that Addie had extended her stay in Kansas City. The two boarded five trains at Palestine looking for her, arousing the suspicions of the stationmaster, who inquired about their business. Emma and John agreed they would try only one more train before abandoning the job. Addie had been on that train. John had spotted her through the window of the coach and had nudged Emma ahead of him onto the car and down the aisle of the car, until he indicated the vacant seat beside Addie. "Sit here," he ordered. "You shan't ride beside a man. You are foolish in the ways of the world, Emma."

Toward morning, Emma got a small nap, but she was up before dawn, and when John awoke, she had saddled the horses and built a fire, since they would be leaving soon. John had said it was a big country and Ned could have gone in any direction, but Emma imagined every minute that Ned was only a few minutes behind them. Still, she believed John when he said that by going west at Pueblo, they would lose Ned. He would go on north to Denver, and when he didn't find them there, he might even continue to Cheyenne. At worst, he would look for them in one of the mining towns west of the capital city. There were hundreds of camps, and Emma believed Ned would search the larger, more notorious ones that were the hangouts of outlaws. He would never think of them hiding in Georgetown, which was every bit as respectable as Galena.

In fact, Emma had chosen Georgetown because its tidy houses reminded her of Galena. Keeping to themselves and having little social intercourse with their neighbors, John and Emma had lived there for four years, in a tiny cottage on Rose Street, with green shutters and a white fence and a lilac bush under the front window. John posed as a mining investor, Emma as his wife, although they had never married. John had asked, but Emma said it wasn't necessary. She didn't love him in that way, and she knew John would never love her quite as much as he had his wife.

John chewed his breakfast of crackers and cheese and dried beef, as Emma packed their things and saddled the horses. She had unstrapped the bundle of money the night before and tried to open it, but the purse was latched, and Emma was too tired to pick the lock. Besides, there was no hurry. Now she put it into her saddlebags. Her ribs chafed where the rough purse had rubbed her skin through the chemise, and she wondered if Addie had tightened the scarf against her ribs on purpose. Maybe Addie had had some premonition that things with Ned were spoiled, and that Emma was responsible. She pictured Addie sitting in the glow of the kerosene lamp, her wrapper hanging open across her sizeable bosom, sniffing over Ned's perfidy. Welcome would be standing in a dark corner, muttering about deviltry. Perhaps Welcome would taunt Addie, but Emma did not think so. The African was not cruel; Emma was sure of it. Still, who knew what was in the heart of a human being who had been tied up regularly and whipped like a dog? Emma had seen the scars on Welcome's back. Maybe Addie had, too.

"Perhaps I can shoot an antelope, and we'll have fresh meat," John said, as he broke off a piece of the tough beef. "Or we can dine in Trinidad and have ourselves a first-rate supper. We should make it there today."

"We can't stay in Trinidad. It would not be a prudent measure. Ned will find us."

So when they reached Trinidad in the early afternoon, they stopping barely long enough for John to exchange their horses for fresh ones. Emma found a store and bought tinned peaches and sardines, and they spent fifteen cents for a piece of watermelon. Then they hurried on and made more than twenty miles that afternoon, and camped under the shelter of some cottonwoods.

They rode for two more days, stopping once at a sign that read BRED FOR SAIL. There they purchased warm biscuits and fresh milk from a farm woman who was doing a pretty smart business with travelers, although she charged thirty cents for a plate of six lumps of dough. But they did not argue about her sharp practice, as they themselves were not without fault in the matter of raw extortion. Finally, on the third day, they reached Pueblo. Emma was nearly perished from the ride, so they left the horses in a livery stable and found a room in a hotel. Emma was so fatigued that she threw herself on the bed fully clothed and slept for twelve hours.

EIGHT

When she awoke after the first night's refreshing sleep in more than two weeks, Emma was lying under a blanket, alone. She could tell from the imprint in the pillow that John had slept beside her, but he was gone now. Her boots were on the floor and her pants on a chair, and as she had no recollection of rising in the night to take them off, Emma supposed that John had removed them for her. She got up then, lazy, and stretched and wondered what time it was, but she could not tell, for she still had wound neither her watch nor Tom's. She pushed aside the curtain, and as she looked into the first yellow streak of day, she was caught up in the memory of that prairie sunrise little more than a week before when she had left Nalgitas with Ned for the ride to Jasper. This morning's early light was only a pale reprise of the fine dawn she had seen from the wagon.

Emma bit her lip as she stared out onto Santa Fe Avenue. Pueblo was a prosperous young city of brick buildings and fine new houses. Just a block away stood a three-story building of dressed stone, with a brick tower reaching into the sky. Across from the hotel, an office block was going up, and beside it, a false-front frame building was being dismantled, probably to be replaced with a more imposing structure. Telegraph and telephone lines were strung from pole to pole down the street. She and John had chosen the hotel from among half a dozen hostelries because it was neither the finest nor the poorest but the most colorless. Emma felt safer, more anonymous in Pueblo than she had since she boarded the train at Palestine, Kansas.

She dropped the curtain, which slid back across the open window, and she let herself wonder then if she loved Ned, perhaps just a little. What matter if she did or not? It was madness to think things would have worked out between them. She had allowed herself to lose control, to daydream about the ranch as the two sat at dinner that evening in Jasper, to soften with reflection in a way that could have made her unfit for the job ahead.

She had loved farming, first as a child at Galena and later on the Eastern Colorado homestead with Tom. John would have been happy to live in a hotel, but Emma had insisted on buying the Georgetown house, where knowing she was too damaged to bear another child, she took solace in growing things. She spent hours in her garden planting lettuce and corn and beans, even though she was not always there to harvest them, nursing flags and heartsease and rosebushes. She had always been partial to the outdoors, in good weather and bad, and knew she would have loved ranching, watching the colts and baby calves grow. She had lost control of her emotions for a little while that night with Ned, but she'd caught herself and had grown curt—for her sake, and for Ned's, too.

Perhaps he would return to Addie. Emma dismissed the jealousy she felt at that possibility. She did not have the right to be jealous. She remembered sitting in the kitchen just a few days earlier, watching Welcome blacken the stove, rubbing the polish onto the black metal with circular motions of a powerful arm. Emma had turned to look out the door and seen Addie run her fingers through

Ned's hair. Ned had grinned at Addie, and Emma felt a longing at the sight of the two of them that had been plain for Welcome to see. Welcome stopped the work to warn, "Be careful what mischief you stir up, or I'll be after you like the devil chasing you with all his forks." Welcome had looked at her darkly then. The African frightened her at times, and Emma wished she knew what was in that brooding heart.

Emma suspected that John knew something out of the ordinary had happened between Ned and her. When John had called a halt beside a clear, pleasant stream the day before, he had watched her as she scooped out water to drink, and he had said, "I believe he cared about you."

It was her good fortune that men often cared about her. That made the job easier. Men in love were not suspicious. John teased her about it sometimes. She had always laughed it off, but this time she let the water run down the front of her shirt and had rubbed her wet hands over her face and had not replied.

John said only, "Perhaps you cared a little for him, too. This was not an easy job for you," but he did not pursue the subject, perhaps because he would not accuse her of what he himself was guilty of. Emma was sure John had had some female company from time to time, for he had an appetite that must be filled, and she was not always passionate. She wondered if John would have satisfied himself with Addie, if she had not been their mark. Fair play, Emma thought, in light of what had passed between Ned and her. But, while John might turn to a prostitute, he hated women of Addie's position too much, and so Emma knew he would not have had connection with her.

Yes, Emma decided, she had loved Ned, more than a little. He had made her heart light. He had awakened in her a feeling she thought had died with Tom. But it did not matter. She would bury it again.

Emma looked through the gauzy hotel curtain into the light, trying to judge the hour—early, she decided, not yet 6 A.M. John must have gone for breakfast or to inquire about fresh horses, since the animals they had acquired in Trinidad had been ridden fast. Maybe he was ordering a bath sent up. His warm heart was always mindful of her comfort. Sitting in a little tub of water would be nice, and perhaps she would have time to purchase some clothes before they left Pueblo. She had only the shirt and pants she had taken with her from Nalgitas, and they were badly soiled. She thought for a moment about remaining in dishabille for John's return, for she was curiously aroused. They had barely touched each other since they had embraced in What Cheer. He would be pleased, and it would be her delight to pleasure him. But there was time enough for that later on. It was not prudent to dally in Pueblo when Ned was only a day behind them, perhaps less. John's instincts were right. They should turn westward and hurry along for a few more days. When they were safely home in Georgetown, they would celebrate at the Hotel de Paris. She would don her best gown, which would please John, and the laugh and song would go 'round. Thinking of home reassured Emma. Georgetown was not a city, although it was a place of some small importance, large enough so that they could come and go without much notice. She and John had been away for too long with jobs that year; she was weary of the gypsy life.

Emma inspected a tear in her pants and considered repairing it. No, she decided, it would be better if she were ready when John returned. So she pulled on the pants, tucking in the shirt she had slept in. A pitcher of water was on the dresser. She washed her teeth, then filled the basin and rinsed her face. The water was dirty when she finished. Emma had not brought along a comb, so she ran her fingers through her hair, then arranged it in a single braid, which she pinned to the top of her head. She was pulling on her boots when John opened the door without knocking and closed it quickly, going to the window and pushing aside the curtain, the way Emma had done a few minutes earlier.

"Ned is here, and he is red hot." He turned to her, his eyes cold, almost sinister, and Emma wondered whether John hoped for a confrontation. There were depths in him she never would understand.

"Where is he?" she asked.

John shook his head. "I don't know. He inquired at the stable if anyone had encountered a man and woman—the woman wearing a man's clothing—riding hard. He said we were old friends whom he had arranged to meet in Trinidad, but we had left a message there that we were continuing on to Pueblo. The livery owner must have expected Ned to return in short order, for he nearly talked me to death to keep me there."

Emma's heart pounded. "Are you sure the man was Ned?" She didn't have to ask. She knew he was.

"Yes. He fits the description. He promised the stableman five dollars if he would locate us. I told him Ned was a quite late pay and gave him ten not to tell."

"And will he?"

John shrugged. "We can hope that Ned will go away only as wise as when he came, but the stable owner is a celebrated old pisser, who is not to be trusted. So I don't intend to wait around and see. After I exchanged our horses, I rode toward the Denver road, but I doubt that I fooled the man."

"We could abandon the horses and take the train."

John considered that option as he spread his blanket on the bed. "We would be too easy to spot at the station—or in the cars, for that matter, if Ned were to board down the line. Besides, with horses, we can go anywhere. Horses will be slower but safer, I think."

As they talked, the two of them quickly gathered their belongings and rolled them inside the blankets they had brought, then picked up the bedrolls and the saddlebags. John preceded Emma down the stairs and out the front door. "He will expect us to retreat down the alleys," John explained. "So we will be bold and use Santa Fe Avenue." They secured their things to the saddles, then mounted. Emma would have raced out of the city, but John slowed her. Two riders at a full gallop would draw attention, so they trotted the horses down the street. They made their way through oxcarts and mule-drawn wagons laden with building materials, past a trolley that had stopped to pick up passengers, until they reached the highway to the west. Then they took off at a smart pace.

They rode westward along the Arkansas River, without talking. John took the lead at first, then Emma, then John again. The mountains with their streaks of white where crevices were yet filled with winter snow loomed up splendidly to the west. Still, the country they rode through was very dull, the road tolerable, although dry and dusty. There had been much travel on it, and the roadside was destitute of vegetation, except for the gray-green rabbit brush with its thick yellow blooms. After a while, John called a halt and filled their canteens with water from the river, wetting the pieces of blanket covering the metal containers to keep the water inside cool. He staked the horses to a spot where grass grew in some abundance— and mosquitoes in superabundance. Then, saying he had known they would not take the time to eat in Pueblo that morning, he produced a loaf of bread and pronounced, "Breakfast!" The wife of the livery stable owner had just taken it from the oven, and he had offered her a dollar for it, he explained, and Emma smiled at his thoughtfulness, as she brushed a mosquito off her hand. But when John broke open the heavy loaf, it was black inside and had a rank, disgusting smell, for it had been made of Mexican unbolted flour, without leavening. Despite their hunger, they could not eat the mess, and they threw it into the river. Emma felt miserable then. She ached from hunger, for she had had neither supper nor breakfast. But she would not complain. John was hungry, too. He had supped the night before, while she slept, but he had not eaten breakfast, either.

"We must keep a sharp eye out for a ptarmigan, and if we shoot one, we will build a small fire at our nooning and cook it," John promised. But they did not find game birds, so when the sun was high and they stopped to rest the horses, John waded into the river to try to catch a trout. He had neither line nor hook, however, only his hands, and he had no luck. There was not time, of course, to go raspberrying. So Emma peeled the skin from a prickly pear cactus and scraped out the pink meat. The pulp did little to satisfy either of them. Other travelers passed by on the road, but John and Emma did not ask them for food, for fear of calling attention to themselves. By the time they reached Cañon City, making excellent time, it had been more than a day since Emma had eaten anything proper.

She was ready to stop for the night then but knew they must push boldly forward. Although both John and Emma believed Ned had gone to Denver, they agreed that it would not be prudent to stay in the small town. They must not dismiss the possibility that Ned had run into someone who had seen them riding west, and if he had discovered that they were in Pueblo, he would have no trouble finding them in Cañon City. They would be more notice-able in the smaller town, and John suggested that since Ned would be asking about two travelers, they ought to separate, going through Cañon City alone and meeting on the other side. He would stop to buy oats for the horses, while Emma procured victuals for themselves.

So she found a general store and bought enough food for two or three days, since it would take no more time than that to get through the mountains and reach Salida. She also purchased a flannel shirt, waiting impatiently as the clerk slowly wrapped her purchases in brown paper and tied them with string. It was not necessary, Emma told him, but he only stopped his work and told her, "That's the way they done things here." Then he took so long making change that Emma almost told him to keep it, but that surely would make the clerk remember her, so she fidgeted while he named each coin as he laid it on the counter.

Although she knew John would be finished and waiting, she nonetheless went two blocks out of her way to ride through the town on a residential street, just in case Ned inquired on the main thoroughfare whether anyone had seen a woman riding astride. When she joined John at the west edge of town, she handed him crackers and cheese, an apple, and some horehound drops, and they ate as they rode the next mile or two at a gallop.

The rail line followed the river, so instead of going that route, the two took to the high ground, where they thought they could make just as fast time without the risk of being spotted by someone on the cars. The river cut straight through the mountains instead of winding around their base, forming pretty rough cliffs that were steep and high. Although the scenery was grand, the ground was very barren. Emma was glad John had purchased oats, for the horses would not have good forage that night. Once, after climbing up a long, steep, and rocky hill, Emma rode to the edge of the cliff and stopped to look far down at the river. It reminded her of the crumpled indigo ribbons on one of the hats she had left behind at The Chili Queen.

They had hoped to gain the summit before nightfall, but not knowing the country, they decided to make camp wherever they were when the light was gone. So as the sky began darkening, they left the main road for a trail so narrow and crooked that Emma could not tell whether it had been made by deer or Christians. The route followed the edge of the cliffs, where the abrupt descent made

Emma shiver, as she recalled the steep trail into the canyon with Ned. When it was too dark to see, John picked a low spot between the cliff and a rock outcropping that hid them from even that narrow trail. They picketed their horses and placed their saddlebags on the rocks. Emma stroked one of the animals. The horses were as tired as she was. They had been ridden too hard, and she and John would have to be easier on them the next day. Then while John made a small campfire, for the night was cool and fall-like and a little rain had fallen, Emma walked to the edge of the cliff and peered into the intense darkness. Although she could not see down into the deep, dark valleys, for the moonlight did not penetrate them, she nonetheless grew dizzy and sick to her stomach from standing on the tremendous height, and she turned and hurried back to the campfire.

John had spread out the supper, and they fell to, eating cheese and pickles and dried beef, then finished with cherries and doughy cookies that made Emma long for Welcome's good spice cake. But John was satisfied with the meal, as he was with most things that came under Emma's purview. "If I had all the luxuries the world could bestow, I would never wish for a better meal," he told her. "Why, it pleases me more than a diamond ring."

Emma thought what an easy companion he had always been and reached for his hand and squeezed it, feeling some of the strain from the day's terrible hard ride leave her. "Well, I would wish for terrapin and peas, although I admit I was hungry enough to eat beef head roasted in the ground." She shivered at the thought.

John picked up the flannel shirt Emma had bought and

handed it to her. "Put it on before the chill mountain air stiffens you up with cold." The wind had picked up, sounding like rushing water as it swept through the trees, bringing the scent of pine needles.

Emma buttoned the new shirt over the dirty one. There would be frost before morning, but even so, she liked this high country better than the prairie. She wondered if Ned's ranch in Telluride were high and cool like this place. As much as she had loved her homestead on the plains, she would sometimes stand in the barnyard there, in the hot sun, looking west and wondering what her life would have been if she and Tom had kept riding toward the mountains and made a farm there. Yank Markham and his men would not have found them. Emma shook her head to rid herself of thoughts of both Tom and Ned and was glad John was stirring the fire and did not see her.

When he was well satisfied that the fire would burn slowly for a while, John got up and brought Emma her bedroll, saying, "I'm sorry these are so lightweight. We shall have to make do for another night or two." He placed Emma's blanket near the fire, then spread his on the other side of her, keeping her safe between the coals and himself. "Do you want whiskey to warm you?" he asked.

"No," Emma told him. "I may go to bed pretty cold, but I will go to bed sober."

"You were on the drink in Nalgitas," he said. It was a statement more than a question, and she did not reply. "I believe Addie was a bad influence. Her kind always are."

"I drank only a little. I did much work around The Chili Queen, as I did not care to get drunk in bed for want of something to do. Besides, Welcome was always there, telling me, 'You wants to live right so the devil don't meet you.' Welcome and Addie got on quite well, I believe, better than I did with either of them. That was odd."

John only grunted in reply and did not invite her to explore the subject. A few minutes later when Emma looked closely at him, she saw he had fallen asleep. She tucked his blanket snugly around him, then sat looking into the campfire, enjoying the solitude of the place. A high wind came up, blowing across the elevated ridge of the mountains and carrying a few drops of rain, and as Emma shivered beside the fire, she suddenly thought it was the gloomiest night she had seen. But she was too tired to dwell on the subject. She wrapped herself in the cover and rolled so close to the fire that by morning her blanket was singed.

They slept until dawn and awoke to a sky the color of slate. It was a disagreeable morning, dismal and cold. The air was oppressive, and clouds rested against the edge of the mountains, obscuring the view. Emma rose from her blanket, despondent. She felt tired and worn, and she tried to shake off the feelings as she shook out her blanket and wrapped it around herself. There had been more rain, and the ground around them was very miry. The fire was out. Emma picked up a handful of sticks from the pile she had gathered the night before and started a small blaze. John got up then, and took out the provisions Emma had bought in Cañon City.

"We can look for chokecherries and wild currants as we ride. They ripen this time of year. Perhaps the bears have gotten to them first, in which case, we should look out for bears," Emma said. When John did not laugh, she glanced up to see if he had heard, thinking perhaps he had slipped off without her notice, to check on the horses. But John was squatting a few feet away, looking beyond her, and she continued. "As for breakfast, I hope you like it cold, for I did not purchase a pan in which to warm it. Perhaps we can toast the bread on sticks." She laughed again, thinking they had not laughed much in the past few days. "Myself, I don't mind a cold breakfast, but oh my, I should like a cup of hot coffee." When John still did not respond, Emma looked at him sharply and realized he had not moved. She felt an unspeakable fear come over her then. She shivered a little, telling herself it was nothing. In a few seconds, John would point to a rabbit hiding beneath a sagebrush or a curious formation of the clouds. But he did not. He remained rigid, his eyes gone paler than usual, and without turning to see what John was staring at, Emma looked about furtively for her gun. Then she remembered they had not slept on their arms that night. The weapons were in their saddlebags.

Suddenly there was a clatter that startled Emma so that she cried out. The yellow-and-white coffeepot Ned had bought for her in Jasper bounced across the ground and landed in the campfire at her feet, leaving bits of flaked enamel where it had smashed against the rocks. Emma whirled around, letting the blanket fall, and faced Ned.

"Try that," Ned said in a tone so measured and cold that Emma thought her blood would clot in her veins. "A picnic is nice duty for a pair of cheating stiffs." Ned was standing on a shale outcropping above the camp, and

Emma thought he must have been viewing them for some time, perhaps all night. She wondered if he had eaten or slept since he left Nalgitas. His clothes were rumpled and dirty, and his hat, which Emma saw was new, was crusted with sweat and dust. Ned lifted his chin a little. His face was gaunt and grime-streaked, and he had a growth of beard. His green eyes were almost black, and his expression was unfathomable. It might have been hate or fury or fear. No, Emma thought, not fear. She did not know what showed on her own face, but what she felt inside was a combination of terror and excitement at seeing Ned again. Her chest felt so heavy Emma wondered that she did not fall face forward.

"Oh, never mind that. We have no coffee," Emma said in a voice that she hoped was as steady as Ned's. "You are looking tolerably good."

Ned stared at her for a very long time, but he watched John, too, and when John started to rise, Ned leveled a gun at him, so John shrugged and remained in a kind of crouch. Then Ned responded to Emma. "Oh, not so good. It appears all my friends have gone back on me."

"Not friends. Merely acquaintances. It is how the game is played. You know it as well as we do," Emma said.

"Then I'll knock the stuffing out of your game—Ma Sarpy, is it?"

Emma jerked up her head at that, but she did not ask how Ned had figured her out. She only knew she had underestimated him. It had been a rash endeavor to take the word of the blacksmith that Ned was too slow and easygoing to be much of a threat. But she should have seen it herself, for she had grown to know Ned far better

261

than had Charley Pea.

Still crouched, John asked in a voice that was steady and slightly amused, for danger made him as cold as mountain water, "What do you want here?"

"What do you think I want?" Ned snarled. "You have what is mine. Give it to me. Then I am going to Telluride, and you may go to hell!"

"Oh, we don't have the money. We left it in Trinidad," John told him, with a slight laugh.

The laugh seemed to unnerve Ned. "And I am Grover Cleveland's horse." He laughed himself then, but the sound was high and shrill and out of control. Emma ached to see his lazy smile again but knew she never would. "You're a damned son of a bitch," Ned added.

Pointing his gun at John, Ned carefully stepped down off the rock until he was on the ground a few yards from them. "Now stand up and be shot like a man, or do you want to die together?"

"You would murder us with one bullet, just like the Minders killed those boys you told me about?" Emma asked.

Pain flickered across Ned's face, then was gone, and he replied to her as if John were not there. "That was different. Those boys never did anything to anybody." He lowered his voice until Emma could barely hear him. "What you did, it wasn't right, Emma. It's not right to steal a man's dream. You said things . . ." He collected himself and raised his voice. "You thieved me out of what was mine, and now you'll pay for it."

He looked at her with such hatred that Emma's hope almost gave way. She said, "We only cheated you out of what you stole yourself. We are no shabbier than you."

"Oh, yes, you are. Oh, yes," Ned said. "Besides, I stole the money fair and square, and now, God damn your souls, I'm taking it back."

The three of them were locked in place, and Emma thought each was waiting for another to make the first move. The scaly situation would have been funny if it had not been so deadly. But no one of them was rash, and so they all remained where they were, while Emma tried to think the thing through. With each job, she and John had weighed the possibility of getting caught, maybe being sent to jail. She had once barely escaped a beating. But she had not expected to be killed. It all seemed unreal to be standing there, yet she had never been so aware of herself or a place. Everything was in focus, just as it had been the day Tom and Cora Nellie were killed, and she wondered why at times of terror in her life, her senses were so sharp. She saw the damp places left by raindrops on the rocks, the aspen leaves shivering in the wind. She made out diseased black spots on the leaves, saw that foliage on a far mountain had already turned gold. She caught the moldy scent of decaying leaves, the smell of horses not far away, the sound of their hooves hitting shale as they moved. The sky was lighter now, the clouds not so black, and in a few hours, there would be blue. She wondered which of them would be alive to see it.

That was an idle thought. She must concentrate. Ned might hate her, and he might kill her, but after what had been between them, he was too decent to do it easily. He would shoot John first. She must be ready to shove John out of the way, catching the bullet if she had to, but she would do it.

"We don't have it," John said in a pleasant voice, turning to Emma for confirmation. As John shifted, Emma saw the rock he held cupped in his hand. She had not seen him pick it up, and she was sure Ned had not either or else he would have ordered John to drop it. Emma felt a surge of relief knowing the odds had improved in their favor. Ned had a gun, but he faced two of them, and John had a good arm. Now it was up to her to draw Ned's attention so that John could kill him. The thought made Emma weak, but she knew there was no choice. If they did not kill Ned, then they would die by his gun. No, no choice, she told herself.

But maybe there was, she thought suddenly. Maybe none of them had to die. "We'll give you your money," she said. "It's in my saddlebags. I'll get it for you." Emma indicated the place in the rocks where she and John had stowed their things.

Ned's lip curled a little as he glanced from Emma to John. He turned back to Emma. "All right, but be easy now. Use your left hand. Keep the right one where I can see it. If you try anything, I'll kill you. You know I will."

Emma hoped Ned did not see her shake as, facing him, she took sideways steps, moving cautiously. She kicked a stone out of the way, and it rolled farther than she had thought, over the edge of the cliff, the clattering growing dimmer with each bounce against the rock wall. The sound made Emma grit her teeth. She glanced at John, who still held the rock, but Ned had been too attentive to give John a chance to throw it.

Both men watched as Emma slowly opened the saddlebag and took out the carpet purse that held the money. "It is just as Addie gave it to me. She locked it." Emma pushed the latch with her thumb to show Ned that the bag did not open. "I don't have the key. We did not take the time to break it apart." She felt panic in her breast, wondering if Ned believed her. It was the truth.

"Give it to me," Ned said.

"No, I'll smash the lock," John said. "Half the money's ours."

Ned laughed again. "Your half's mine now. Like you said, it's how the game is played. You dunned a man and got nix. It's my turn, and I'll take it all. First the money and then your horses." He almost sneered at Emma. "But I won't take you. I don't want you anymore."

Emma already knew that, but the vehemence in the words gave her chicken skin.

Ned glowered. "If this is a trick, why then, I'll take your lives, too." He turned to Emma. "I told you once, I'm not much for killing, but I do it now and again when I have to, and it rests easy on me. Just like it does on you." He stared hard at her. "Now, I've had enough of your windy talk. Set the bag on the ground and push it to me with your foot."

Emma put the bag down as she sent John a pleading glance to tell him it did not matter if Ned beat them. But the look on John's face, his eyes almost white with fury, warned her he would not have it so. He bent his arm back a little, as he said to Emma, "Why, sonny here has robbery on the brain, and a very small brain it is, from what you have said." She knew John was trying to make Ned imprudent, and it was a good bet he would succeed, for after what had happened between Ned and her, Ned's pride was at stake.

But she did not want the two of them to go after each other. She would calm both of them. First, she would save their lives by restoring Ned's self-respect. After that, she would temper John's rage. Suddenly, she knew the solution. "Take it then. Take it all. You have outsmarted us, and you win the prize." Emma dropped the money purse on the dirt, then turned to John. "It is not fabulous riches and not worth so much to me as your life. Do this for me, and I shall make it up to you." She shoved the carpetbag toward Ned and stepped back.

Ned looked surprised, then wary, as if unsure why she would give up the money so easily. But it was John whom she had misjudged. Perhaps, Emma thought afterward, she had not realized John's honor was at stake, too. When Ned reached down for the bag, John straightened and raised his arm. Then he threw the rock.

Ned turned just in time to dodge the missile, but it threw him off balance, and he fired twice, the gun slipping from his hand as he fought to regain his footing. "You tricked me! I'll stomp you!" he said. His face was contorted and terrible to look at. He groped for the gun, but it had slid out of reach, so howling like a madman, he set upon John.

Emma did not know a man could move so fast. John's arm was still in the air when Ned hit him, smashing his fist into John's face and sending him reeling against the rock escarpment on which Ned had been standing only minutes before. "You are dead!" he cried.

John caught himself and did not fall, and he laughed at Ned. "You'll have to be better with your fists than your gun. Not a scratch hit me," he replied. He hurtled himself at Ned with such force that Ned was knocked to the ground. Before Ned could rise, John was on top of him, encircling Ned's neck with his hands, sinking his strong fingers into the flesh. "The gun. Get the gun," John called over his shoulder to Emma.

But she had the weapon already. She pointed it at the two men, but they rolled over and over, making her fearful that if she shot, she would hit John. The men slid across the shale, which shattered into pieces under the weight of their bodies. One kicked the other with his boot—Emma could not tell which one did it—and there was a thud and a cry. John broke free and rose to his feet. "Kill him," he called to Emma. She raised the gun, but she could not pull the trigger. She could not kill Ned any more than she could have shot John.

But it did not matter, for the chance was gone. John was between her and Ned, the two men circling, waiting for a chance to strike. There were long scratches on Ned's face, and John's back was bloody under his torn shirt. The two men were evenly matched. John had more control, but Ned was faster, more spirited. Ned's fists moved in and out, striking John's chest with quick hard punches. Then John landed a massive blow square in Ned's face, and Ned's head snapped back. He spun backward shaking his head from side to side. John lunged forward to finish him off, but it had been a trick. Ned swiveled away to avoid the blow, sending John off balance, and he fell onto the ground.

Emma watched them, frantic, shouting for them to stop. "Take the money! Take the money!" she screamed until her throat was tight and raw, but neither man heeded her.

Ned kicked at John's head, striking his ear, and John grunted in pain. Emma thought she saw fear on John's face, but she was not sure since she had never seen John afraid of anything. Then Ned struck out with his boot again, and John grabbed it, grabbed Ned's leg, and pulled him down. They rolled nearly to the edge of the cliff but stopped short of it, Ned on top, locking John between his knees. Ned's face clouded with hatred, as he reached his thumbs to John's eyes.

"No, Ned! No! Take it. Here's the money!" Emma shouted, picking up the carpet purse and throwing it along the ground toward the two men. They heard her then and turned to see the bag spin toward them, gain momentum, hit the slippery rocks, and slide over the cliff. The two men lunged for the pouch, rolling together, a ball of arms and legs, and plunged over the side after the money. There was the thud of impact, then a long animal-like scream, loud at first, then faint. Emma did not hear the bodies land and realized with horror that they must have fallen a thousand feet and lay smashed on the far rocks.

Forcing herself to move, Emma turned slowly toward the cliff, willing herself to put one foot in front of the other. It was as quiet as the grave when she reached the edge of the cliff. The giddy height made her sick, but she forced herself to look down, to search for some sign of either man. She could not see a body, only a piece of coat—Ned's coat, for John had worn only a shirt— attached to a rock.

Then her eye caught something human just a foot or two below, flat against the cliff, a hand straining upward. A man stood on a tree that grew perpendicular from the rock wall. She heard a strangled human sound and saw the hand reach higher. Her heart beating wildly, Emma lay down on the ground, bracing herself against a rock and holding onto a stunted pine tree. Then she extended her free arm over the edge and felt a hand grasp hers. She gripped the man's wrist and slowly pulled him up. The only sounds were her gasps and his boots striking the rock as, holding onto her, he walked up the canyon wall. She did not know if the life she was saving was John's or Ned's.

welcome

NINE

The fine-looking Negro in the derby hat and flowered waistcoat was the last passenger to board the Colorado Central cars at Golden, just outside Denver. He looked about for a suitable seat, one that would allow him to sit by himself or beside a man, but there was neither, so he took the only place available, next to an elderly woman, careful not to brush against her. He removed his hat and the yellow gloves. The woman looked at the gloves with amusement but said nothing, and he ignored the snickers of two men a few seats away. Nor did he react when a boy called, "Lookit there at that prissy darky," although with the back of his powerful hand, he could have knocked the kid across the car. The insult was as nothing compared to what he had endured before. Ever since his boyhood in slavery days, when he had been sold from his mother, just as the calf is sold from the cow, he had learned to let the insults roll off him. It kept him from bitterness. He was not an unhappy man. Far from it. He was a man of strong emotions, and he enjoyed life hugely. It amused him. Why else would he risk embarrassment by wearing gloves that made his hands look like two fat lemons?

After looking over her seatmate, the old woman ignored him and began fanning herself, for the coach was stifling. Then she got up to open the window, but he said gently, "Madam, may I be allowed?" and raised the window for her. She dipped her head in recognition but did not thank him.

Just as the train started up, a woman boarded and looked for a seat. The men in the car stared out the window or busied themselves with their newspapers, but the black man rose, and with a slight flourish, he indicated his place. The woman sat down without acknowledging him. As the train jolted out of the depot, he went to the observation deck and lit a cigar. Although there would be stops along the way, the ride was not a long one, and anyway, he would rather be outside, where he could breathe the clean mountain air, than confined to the stuffy coach. It was getting on toward fall now, although the weather was still filled with sunshine. The aspen were streams of gold in the mountain crevices, so brassy and bright that they almost hurt his eyes. He hoped the clear air would calm him, and it did for a time. But later, when the train slowed down on the flats just outside Georgetown, he felt the turmoil rise again in his breast.

He went inside the coach to collect his hat and carpetbag, which were stowed on the rack above the seat he had given up, and he waited until the other Georgetown passengers had disembarked before stepping back onto the observation deck and looking around.

He saw them right away, of course. There were only two persons who were still waiting for passengers. Emma stepped forward and grasped his hands. She was too aware of propriety to embrace him, and perhaps she would not have done so under any conditions, but she gripped his hands firmly, and he could tell from the joy in her eyes that she was pleased to see him. Or, at any rate, that she was happy about something. She seemed to have recovered, and he did not know if he was glad for it.

"My friend," she said, still holding his hands.

"How are you, Emmie?"

"Well." Her blue eyes clouded for a moment, and the smile faded. "Passing well." She looked down at his hands, squeezed them again, then let go—reluctantly, he thought, although he was never sure about her. She had been a performer once, just as he had been. And still was, he thought, as was she. Emma said, "You know Ned, of course."

The Negro gave a slight nod of recognition.

"And, Ned, you are acquainted with Jubal Welcome."

Standing just behind Emma, Ned stared flint-eyed at him. "Not as a man, by zam," he replied, looking from the yellow gloves into Welcome's smoky eyes.

Neither man laughed. Instead, they regarded each other warily, while Welcome thought that this was awkward for Emma, awkward for all of them. Still, he would not make the first move. He had liked Ned well enough, better than he'd expected to, but that was before. The thought of what had happened since the two last met made Welcome go distracted for a moment. He blamed Ned, and Ned surely resented him for being part of the plot to steal Ned's money. Perhaps Ned, too, was refusing to make the first move.

But at length, Ned extended his hand, and grinned. "No hard feelings," he said.

Welcome took the hand and shook it, but he did have hard feelings. How could he not? John Roby had been his best friend, had saved his life when he was set upon by bullies, had always treated him like a man. Welcome would have sacrificed his life for John, but he had not been given the choice. He wondered if Emma had been given the choice, but that was unfair. While she had always been curiously dispassionate, she was as loyal to John as Welcome was. But now John was gone, and Welcome knew Emma would never give him the same devotion; nor would he give it to her. Welcome liked Emma, admired her, and she had treated him fairly. But they had maintained their distance from each other. There had been words between the two of them in Nalgitas when Welcome thought Emma had grown too fond of Ned. Welcome had not cared so much that their game of buncombe might fail as he had that she would do something foolish and so cause John pain.

He saw that Ned and Emma were staring at him, waiting for him to say something, so he replied, "No, no hard feelings."

"You received the dispatch I sent by way of Charley Pea?" Emma asked.

"Yes."

"And you understand there was nothing we could do. John threw the rock that started the fight, and then he could not be stopped. You know how he could be when he was taken up in fury." Welcome knew, and he dipped his head in acknowledgment.

"I guess that doesn't matter, does it? Ned and I searched for his body all that day and finally found it on a ledge. We tried to retrieve it, but we could not reach it. The body was caught halfway down the face of a sheer cliff." Emma shuddered. "We could not have brought it up under any circumstances."

"No," Welcome said. He knew what an effort it must have been for Emma to look for the body, for she was greatly afraid of high places. It didn't matter to him where the body was, only that John was dead. "And the money?" he asked.

Emma glanced around. They were alone now, but she was cautious. "Let us walk. I have made arrangements for a room for you at the Frenchman's. I think you would be more comfortable there."

She would be more comfortable if he spent his nights there, Welcome thought. Still, he himself did not want to stay at the little house with Emma, not with Ned living there in John's place. He wondered how Emma had explained that to the neighbors, but the neighbors came and went, so perhaps they did not know that John had been replaced by Ned. That was a bitter thought.

The three of them walked in silence from the depot along the street into town, past the white houses with their fanciful trim and dried yellow roses and wire fences that reminded Welcome of Emma's hairpins lined up on the bureau at The Chili Queen. Hurt spilled over Welcome as he remembered strolling along the street with John, the two of them chuckling over a scam. At first, Welcome had played only a small part in John's and Emma's games, pretending to be a porter or drayman. But he quickly became indispensable, for he had a knack for playacting, and nobody ever suspected him. Welcome loved that. Their victims wouldn't admit even to themselves that a Negro was smart enough to trick them. When the blacksmith wired Emma that Addie had lost yet another housekeeper and Welcome had hurried to Nalgitas and knocked on The Chili Queen's back door asking for work, Addie had only congratulated herself on having good luck. It was just the way the three of them had planned it. Welcome had had plenty of time to assess the situation before Emma showed up. If the setup had been different from what the blacksmith told them, Welcome would have disappeared, and the scam would have been called off. And John would be alive, Welcome thought then. But that wasn't the way it had turned out, and what was done could not be undone, Welcome thought as he and Emma and Ned turned in at the little place with the green shutters on Rose Street.

"There were lemons at Kneisel & Anderson, so I have prepared lemonade for your pleasure," Emma said, as she untied the strings of her bonnet and hung it on a hook beside the door.

Welcome nodded. He himself would have preferred a drink, but he was mindful that Emma had got on the drink again in Nalgitas, and he knew that that had concerned John. He set down his valise, then took off his coat and waistcoat, and looked around. He thought there might be some sign of mourning, gauze draped over a mirror or a black ribbon across the framed sampler that Emma prized so highly. But Emma was not much for sentiment. Everything was exactly as it had been before, except for a battered yellow-splattered coffeepot that sat on the stove. Welcome wondered where that had come from, but he didn't ask.

Emma chipped ice into three glasses and set them on a tray with a pitcher from the icebox and a plate of oatmeal cookies. Ned carried the tray into the backyard and placed it on a table. Emma picked up her work basket and followed him, but Welcome stood in the doorway a moment, looking out past the school that loomed like a mountain over the yard, to the square stone tower of the Presbyterian Church beyond. He was fond of the church. Emma was not a churchgoer, but for whatever reason—perhaps a fear of hell, for Welcome knew things about him that Emma did not—John was among the faithful. He had taken Welcome to church with him, where, to the black man's surprise, the preacher insisted that Welcome sit next to John in the front of the church, instead of in the back row. When one of the congregation complained that the Bible did not approve of the mixing of the races, the preacher had replied, "The Good Book, like the fiddle, can be made to play many tunes."

Emma turned to see Welcome staring at the church, and she said, "I told Pastor Darnell that John had passed, and he has offered to hold a service, with just us present. I said it would not be necessary, but he thought it might make you easy in the heart. Do you want such a ceremony?"

Welcome nodded. He was not much more religious than Emma, but he thought a service would bring a proper ending to John's life.

"And a stone? We could buy a stone."

"To mark what?" Welcome asked.

"Quite right," Emma replied.

Welcome went to the little table under the trees and accepted a glass of lemonade. "The money," he said. "Now tell me exactly what happened."

Emma exchanged glances with Ned, then passed the plate of cookies to Welcome. They were made from the same recipe Welcome had used at The Chili Queen, but Emma had replaced the raisins with nuts. Welcome did not think they tasted as good. "It was just as I wrote you," Emma said. "The bag with the money in it went over the cliff. We searched for it all the while we were searching for John's body. It must be caught in the rocks, too, or maybe it fell into the river. At any rate, we never found it."

Welcome looked from Emma to Ned, who leaned forward, his forearms on the table, and said, "That's the God's truth. The whole thing, just . . ." He raised his hands in a helpless gesture. "It went over the cliff."

"It was my fault," Emma interrupted. "I threw it. How

could I know it would slide so far? How could I?" She and Welcome stared at each other for a moment, and Welcome knew they both were thinking if she had not thrown the money, John would be alive. "We would not hold out on you. I believe you know that." She reconsidered. "I suppose you do not know Ned well enough to assess his intentions, but you know *I* would not cheat you. That would dishonor John."

The sound of the school bell across the yard startled them all. There was shouting, the sound of doors slamming. The three sat for a few minutes, listening as the children rushed out onto the streets, and the din died away. Emma took out her sewing. She pinned two small triangles together and began to stitch. Emma had tried to teach Welcome how to sew, but he couldn't do it. His hands were too big, and he could not thread a needle.

Welcome looked at the yellow aspen leaves that were sprinkled about the yard like ten-dollar gold pieces and asked, "You never even counted the money?"

Without looking up, Emma shook her head. "Why would we? You saw Ned and John count it at the station. Besides, there was no opportunity. John and I were in the saddle every waking moment from the time we left What Cheer. Besides, the purse was locked, and I had no key. The money's gone. Ned's money, ours, all of it."

Welcome was satisfied they were telling the truth, and he reassured Emma, "I don't doubt you. I do not believe you capable of calumny where I am concerned."

"You talk different," Ned said abruptly.

Welcome grinned. "I told you once, I got the bejesus in me to talk like an old granny, Lord have mercy on me,

yes, but I can talk every bit as high-class as Emmie, too."
Welcome was proud of his refined language, which, in
fact, he had acquired only after careful study. His natural
speech was that of the plantation, and when he was not
careful, he slipped into it.

The three of them lapsed into silence again, a little
uncomfortable in one another's presence. Emma snipped
a thread with her scissors, then fished more little yellow
pieces from the basket, fastening them together with pins
she took from a copper-colored candy tin. She knotted the
thread by winding it around her finger, then rolling it off
into a tangle that she pulled until it was a fat knot. She
selected a finished square from the basket and flattened it
on the table. "This is what I'm making—Georgetown
Puzzle. I suppose I picked it for the name, although I am
fond of the design," she told him.

Welcome nodded his approval, then Emma returned to
her sewing, and he watched the point of her needle dart in
and out. When he tired of watching, he turned to view the
yard. Tansies and late daisies were in bloom, but the little
vegetable garden he had helped Emma plant in spring had
died out, for no one had tended to it while they were away.
Then he leaned back to look at the mountains that walled
the town on two sides. He would miss the mountains.
There was peace in this place for John and Emma and
him, or there had been before John died. Perhaps Emma
found solace here still, but for Welcome, it would never be
the same. He would miss Georgetown, but his decision
had been made before he left Nalgitas, and he did not
regret it. Oh, no. The past had been important to Emma
and John. Welcome had always looked to the future.

Emma set her sewing in her lap and glanced at Ned, but before she could say anything, Ned asked, "About Addie, is she all right?"

The question vexed Welcome. Ned had deserted Addie, and Welcome didn't feel like salving Ned's conscience by telling him that Addie was fine, better than fine. So he replied, "The day you left, she lined up her bottles of rot and got full after noon and was on it big for four, five, six days, drunk early and late. Whilst she was on the bender, she had a row with the girls and gave Miss Belle a swelled nose. Then Miss Addie locked the girls out of the house, and Miss Tillie got stung on the lip by a scorpion when she lay down on the porch. After that, the whores lit out, and Addie shut down The Chili Queen."

Emma looked uncomfortable, and Ned said, "You should have stopped her."

Welcome wanted to reply that if Ned had not deserted her, Addie would not have gone on the spree. Besides, Welcome *had* stopped her. "I guess she'd still be reposing there till now if she hadn't got sick from drinking and eating bad mutton and sent me out to the chemist for laudanum. So short of reason was she that I feared she would kill herself, and I told her no shiftless road agent was worth it." Welcome was enjoying himself, but Ned winced, and Emma looked stern, and although what he had said was the truth, Welcome decided it best to end the recitation. "Miss Addie thought that over and said she was tired of being indisposed. Shortly, she was in much better order and went out and found a man to buy The Chili Queen for an eating house. Then she packed up and got on the train." He turned to Emma. "Your roses died."

"I'm glad to hear she is all right then," Ned said. "Where did she go?"

Welcome shrugged. "She didn't say, and I didn't ask. By then, I was in receipt of Emmie's letter, with such terrible news as I have never before received." Welcome stopped and removed a silk handkerchief and dabbed at his eyes, annoyed at himself for the tears. "I got on a train myself and came here."

Emma nodded and glanced at Ned, who dipped his head. She cleared her throat and said, "There is no reason we can't go on, the three of us. Of course, we have no choice, since with the money gone, Ned cannot buy the ranch in Telluride. I suppose you know that is what he planned to do with the money." Emma looked at Welcome, who did not respond. Of course, Welcome knew it. There wasn't much that had happened between Ned and Emma that he didn't know, except for what had gone on during the trip to Jasper. Emma had returned from it much troubled in her soul, and she and Welcome had had an unpleasant exchange over her refusal to discuss it.

When Welcome didn't reply, Emma cleared her throat. "So we must all earn our living once more." She looked at Ned again. "I have learned that there is a man in St. George, Utah, a Mormon with three wives," she began.

She stopped when Welcome began to shake his head. "I cannot."

"But, of course, you can, Welcome. We are a team. You and John and I have played it all so well before. We need Ned. He will take John's place."

Welcome stiffened. "Never for me," he said.

Emma thought that over. "No, I suppose not." She

lapsed into silence. The sun had touched the edge of the mountain, and shadows covered the yard now. She shivered, and Welcome, too, felt the fall chill, so different from the heat of New Mexico. "You must be tired," Emma said, standing. "Tonight, we will enjoy a fine dinner at the Hotel de Paris, and tomorrow, I shall see to the service for John. You must go through John's things. I set his diamond stickpin aside for you and his watch. Anything else you wish to have is yours."

"Thank you."

Ned stood, too, coming up behind Emma and clasping her about the waist. "You best tell him," he said.

Emma smiled at Ned, and she covered his hands with her own. Welcome never had seen her so happy. In fact, he was not sure he had seen her truly happy at all. Emma blushed and held up her hand so that he could see a gold ring with a red stone. "Last week, Pastor Darnell married Ned and me." She added shyly, "I need Ned."

Welcome stared at her for a long time, wondering why it was necessary that she marry so quickly. After all, she and John had been together for years, and they had never had preaching over them. He looked at Ned, who grinned like a school boy, then back at Emma, who seemed as eager as a child for his approval. "Well," he said. "Well, I guess that's fine. I guess that's just fine." Emma stepped forward and kissed Welcome on the cheek, something she had not done before. Then Ned shook his hand, and Welcome said again, "That's just fine." And when he thought it over, Welcome decided it was fine.

In the end, Welcome agreed to participate in one more

job. Emma said she understood why he did not want to be partners with Ned, but they had designed this job with a part for Welcome and could not pull it off without him. Besides, she pointed out, Welcome's cut of the Nalgitas job had gone over the side of the cliff, too, and he must be short of money. They would divide the pickings, with Welcome getting one-half, and she and Ned the rest. That would give Welcome a start, she said. He did not want to work with Ned and Emma, but they would think it odd, might even grow suspicious, if he turned down such a generous offer. After all, John had paid him a fourth. So at last, Welcome said he would join them.

He stayed on for another day so that he could attend the service for John, then finalize the scam. Emma took charge. She always had been in charge, Welcome thought with surprise. He had not realized until then that John had done her bidding, not the other way around, and so would Ned. The two of them would do well together. They did not need him.

Since the job would not begin for a month, Welcome told Ned and Emma he had business to attend to and would meet them in Utah. Emma replied that he did not need to leave Georgetown, that any differences among the three of them were resolved, but Welcome insisted. So Ned and Emma took him to the depot and waved him off. When Welcome reached Denver, he took a train south.

He reached San Antonio in the early evening and walked from the depot to the Plaza de Armas under a darkening sky, where the rays of the sun were like shavings of gold. He had packed away the bright gloves and waistcoat and put on plain clothes, for Texans were not as tolerant of a Negro who stood out as the Coloradans. He had thought of donning a dress but decided against it, for he wanted to be a man when he met her.

The air was still hot in the dusty plaza, but he was used to the heat and barely noticed the cooling breeze that carried the smell of roasted meat and spices. He passed a long table covered with bright oilcloth and smiled at a chili queen in a short red dress. She called to him in a language he didn't understand, but he took her meaning and shook his head. He passed fires of mesquite and charcoal where women broiled meats and boiled buckets of coffee. The chili queens cried, *"Tamales y enchiladas, menudo y tripitas,"* as he strolled by the rows of tables. A woman with peacock feathers in her hair grabbed his hand, but he pulled it away and kept on until he saw Addie.

"I have agreed to one more job," he said. "Then it's over."

Addie nodded, then dipped her head at the tables in front of her. "All these here, they're mine. I bought them," she said. "And they didn't cost hardly anything. When I get settled in, I'll open us a restaurant, maybe buy one of those buildings over there." She nodded at the smart brick and stone business blocks going up among the adobe buildings on the edge of the plaza.

"You are a shrewd businesswoman." Welcome meant it.

"It was always my dream."

Welcome squeezed her hand and said, "You have been tried by pain and disloyalty and heartache. It is high time you try something else."

Addie was still a moment, as she gazed across the plaza at the back of a church. "Did you see Ned?"

Welcome had expected the question. "He asked about you."

Addie waited.

"They are married."

She didn't say anything for a long time. Then she gave a deep laugh that thrilled Welcome, and said, "There but for the grace of God . . ."

Welcome said, "They're happy."

"I don't mind. I never was one to bear a grudge. Besides . . ." She didn't finish but turned to him again with a smile so sensuous that Welcome easily took her meaning.

There was a commotion at one of the tables, and Addie got up and went to see about the trouble. She inspected the arm of one of the chili queens, then went to a tub of water used for washing dishes. Addie dipped a rag into the water and held the wet cloth against a burn on the woman's arm. She tenderly wiped away tears on the chili queen's face, and led her to a bench and told her to rest. Welcome felt a happiness that Addie was so kindhearted. He was not only lucky but blessed to have found such a woman.

In a minute, Addie returned with a bowl of chili and handed it to Welcome, who used a tortilla to scoop it into his mouth. The stew was rich and greasy, and Welcome savored the heat and bite of the seasonings. He was glad Addie was a woman of hearty tastes.

"What about the money?" Addie asked.

Welcome chuckled. "They never even opened the bag."

"Katy, bar the door!" Addie said. She was so tickled that she began to laugh, and she reached out and linked her arm through Welcome's. "Not ever?"

Welcome shook his head. "Never. You read her letter, where she said the purse had gone over the cliff. She tried to open it often. Ned caught up with them, but the bag was locked, and you forgot to give her the key."

"Well, I guess I did at that," Addie said. Welcome could see the glow in her eyes as she turned to him and winked. "I guess I forgot to give them the money, too."

"Are you sorry they didn't find out?"

Addie's eyes grew misty, and Welcome patted her hand. "You have such a tender heart," he said.

Addie sniffed and replied, "I wanted them to find out, of course, wanted them to know *I* had outsmarted *them*. I have that right, you know. They betrayed me, both of them. But that was before . . ." She stopped and chuckled. "Now, I think it's better this way. You know, and that's enough for me."

"It was the cleverest switch I ever saw. I almost could not believe my eyes."

Addie cocked her head and said proudly, "I told you I used to be the best there ever was. I guess I still am."

"I was mightily conflicted at the time," Welcome said, but, of course, Addie knew that. They had talked about it before. At first, when he had seen Addie switch the money that she had wrapped in a handkerchief, for a packet of newspaper tied up in a similar handkerchief and hidden in the waist of her dress, he had wanted to warn John. John had not seen the switch, nor had Ned, because Addie had ordered both of them to look away. But revealing Addie's treachery there at the station would have spoiled John and Emma's bunco game. So he had kept quiet, intending to find out where Addie hid the money and then take it to John himself.

So he had stayed on at The Chili Queen. But even if he had found the hiding place—and he never did—he couldn't have left Addie then, for she was in pain and drunk as a lord, and abandoning her would not be a manly thing. Then Emma's letter came, telling him John was dead and Ned was with her in Georgetown. And by then, he had developed such feelings for Addie.

The remarkable thing was that Addie wasn't surprised when Welcome told her he was a man. She'd said that all along she'd had an idea he wasn't any woman.

"La!" she'd said, she'd always appreciated a dark man.

"Plenty of white men will be willing to look after you now that you have money," he'd said.

"Now that I have money, I can choose the man I want to look after me," she'd replied, reaching for Welcome. "And the man I choose is dark."

The memory of that gave Welcome a warm feeling. He put down the empty bowl and he slid across the bench until his body touched Addie's. She ran her hand along the warm muscles of his arm. She took his hand, and they stood. Then in the Mexican twilight, they strolled across the plaza, where the air was sultry with the scent of chili and melodious with the calls of the chili queens.